MW00475169

Camden

Photo by Katherine Yearwood Klegin

SOUTHERN STORIES FROM  PORCH SWING

Tales of Friends, Family and Faith

JANET MORRIS BELVIN

BOOKBABY PUBLISHERS

DEDICATION

Many years ago, I began thinking about this book. But life got in the way as it sometimes does. Finally, though, I found I couldn't go on without capturing my memories, so here they are, presented to all of you who have supported me through the years.

To LOUISE, who nagged me and asked me why I hadn't published,

To MARTHA JEAN, who, like me, has a journal entry for almost every day of her life,

To JERRY, my womb-mate, who has loved me through thick and thin,

To my friends, too many to name, whose cheers encouraged me to keep on,

To my children, TOM, KATHERINE and CAROLINE, the best work I've ever done, and *to their spouses*, JULIE, SHON and BEN, *my bonus children*,

To my grandchildren LEIGHTON, NOLAN, NAOMI, MASON, WILL, HUDSON, and HENRY – who fill my life with joy,

To PAUL, the love of my life, who opened the doors and made it all possible,

And finally, to the memory of the three I miss most of all –

To CAMDEN, my tiny grandson whose smile brightened my life and the lives of so many others – and still does,

To MAMA, who reminded me to remember where I came from,

And to DADDY, who, when I told him I was writing a book, said to everybody, "She's writing a book and we're all gonna be in it,"

This book is humbly dedicated. I finally did it, Daddy.

CONTENTS

Preface   xiii

Peach Ice Cream   1

Reason #537 Why I'll be Living in the Low-Rent District of Heaven   3

My Family   4

Southern Things   5

Going to the Beauty Parlor   9

Turtle Eggs on Wilmington Island   11

Christmas Gifts from Mama and Daddy   14

Country Ham   16

The Basement   18

Sisters   20

The Books that Changed my Life   21

Daddy's Hands   27

Thoughts after a Funeral   27

My Fortieth College Reunion   29

Mama   32

No Room for a Pump Organ   35

I Hate this Date   37

I Heard My Mother's Voice   39

My Day at the Spa, or "A Mule in Horse Harness"   40

A Love Letter to America   43

Toys from my Childhood   45

Iney's Coin Purse   48

Beach Thoughts   52

Finding Blessings on a Country Road   54

The Blessings of Being Born in the South   57

15 Reasons I'm a Dinosaur   58

Digging Peanuts   61

Thoughts on Falling Leaves   63

My Father's Love   65

Happy Birthday to Tom - a Note of Appreciation   67

Here Comes Nolan "Trailing Clouds of Glory"   68

My Mother's Moment of Fame   71

Paris Memories   74

Hog Killing   76

A Good Day   77

Savannah High School Class of '66 - Our 45th Reunion   78

Nolan's Dedication Service   81

A Visit from Three Angels   83

Advice from Nana   85

Till Next Thanksgiving Day   87

The Cottage   90

Home for Christmas   93

Mama and Her Sisters   98

Beulah Jane Smith Morris   100

Dusty's Saddle   104

Thinking about Mama   106

How Daddy Came to Be a Minister   107

How Mama Met her Grandchildren   109

Slacker Inventions   111

Daddy the Outdoorsman   113

How Daddy made me feel special   115

A Lump of Coal   118

How Mama and Daddy fell in love   119

"God Always Bats Last"   123

Comic Books   125

Daddy Tells a Tale   127

Slats   128

A Love Story   130

Washing Dishes   133

Shopping - Grrrrr   134

Friendships   136

Eighty years later   137

A Thank You Note to Mama 139

Just One Name 141

Outer Banks Memories 143

Daddy 146

Summer Days 147

The Cars in my Life 149

What Daddy Missed 150

My Southern Mama 151

Remembering a Fire 154

Following the coffin 156

Grandmama's Ironing Board 158

Grandmama's Pantry 159

Daddy Talks about his Childhood 160

Christmas Carols 164

Christmas List 166

Mama's Bed 167

Yoga Lady Returns 169

The Spa as Sanctuary 170

A Sad Birthday 172

Nana's Eulogy for Camden 174

Thanatopsis 178

Letters from Mama and Daddy 179

Destination Savannah 181

Parker's Barbecue 184

Fifty Years 185

The Class of 1970 - Forever Strong 187

The Sound of Music...again 189

Savannah Safari 191

Horseback Riding with Daddy 194

Barn Love 196

Home 200

My Baby Loves the Western Movies 201

The Home Show 204

A Memorial toTheodosia Ellen Dever Morris 205

That Terrible Day in 1963 210

Jerry and Larry 211

Mama - the Good Sport 213

Mama and her Grandchildren 214

Mama leaves home 215

I Interview My Mother 217

Southern Storytellers 221

Fakebooking 222

The Shepherd Boy's Christmas 223

My Childhood Christmases 228

Daddy's Knife 231

Leigh Street Baptist Church 233

Dedicating Baby Will 235

Books of My Life 237

A Visit with Camden 239

Why I Pray 241

TV's Golden Era 242

My Mother 246

What Mama Missed 247

...So God sent us Henry 248

Mama in Her Chair 250

The Country Store 252

Holding the Rope 254

A Day with My Father 257

Saying Thank You 259

Old Hymns 260

A Veteran's Day Roll Call 261

Being Retired 263

Laughter 264

Grace 265

Photo Albums 267

Holding onto Memories 269

PREFACE

In the space of little more than five or six years, the world lost Roy Rogers, Dale Evans, Clarabell the Clown and my mother. All those people were important to my growing up, but, of course, only my mother was real to me. Still, the realization that they were no longer on this earth changed me somehow. I realized, finally, that time was not infinite.

Time is the one thing I've never had enough of. Ever since I was a small child, I've been conscious of how quickly time passes and have wanted to slow it down somehow. Of course I never found out how to do it, but it's worried me nonetheless. About the only way I have found to hold on to time is to write down my thoughts. So I began keeping a journal when I was fourteen. Of course I didn't call it a journal back then. It was "Dear Diary." My mother subscribed to Ladies' Home Journal and that January, the magazine gave away a free mini-datebook for the New Year. Mama said I could have it so I began sporadically recording my thoughts and activities. Some of the entries I now find laughable or embarrassing. I was a middle school kid after all. But that diary set me on a path of recording the events of my life that I have followed for many decades since then. The paragraphs in this book grew out of that idea.

In the years since I began writing in my journal, I've experienced the pain and exhilaration when three tiny newborns drew their first breath and cried for the first time. And I've wept at my mother's bedside when she gasped her final breath. In all the years I have lived, I have experienced the full gamut of emotions – from great joy, to great sorrow. I have laughed and I have cried. But throughout it all, I have been thankful to God for life and all of its blessings. I hope I haven't wasted it.

"God gave us memory so that we might have roses in December."

– J.M. Barrie

PEACH ICE CREAM

I was born in the little town of Gaffney, SC. It's in the northern part of the state very near the North Carolina border. Gaffney prides itself on the peach groves surrounding the town. The growers bring their sweet produce to the peach sheds on the outskirts of town. If you've ever traveled south on Interstate 95, you'll know when you've come to Gaffney, because of the large water tower alongside the interstate. It's shaped and painted to look exactly like a peach, but if you are immature enough, you can make a lot of jokes about the fact that it also kind of resembles buttocks. I know our family has gotten a lot of mileage out of that.

My daddy was pastor of the First Baptist Church of Gaffney when I was born. Although we lived there only seven or eight years, he never got over his love for the little town. It seemed that no matter where we were headed, be it Asheville, NC or Lexington, KY (I would have said Gravel Switch, KY but only a couple of you would know where that is - more on that later) or eastern North Carolina, we had to go through Gaffney.

When we visited there, we stayed at the La-Dell Motel or, later the Shamrock Motel, both now victims of the interstate. While there, Daddy made stops at his favorite places – first to Charlie Jennings' store, then to WGAI, the local AM radio station where, in the middle of the swap meet broadcast or the Arthur Smith show, the station general manager Raymond Parker, would put my daddy on the air impromptu. It seemed Daddy was a regular celebrity. Then we'd stop by the old neighborhood to see Mrs. Clarkson, our next door neighbor and her children Nancy and Tom, our old playmates. We'd see Mrs. Cooksey, Daddy's old secretary, and Zeb and Nora Whelchel, local Gulf oil dealers. Finally we'd make our way to the Sunny Slope peach shed where, no matter how much luggage we were carrying, Daddy would always make room for a couple of half bushel baskets of peaches.

Raymond Parker interviews Daddy.

It was always a great delight to my grandfather in Kentucky to see those baskets of pink beauties in the back of Daddy's sedan. Though it meant my grandmother had to peel peaches and cook the custard and my teenaged cousins (usually Buddy and Billy) had to turn the hand crank of the old wooden churn, the peach ice cream that followed was reward enough. We ate it outside on metal lawn chairs under a big Kentucky moon. I remember having brain freezes because I ate mine so fast.

After the ice cream, the aunts and uncles sat in the twilight and told stories and jokes and memories. We younger kids lingered at our mothers' feet or ran around the pasture in front of the house to catch lightning bugs. Soon enough it was bedtime and we climbed the stair, past the diamond-shaped stained glass window at the landing and into our beds, our stomachs full of peaches and our heads full of stories.

Recently Paul and I got some good-looking peaches at Costco. Of course my daddy wasn't there to haggle with the peach shed owner over price; there was no peach shed with its baskets and trucks and scales and bags. My mother wasn't there to pour in just the right amount of cream and eggs and sugar and vanilla. And we used an electric White Mountain churn to do the work. We have a hand cranked churn which I insist makes better cream, but Paul refuses to use it, so I gave in and we got the electric one.

Things are different now. My parents are gone, my sisters and I are all grandmothers, and our children are spread far and wide. So things are different. Not worse, not better - just different. The peach ice cream we make now may not be as good as that in my memory. But as a way to close out the summer, it'll do.

REASON #537 WHY I'LL BE LIVING IN THE LOW-RENT DISTRICT OF HEAVEN

I went to the CVS to get some prescriptions filled recently. Just as I neared the curb, I saw a busload of senior citizens disembarking from the Heatherwood Senior Living Center bus, all headed like a bunch of slow-moving turtles ahead of me toward the door of the drug store. Of course it was obvious what was going to happen – they were all aiming directly for the prescription counter like me, only they were pushing walkers, wheelchairs and canes, and they were moving like molasses in January.

"Oh crap, that's going to add another 15 minutes to my trip if I get behind them," I thought.

I tried to go around them but couldn't find a path. As soon as I entered the building, sure enough, there they were, headed for the prescription counter like a line of ants. Suddenly – inspiration! Light bulb going on above my head! I took a detour around Greeting Cards and headed up the Pampers aisle. Surely they wouldn't be going that way. I skidded into first place at the prescription counter just ahead of a grey-haired gentle soul and thrust my prescription in the pharmacist's face. He looked around for a while to see if what I needed was in stock. The whole time I wanted to crawl behind the sign which read, "Stock up on cold and flu supplies before cold season!" In a few minutes the pharmacist told me my order would be ready tomorrow. I sheepishly thanked him and slunk away, fifteen minutes ahead of the game but awash in guilt.

Parting thought – it has occurred to me that, like those slow-moving souls I zoomed past, I am officially a senior citizen going to the CVS to get my prescriptions filled. Only difference between me and the grey-hairs from Heatherwood – no cane or walker for me and I color my hair. How long before some young whippersnapper dashes ahead of me in line?

MY FAMILY

I'm thankful today for my family. I was the third born of four girls, each of which grew up to be very different from each other. But we all married and had a passel of kids which brings me to this point. I just love my family. My parents had ten grand-children from the four of us, and those ten grandchildren have had, so far, 23 great grandchildren. We're a very prolific family! For many years we got together every two years for a big Thanksgiving celebration which one of the four families hosted. On the off years, our children can visit with their in-laws (or outlaws, as my Daddy used to say.) When we did get together for our big Thanksgiving celebrations, we usually rented a giant house at the beach and everybody (I think the count is now up to about 39) piled in for a week. While we were together, we took a family photo, had competitions, games, tournaments, and we ate! Boy did we eat. Two of my sisters, Jerry and Martha Jean, are fantastic cooks as are the younger girls (our daughters and daughters-in-law.) Louise and I are very appreciative of their efforts! Before, during and after the giant feast, we enjoyed spirited contests between what we shamefully call the Crips and the Bloods. (The Crips are those who have married into the family and the Bloods are those favored souls who were born into the family.) Last year, we divided up into groups and had a scavenger hunt. Other years we have had the Frank Morris Memorial Rook tournament dedicated to my daddy's favorite card game. There's usually the Theodosia Memorial Bake-off (my favorite contest!) and last year, a volleyball tournament on the beach. My favorite part of the week was when everyone was arriving. We oohed and ahhed over how much the children had grown and looked over the new babies. The men generally checked out what the others were driving and the women got everyone settled in. For the last few years we had a 5 K race which most of us participated in. I am proud to say that I came in first in my division the last year. (Of course there were only two of us but I totally schooled you, MJ.) The saddest part of the week was when you began to hear mumblings of when people are leaving. You know that things may be different when you reconvene. But we left, nevertheless, to go back to our lives, strengthened by the bond of family that can never be cut, no matter what.

SOUTHERN THINGS

I have lived here in northern Virginia for over two decades now, and although, technically speaking, Virginia is a Southern state, it really doesn't feel that way, being so close to Washington, DC and all – too many dadgum guv'mint lawyers, one of whom I'm married to. (I love you, Pablo.) So every once in a while I get a hankering to be surrounded by Southern things, Southern accents, Southern foods,

Southern people. Here, in case you ever long for them too, are some of the things I love about the South.

SWEET TEA – I never, and I mean never, am without one and sometimes two pitchers of sweet tea in my refrigerator (or as my grandmother called it my Frigidaire.) Served in a clear glass (it's just not as good in plastic or Styrofoam) this cognac colored elixir of the gods has been called the house wine of the South with good reason. I drink it for breakfast, dinner and supper. (And yes, those are the three meals down South, not breakfast, lunch and dinner.)

MULES – Yes, I know mules aren't strictly Southern animals, but I associate them with the South and specifically, my past. Because, unfortunately, that seems to be the way they are going – into the past. I remember visiting my grandparents in Gates County, NC and seeing their barn full of mules used for working the garden and fields. There is just something about their strong Roman noses and the ears perked up that make me happy. I like the brown leather harnesses they wear, soft and scuffed from years of use, and the wagons or tobacco sleds they pulled. William Faulkner said, "A mule will work for you ten years for the chance to kick you once." But I still like them. You don't see them much anymore.

BANJOS - I have always liked the sound of a banjo, whether it is plucked or strummed. When I was a child, I used to see my daddy's pleasure on hearing a bluegrass song on the radio and I cringed a bit. That is so old-timey, I thought, in the way that only a self-important pre-teen can think. We'd go to Kentucky to visit my grandparents and listen to the hick songs on WCKY in Cincinnati – O-HI-O as far as the static-y radio in Daddy's car would allow. One of his favorites was "Fraulein." When I was in my forties, I bought a banjo at a pawn shop and a couple of books to teach myself to play. But almost as soon as I did, I got pregnant with my third child, who's now in her thirties, so I put it aside. It sits there in the corner still, guilting me into making promises to pick it up again someday. I was pretty good on "Buffalo Gals" so maybe I'll try it again someday. You just can't play a sad song on a banjo and I like that about it.

SCREEN DOORS – I particularly like the old fashioned Victorian kind that I used to see on my grandparents' porches with all the turned spindles. And they have to sing a little with the rusty spring sound that says "I've been here a long time and I'll be here when you're gone." I like hearing it bang behind me when I go into the house to get a cold drink. Speaking of that…

ICE COLD SODAS IN GLASS BOTTLES – When I was a young girl, I'd visit my grandmother Beulah Morris in North Carolina. She was crazy about Dr. Pepper. At that time, they had kind of a clock face on their glass bottle with 10-2-4 on it. My grandmother always said that was when you were supposed to drink Dr. Pepper for its medicinal properties to take effect, so she did! I can still remember the taste of a cold Dr. Pepper on the porch swing on her front porch. Speaking of which…

PORCHES AND PORCH SWINGS – All around me I see nothing but McMansions going up. Almost none of them have any kind of porch. A porch, screened or not, was an invitation to relax, visit with your neighbors, relax in the hammock, or watch from your rocker as the cars went by. I remember shelling butter beans in an enamel pan on my grandmother's front porch swing. My grandmother Beulah lived up a long dirt lane and every evening after supper, we'd sit in the rockers or on the swing to watch the cars on the highway. Occasionally one would turn in and it would seem to take forever to make it down her rutted lane. "Who do you reckon is in there?" we'd say. We'd be sitting in the dark, because turning on the porch light drew bugs. It was a little spooky but very cool to sit in the comfort of my daddy's lap out on the porch on a hot summer night.

Y'ALL AND OTHER SOUTHERN PHRASES – Sometimes when I told my students to "cut the light off" if we left our classroom, they'd give me the funniest look. Then I remembered that this far north you have to say "turn the light off." I'm sorry, y'all, that's just wrong!

SIR AND MA'AM – Children here don't have to say this and it irks me. They often don't even respond to me with "yes" – just "yeah!" I often reminded my students that they must respond to me with "yes" or "yes, ma'am" but "yeah is never gonna cut it. Yes, ma'am, I'm old school.

PULLING YOUR CAR OVER TO THE SIDE OF THE ROAD FOR A FUNERAL – Once when I attended a funeral in South Carolina, they even had policemen with black arm bands directing the traffic. It's just common courtesy and one last bit of respect you can pay to honor a life.

COUNTRY HAM, DEVILED EGGS, CO-COLAS (THE SOUTHERN PRONUNCIATION) AND PECAN PIE. I believe when I get to Heaven, I will be served these foods on a daily basis.

A MESS – Knowing how much is in "a mess" of collards or "a mess" of butter beans (another one of my Heavenly foods) is an important Southern bit of knowledge.

BEACH MUSIC – There is nothing so wonderful as shagging to "Miss Grace" or "My Girl" or something by THE TAMS with the wind off a sand dune blowing your hair and your boyfriend's arm around your waist (even if you color your grey, not that mine is, of course) and your boyfriend is your husband of many years.

BARBECUE, HUSH PUPPIES, COLE SLAW AND BRUNSWICK STEW – all preferably from an eastern North Carolina hole in the wall kind of place.

POURING A PACK OF SALTED PEANUTS IN YOUR GREEN GLASS BOTTLE OF CO-COLA – Then after you finish it, check the bottom to see where the bottle is from. The person with the farthest city is the winner.

THE COMBINATION OF AN RC COLA AND A MOON PIE – That's an obvious one.

HAVING A FIRM GRASP ON WHAT IS AND IS NOT "TACKY," – clothes, make-up and lives!

AMAZING GRACE – The old hymn is my favorite and, though it is sung all over the world, it feels particularly Southern to me for some reason.

Amazing grace, how sweet the sound,

That saved a wretch like me!

I once was lost but now I'm found,

Was blind but now I see.

GOING TO THE BEAUTY PARLOR

I recently went to the salon to get my every-four-weeks touch up. I've been coloring my hair now for about fifteen years and it's amazing what a boost it gives me to have it done. When I first started, I had very little grey hair. I wonder what's under there now! Going to the salon always reminds me of going with my mother to what we called the "beauty parlor" when I was a little girl.

In Gaffney, SC where I lived until age 5, I went to Mrs. Sam Miller's shop. In Savannah, I went to Mrs. Lillian Knight's shop, gloriously named the Eugene-Waltann Beauty Salon. The smells of both shops were the same - an acrid, unforgettable odor which came from the permanent wave solutions. Mrs. Miller's shop was in an upstairs suite of rooms and I seem to recall that each beautician had her own room with frosted glass halfway up the walls to the ceiling. The beauticians all wore white uniforms and white shoes. Whenever I went, Mrs. Miller would get my sister Jerry and me a small Coca-Cola in the green glass bottle while the permanent wave solution did its work. I remember sometimes we would walk into a back room of the salon which had a wide warehouse-type door that for some reason stayed open to the outdoors. I remember edging carefully to the threshold and looking out on the railroad tracks a full story below. It was very frightening, yet thrilling to a little girl.

My permanent wave – didn't I look snappy?

After the haircut and the shampoo and set, you had to sit under a hair dryer for about a thousand years. There was a large room for the hair dryers which were huge silver helmets on chrome stands. The seats beneath them were black leather arm chairs with chrome tube arms. Most of the chair arms had ashtrays built in. Low glass tables bore stacks of "TV Radio Mirrors," or "Ladies Home Journals" or "Photoplay" magazines. I remember squirming and whining because the metal curlers got very hot from the heat of the dryer.

After the dryer, there was the comb out after which Mama paid Mrs. Miller. I don't remember there being a cash register, just a cash drawer. When our curls were complete, we emerged from the relative darkness of Mrs. Miller's shop to the bright sunlight of the town's streets. It was time to get into Mama's Mercury and drive home to 351 College Drive.

TURTLE EGGS ON WILMINGTON ISLAND

I think everyone has a secret club when you're growing up. Mine was the Bones Club and it lasted far longer than most. Oh, there was that little fling with the Pat Boone Fan Club (remember him?) which met a few times in Eleanor Hendry's garage next door. The big draw for that was that we lit a candle and looked at pictures of Pat Boone from the pages of *Photoplay* or *TV Radio Mirror* magazines. But the club that lasted was the Bones Club.

The founders of the club were my sister Jerry, otherwise known as J-Bones, our neighbor across the lane Terri, otherwise known as T-Bone and me – Hambone. We called ourselves the "Originals." Later members, obviously given a lesser status, were known as the "Commons." We published a newspaper called the *Bones Review*, made up a strict code of behavior, and had our own songs, brazenly plagiarized from *The Baptist Hymnal*. When the hymns from which we stole were sung in Bull Street Baptist Church, Terri, Jerry and I would look at each other and snicker, then sing our Bones Club words to the tune, while, all around us, ardent Christians sang the true words, glorifying God.

Each summer Terri's dad, E.K. Bell, took his wife Cleo and Terri to the General Oglethorpe Hotel on Wilmington Island, Georgia for conferences sponsored by his job. It was a working vacation for him and Terri and Mrs. Bell got to see some new scenery.

Terri was an only child. Jerry and I came from a large family of four girls with many cousins on both sides of the family. I think the three

Originals secretly wanted what the others had – Jerry and I wanted to be only children who got all the attention and Terri longed to be part of a big, noisy family. So we kind of adopted each other and absorbed some of the best of both worlds.

Because Terri didn't want to be alone on Wilmington Island with her parents who were older (probably much younger than I am now,) she was allowed to take friends with her, and Jerry and I were often chosen. We pretended that these trips to the elegant General Oglethorpe Hotel were our annual Bones Club conventions and renamed the hotel the General Bonesythorpe Hotel. We ran around the hotel, pretty much on our own, self-assured little girls of eight or nine with no worries, no thought of kidnappers, or other dangers of any kind. That's simply the way it was to grow up in the 1950's, a glorious, unfettered, simple time. How lucky we were and how different it will be for my children's children.

Mrs. Bell was rather formal and gave Terri the classes and personal attention I craved from my overworked, tired mother. Terri had ballet classes, dolls of every kind and the biggest bedroom in her house. Mrs. Bell didn't joke around but spent every opportunity with us finding teachable moments. I can imagine what a challenge that was because I know how empty-headed I was as a child. But still Mrs. Bell soldiered on, buying classical albums for us to play on Terri's stereo, watching our living room performances, and teaching us the proper way to make a sandwich ("Always get two pieces of bread that are side by side in the loaf so it makes a prettier sandwich, girls.")

One starlit night on Wilmington Island, the three of us girls had finished dinner in the grand hotel dining room (at Mr. Bell's expense!) and Mrs. Bell, normally an inside type, suggested a walk on the beach. I remember it as clearly as I remember yesterday. The islands along Georgia's coast then were pristine and relatively undeveloped. The moon that night was so big and bright that it almost seemed like daylight.

We walked along the water's edge, skittering in and out of the water while Mrs. Bell called to us to examine some shell she'd found or name some constellation in the sky. Suddenly she lowered her voice to a whisper and called the three of us to her side.

"Be very quiet," she cautioned. "Look over there."

Ahead of us on the beach, we saw two large sea turtles lumbering up onto the sands of the beach from the ocean, the tracks of their flippers looking for all the world like tire tracks from a tractor. Breathlessly we watched as the turtles came ashore and dug a pit using their front flippers. Then, slowly, they turned around and using their back flippers, dug a smaller hole for the eggs.

A few moments later, we watched them deposit the eggs into the cavity – small ping pong ball-sized eggs that seemed like hundreds at the time, though probably the number was much smaller.

Finally, their work done, they covered the nest with sand and waddled back out to sea. When the turtles were back in the ocean, we girls gulped and looked to Mrs. Bell for an explanation.

Mrs. Bell taught me many things – an appreciation for classical music, an orderly house, and the finer points of etiquette, but the thing I remember most about her was what she taught me about the cycle of life on that beach.

"You'll never forget this night, girls," was all she said. And over fifty years later, I never have.

CHRISTMAS GIFTS FROM MAMA AND DADDY

I was driving home from work today when the Glen Campbell version of the song "There's No Place like Home for the Holidays" came on the radio. It was on an album (yes 33 and 1/3 rpm!) I inherited from my Mama and Daddy after their passing, and whenever I play it, their faces come to mind. Though I miss them all the time, I never miss them more than at Christmas, a time when we were all at home.

For the first 16 years of my life, home was a parsonage in Gaffney, SC or Savannah, GA. But for the last years of their lives, Mama and Daddy lived on a 33 acre farm in eastern North Carolina. Daddy raised hogs and had goats, turkeys, geese, chickens, and a herd of ponies. Our good friends Randolph and Leon Umphlette farmed the land raising corn and soybeans there.

Every year Daddy had a huge garden and brought Mama prodigious amounts of vegetables to can and freeze. We enjoyed them all winter long. I'm thinking right now of the beautiful jars of canned tomatoes Mama put up year after year, sitting jewel-like on shelves and waiting to be turned into sauces and casseroles of all descriptions. Today when I fix my mama's spaghetti sauce recipe, the best I can do is open a can of Del Monte tomatoes and hope for the best.

Mama was an outstanding, self-effacing cook, mostly self-taught, as her own mother died when she was four. Her fried chicken was legendary and every night, EVERY NIGHT, she prepared a full, hot meal from scratch for my father. She made breakfasts of sausage and eggs every morning, (from the farm, of course) and lunches warmed over from the meal the night before. Every once in a while, she and Daddy would take Tom and me to the McDonald's in the nearby town of Ahoskie and she thought it was a great treat. Now I understand. She was worn out from all that cooking! But it was her gift to us all those years. We never went hungry as long as my Mama was alive.

Daddy's gifts were precious too, but very different. He gave us the gift of joy! I rarely recall seeing my father without a smile on his face or a story to tell, especially when he was with one of his ten grandchildren. He had a couple of brothers who had no children and he always invited them over to spend Christmas with the family. There was never a worry about there being enough food – Mama always had plenty. She'd simply set another couple of places at our already cramped table and sit back quietly to watch the chaos.

Daddy had a funny nickname for everyone. Occasionally on Christmas, he'd walk around with a Santa hat on his head and a handful of cookies or a bite of ham for the grandchildren. He was never happier than when we were all together. After the great day was over, he was always a little sad and glad to get back to his regular routine.

I never really appreciated Daddy until the first year I was married. My new husband had never had the custom of hanging stockings in his family, so he asked Daddy what he should fill mine with, as he knew I was filling a stocking for him. Daddy took him shopping one night to give him some assistance. What he chose surprised and disappointed me at first. On Christmas morning, I opened my stocking to find not the jewelry and trinkets I had expected, but an orange, an apple, a box of a ball and jacks and - horrors – seed-filled raisins, still on the stem! I could barely contain my disappointment. Still, I tried to act pleased, and gamely ate the fruit, although I could never stomach the raisins.

Years later I came to an understanding of what those stocking contents meant. My daddy grew up in the teens and twenties of the last century on a farm with eight brothers and sisters. Fruit and toys were great luxuries to children of his time and in leading my husband to give those to me, Daddy was saying, "Give her the best you can, son." In so doing, he also gave me a little bit of his past.

I've often thought of those rows of canned tomatoes and that stocking so many years ago. On days like today, I remember my Mama and Daddy with great tenderness and long to see them. If I don't get to be with them this Christmas, I'm glad they get to have Christmas in Heaven with the Master.

COUNTRY HAM

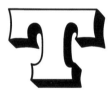

he country ham arrived by truck yesterday and now sits, encased in a cloth bag, in my refrigerator waiting to be sliced. The paper thin slices I cut with my super-duper electric slicer are so good that, even writing this down, I am salivating at the thought.

I was introduced to this most elegant of Southern delicacies at my Mama and Daddy's table. Mama and Daddy, both having grown up in the years just before the Great Depression, had been farm children, and when there was no extra money, there was always plenty of home grown food. At the top of the list was pork in its many varieties.

My daddy was a great connoisseur of pork, and in his later years, raised hogs on his small North Carolina farm. I lived nearby on a peanut/soybean farm and, on occasion, was called into service to help him "trim pigs" as he called it. This was his euphemism for turning young male hogs into young eunuch hogs! They were easier to keep and, I believe, tasted better. If I sit for a minute, I can still hear the pigs squeal and grunt for a few seconds until the operation was over and done with. You'd think that having been witness to such brutality, I'd never want to eat another piece of pork. But like St. Peter in the Bible (Acts 10) I found that all foods were good and never in all the years since have turned down a slice of crisp, salty bacon because of what I saw.

But my most prevalent memory of pork is watching my daddy slice a country ham for my mother's Christmas dinner table. Daddy butchered his own hogs (I even helped out at a couple of hog killings on days so cold you could barely feel your fingers.) First Daddy would carry his rifle back to the hog pen deep in the woods behind the house and kill the hog he'd selected previously. Usually he'd take the carcass to a nearby meat processing plant but then he'd bring the carcass and string it up, head down, on wooden scaffolding. Nearby was a huge black iron cauldron beneath which burned logs of first growth oaks he'd gathered from his woods.

Before beginning, Daddy would have spent what seemed like hours sharpening his butcher knife on a carborundum stone until it was finally honed to a dangerous edge. About this time, cars and pickup trucks would start arriving bearing country boys in bib overalls and wearing gimmee caps. Men and women, boys and girls, loved standing around and talking while the work was going on. Soon the meat which could not be preserved, like tenderloin, was cut up and wrapped for the freezer. Next, chitlin's, livers, knuckles and brains were divided up among the workers. Then the leftover fat was tossed into the kettle to make lard for cooking. What was left over after all the boiling was done were cracklin's, kind of like potato chips but with a ham taste. Daddy put the scraps of leaner meat into sausage casings with lots of pepper, sage and other spices. But the better cuts of meat like ham, shoulders, and sides of bacon were buried in salt in a bin and later hung to cure in the smokehouse.

It was one of these hams that my daddy sliced each Christmas morning. With all of his grandchildren gathered around him watching the delicate operations, Daddy would make the first slice and hold it up to his nose for a whiff. He'd shake his head and wink at us with that dimpled grin of his to let us know what a treat lay ahead of us. My sisters and I would be scurrying around in the kitchen while our children would be looking surreptitiously at the ham.

In my mind's eye, I can see my son Tom, a lad of three or four, cupping his hands to receive a taste from Daddy who was slicing the ham minutes before dinner. Daddy would peel off a slice so thin you could almost see through it, and place it gingerly in Tom's mouth.

"Don't tell your Mama," he'd say, and Tom would grin and run off, his mouth still savoring the salty delicacy. I pretended not to hear and waited for my turn to do the same. He'd put a piece of ham smaller than Tom's serving in my hand, smile at me and say, "Don't tell your Mama."

I didn't. It was always our little secret. The ham I'll serve this Christmas will be delicious though Daddy didn't raise it or prepare it. But I'll appreciate it all the more because of the time I had with my mama and daddy here on this earth. And if I can, I'll try to slip a little piece into my grandchildren's mouths and whisper, "Don't tell your Mama."

THE BASEMENT

I've been trying to clean up my basement lately, in preparation for returning all the Christmas things to their storage bins for another year. It's a large unfinished basement with no walls covering the entire footprint of our house. There is a corner for Paul's workshop and all his stuff like circular saws and other things for which I don't have names – big things. There's an area dedicated to my sewing machine with a large L-shaped table, a big dress form (to suit "generously-sized" women like me) and bins of quilt fabrics, sewing notions and patterns.

There's a seating area with a couch and several chairs as well as a sturdy wooden nursery table and four chairs bought from Forest Hills Baptist Church when they were getting rid of old things. Two end tables Paul's daddy made are there, too, as well as a crooked table my grandmother made out of rough pine boards and painted fire engine red. It stood for years in the unheated bathroom in her old farmhouse. It's as ugly and rough as can be but I wouldn't part with it for millions.

There's a large television and walls of bookshelves loaded with books of all descriptions, videos and DVDs, toys and games, and photo albums from fifty years ago. Finally there's an area where junk is stored (kind of like the lumber room in Scrooge's house in *A Christmas Carol*.) As I said, it's an unfinished basement and the walls are rough and unpainted. The floor is concrete except for a few scraps of rugs I've placed here and there to add warmth. It's altogether different from the finished, well-ordered rooms above it. Yet, curiously, it's probably my favorite place to be in the house.

Here is where I go to create. I set up my quilt frame or sew, or I take a yellow legal pad and write stories. Sometimes I grade papers down there. But most of all I'm surrounded by things from my past. On one shelf there's a large Mason jar containing about a quart of dirt I dug up from my Mama and Daddy's farm in Gates County, NC, just before they sold it. That land was sacred ground to me and I always wanted to have a piece of it with me. In another corner is the crib I slept in as a baby, now filled with cast-off dolls and stuffed animals from when my own children were small.

On the shelves are left-behind toys, the detritus of Christmases past. If I close my eyes, I can still hear the shouts of joy as Tom, then Katherine, and finally Caroline, discovered them under the Christmas tree, a half-eaten plate of cookies nearby as proof that Santa had been there. When I'm not using the dress-form, I hang one of my Daddy's old sport coats on it and can pretend he's there watching over me. It's a dreadful brown polyester coat straight out of the seventies, but he wore it and wore it and I can't bear to part with it. There's a crocheted afghan he brought my mother in the hospital after she had her stroke. She couldn't communicate with him anymore but he loved her so and wanted to keep her warm and safe as he always had. So he brought her the cream colored afghan and wrapped her in it in her hospital bed.

I've asked my children to take some of their things home with them but they put me off. They can't be bothered with them. In fact, they've often told me to throw them away. But somehow, I can't. That would nullify all the memories they call to mind. It would be like saying "all those Christmases I helped Santa to create weren't good enough to hold onto. The memories of my Mama and Daddy don't matter. The years we spent on that farm in Gates County didn't matter. Only today matters."

Somehow I can't do it. I can't bring myself to throw all those things away. So I hold onto the toys and Little Golden Books and afghans and memories for another year and occasionally go down to the basement to clean it up.

SISTERS

aul and I are having visitors - my twin sister Jerry and her husband Larry are coming to spend the weekend with us. I'm so happy to have them here because the four of us have a lot of fun together. I'm lucky to have three sisters. I don't get to be with Louise or Martha Jean so much but when we all get together, we really have stories to tell. Growing up in a house full of women was pretty hectic and a lot of fun. There was always a boy coming to pick up Louise or Martha Jean and Jerry and I were always making up some club or business – the Bones Club or our many playhouse businesses – the restaurants we had on our toy stove, our used comic book or lemonade stands. (Our parents and the mailman were our best customers.)

When I was growing up, our Father was pastor of large city churches and our Mother usually accompanied him to meetings, class socials, and church programs so our older sisters were often tasked with babysitting their younger sisters, not always their favorite thing to do. I remember one night in particular when they were watching us. Louise drove Martha Jean, a couple of their friends and Jerry and me to Our House, a local restaurant located on Victory Drive. Victory is a beautiful avenue in Savannah lined in the center with magnificent palm trees. Louise was driving our daddy's 1951 burgundy Mercury Sport Sedan with the suicide doors. An anachronism even then, it was a charming reflection of our daddy's fun-loving side. He LOVED cars! The four older girls were at their most devastatingly beautiful, their long hair windblown, not a care in the world. Pulling up to a stoplight, I glanced over to the other lane of traffic and saw a carful of teenage boys looking at my sisters with big grins on their faces. The light changed and Louise pulled away from the stoplight just as one of the boys yelled to her, "Hey babes, what's your story?" They clearly couldn't figure why four gorgeous teenagers were saddled with two little brats. Jerry and I stuck out our tongues at the boys and slid down in the seat. Now this is not an important story but it reminds me that my sisters and I have been together for a very long time and we've had lots of adventures together. I'm thankful today for my sisters and all the fun we've had.

THE BOOKS THAT CHANGED MY LIFE

ixty years ago or so, I was in Miss Bess Bruce's first grade class at Central Elementary School in Gaffney, SC, a two story white clapboard building probably at least fifty years old already and next door to my home. Two of the main features I remember from the building were the impressive tall swings on metal poles sunk in concrete and the metal pipe attached to the side of the building which served as a fire escape. We used to climb inside the pipe as far as we dared and slide down. Our class was in the "new" portion of the school, a one-story brick portion from the early fifties. I remember our room had low tables and we children were given pegboards to play with. The idea was to insert tiny houses, trees, and cars into the holes to make our own little village – quite a different educational beginning from the test-driven forced march children are started on today.

We did have a textbook, *Our New Friends*, which led me into the adventures of Dick and Jane and their little sister Sally. They lived with their parents in an apparently all-white town with their dog Spot and kitty Puff. Dick and Jane had many adventures – building with blocks at school, having birthday parties and leaving toys out in the rain. Mother and Father never lost their tempers and everything turned out well in the end. I moved on to Charles Ellis Elementary in Savannah, GA where Mrs. Cephise Thompson introduced me to my next reader, The new *More Friends and Neighbors* in which I learned of Mother Bird building a nest in Nancy's mailbox and Nancy and her friend from the city riding the pony named Sam to Uncle Dick's store at Four Corners. Each reader had a list of vocabulary words to learn as well as word attack skills for the teacher to use. These, of course, meant nothing to me. I was more interested in the colorful pictures at the top of each page.

Now of course, I rarely read books with pictures – the pictures are all in my mind. Somewhere along the way, Mrs. Thompson or Mrs. Guerry or any one of the other wonderful teachers I had through the years opened the door for me into a wonderful world where I found *The Mirrors of Castle Doone* (my first mystery,) *The Secret Garden, Peter Pan, To Kill a Mockingbird, Romeo and Juliet, A Christmas Carol*, or *Bleak House*. Books allow me to live other lives in other places that otherwise I'd never know. I can be Augustus McCrae, the wonderful cowboy in *Lonesome Dove* who followed a herd north. I can be Scarlett O'Hara, the strong, impetuous, headstrong heroine of *Gone with the Wind* or Matthew Shardlake, the kind and compassionate hunchback lawyer of C.J. Sansom's many layered masterful detective stories.

In addition to changing and entertaining me, books have educated me. The biography of *John Adams* by David McCullough taught me more about the early days of our country than I ever learned in a classroom. (Sorry, Mrs. Boney, my history teacher!) I love photo essays such as one I recently discovered, *Civil War Battlefields Then and Now*. I have learned about the sport of thoroughbred racing through Laura Hillenbrand's great *Seabiscuit*.

When I was a child, we had a modest home library, filled mainly with maroon covered ancient copies of *Encyclopedia America*, a beautifully bound six-volume set of Sandburg's *Abraham Lincoln*, a large collection of Bibles and Biblical commentaries, as well as a few dusty copies of such books as *The Bobbsey Twins* or *Nancy Drew* series; *Cherry Ames, Student Nurse*; Defoe's *Robinson Crusoe* and Du Maurier's *Rebecca*. I recall hiding in the upstairs hall closet of our house in Savannah to find a quiet place amidst the out of season clothes to read, escaping for the moment my mother's call to pick up my toys or wash the dishes. Even now, sometimes I still long to hide myself away like that to read.

I'll never understand the appeal of newfangled contraptions like Kindles or Nooks, as my husband does. I prefer the heft and feel of paper, the smell of dusty books opened for the first time in years, the soft leather bindings of old volumes standing at attention on my shelves. Books have always been magic carpets for me.

I love children's books – who wouldn't want to be transported to Victorian England and fly with *Peter Pan* or to Prince Edward Island to live the life of *Anne of Green Gables*. I devoured all of Grimms' or Andersens' fairy tales and fell in love with my very first mystery novel, *The Mirrors of Castle Doone* by Elizabeth Kyle.

The Savannah Public Library

When I was a little child growing up in Savannah, GA, one of my very favorite things to do was to go to the public library. The Savannah Public Library on Bull Street was a massive building of stone with huge Ionic columns in front.

Inside the tall doors was a beautiful tile floor leading up to a paneled wooden circulation desk. To the right was The Children's Room, the most magical place ever. The walls were covered with a painted mural featuring characters from literature, I believe. Helped by the head librarian, a woman I knew only as Miss McCall, I came weekly to enter another universe. My particular favorites at one point were the fairy tales collections. I read every book in that section. Then I graduated to mysteries, *The Mirrors of Castle Doone* being the one I remember most. (A couple of years ago, I found a copy on Amazon, bought and reread it. Instantly I was transported back to 1957.) Miss McCall took my large tan library card each week, stamped it and congratulated me on my selections. Occasionally she'd introduce me to a new genre and I'd be off on another flight of fancy. Through her gentle guidance, I became a lifelong reader with such affection for books that I always have at least two going at once.

These were some of the children's books that started me on my love of reading:

- *The Secret Garden* - started me on my love of gardening

- *The Wonderful Wizard of Oz* - witches, munchkins, flying monkeys? Of course

- *The Wind in The Willows* - I wanted to be as unafraid as Toad was

- *Peter Pan* - I held on to this book long after I left childhood which I'd found to be so brief and precious

- *Horton Hatches the Egg* (and a whole host of other Dr. Seuss books) taught me about responsibility

- *Grimm's Fairy Tales* - short, magical stories in which the princess always married the prince

- *Mystery in the Old Red Barn* and other mysteries by Helen Fuller Orton - I wanted to be a kid detective!

- *To Kill a Mockingbird* – As a child of the South, I grew up with the typical prejudices that came along with that era. I judged people first for the color of their skin and the appearance they made rather than, as Dr. Martin Luther King, Jr. said, "the content of their character." It's to my everlasting shame that I admit this. But this book made such a difference in my outlook that, slowly, gradually, my feelings began to change. That's the importance a well written book can bring to a generation of readers.

- *The Travels of Babar* - an elephant king and queen who wore crowns and had adventures

- *The Secret of Red Gate Farm* and other Nancy Drew mysteries - I wanted a roadster and the freedom to solve mysteries with my boyfriend Ned

- *Hitty, Her First Hundred Years* - a doll's story helped me gain an appreciation for history

- *Little Women* - where I learned I was to become a writer. I wanted to write in a garret like Jo

- *The Bobbsey Twins Series* - I was a twin so these books were naturals

- *Eloise* - My sister Louise, who had a flair for the dramatic, acted it out for me.

- *The Complete Tales of Uncle Remus* - as a Georgia girl, this was must read material

- *A Christmas Carol* - I have read it every year since I was about 10. Scrooge's transformation is wonderful magic every time

- *Gone With the Wind* - again, no Georgia girl could NOT read this

- *My Friend Flicka* - started me on my lifelong love affair with horses

- *Uncle Wiggly's Automobile* - seriously - a rabbit with an old lady nurse - Miss Jane? I loved it.

- and finally *Our New Friends* , my Dick and Jane reader from first grade - the book that started it all.

DADDY'S HANDS

I woke up this morning at my usual time (5:06) and had been dreaming of my daddy's hands! He was retelling, in my dream, a story he'd told me many times while he was alive. He was in an oyster bar and a young boy was shelling oysters for him as they did back in the fifties. The boy took one look at my daddy's big hands and said, "Mister, was you a prize fighter?" The contrast between prize fighter and minister struck Daddy as funny. I've thought about his hands all day and wished I had a hug from him.

THOUGHTS AFTER A FUNERAL

I went to a funeral today for my brother in law Hines Adams, who married my sister Martha Jean over fifty years ago. The service was held in a small white-framed country church where Hines was pastor. It was a beautiful spring day and the funeral had all the earmarks of a typical Southern funeral - a minister in robes who read Scripture and offered prayers and comforting words, little granddaughters dressed in flowing white dresses, lots of cousins and other family members including my three sisters (all of us old women now in our 60s and 70s,) and sweet hymns. As we sat in the wooden pews, the silence was punctuated by the rhythmic tick tock of a lovely antique clock on the wall near the family. After the service, the ladies of the church prepared a typical

Southern funeral meal for us - fried chicken, salty ham slices, potato salad, deviled eggs, pimiento cheese sandwiches, cakes and pies and lots of sweet tea. There were reminiscences and laughter and a few tears. After lunch we moved to the lawn of the church where we looked at who had a new car, watched the children run and told more family stories. We lingered a good while, reluctant to leave each other to go our separate ways. Who knows when we'd see one another again?

Last night Paul and I went to the family cemetery in Gates County where my parents rest today and where Hines is buried. I was struck by how many visits I'd paid to that cemetery over the years - too many to count. I remember walking there with my Mama and Daddy and telling them that it was where I wanted to be buried someday. I think it is a comforting thing to know where you'll meet the Lord.

I thought about my mama who had grown up in Kentucky over a hundred years ago, and my daddy who had grown up in Gates County, near his final resting place. I saw the corner (Eason's Crossroads) where Daddy told me he'd worked at a country store as a lad. Now it's an empty lot. My Father has been gone nearly 28 years, my Mother 18. I saw the high school where I used to teach, my parents' old house, a farmhouse that had been built by my great grandfather Ephraim Morris, and the fields surrounding it where Daddy used to plow a big garden with his little pony Dusty.

This morning on the way to the funeral, Paul and I ate breakfast in the Tarheel, a country diner near Gatesville. While we were there, two of my former students from 30 years ago came up to me and said hello. I love that about living in the country - you seem to matter to people because there are so few people around. So everyone counts. Even the organist at the funeral was a former student of mine. It was amazing to see them all now grown and middle aged and contributing to the community.

I thought of all these things this morning while sitting in the church listening to time passing as measured by the ticking of that clock. And I thought of how important we are to each other. I thought of all the children

I've taught through the years, of all my friends from Chowan College and Meredith College, from Savannah High School and Hampton High School and Richard Arnold Jr. High School and even Charles Ellis Elementary and even a few from Gaffney SC, where I discovered America as my daddy used to say. I thought of old friends from all the churches I have attended and all the jobs I have ever held. And most especially, I thought of all my wonderful family - sisters, brothers, nieces, nephews, daughters and son and grandchildren from the oldest to the very youngest - those beautiful faces!

And then I thought of this - each of those people touched my life in some way and I am better for it. Though there are few people alive today who even remember my Father and Mother's names, I remember them and all of you who have been in my life. Thank you for any kindnesses you have shown to me and my family. Thank you for touching my life. As long as I am alive, you will never be forgotten.

MY FORTIETH COLLEGE REUNION

In my real life, I'm a 70 year old wife, mother of three, grandmother of eight adorable grandchildren (I've got pictures!) and retired school teacher. But for about 48 hours this weekend, I was transported through some odd space/time continuum to the years 1968-1970, the years when I was a student at Meredith College in Raleigh, NC. (I had transferred in from Chowan which was then a two-year college.)

It's a funny thing about going to a girls' school (nowadays they call them "women's' colleges" but I'm Southern and old school, so "girls' school" it will be for me.) There's just a special bond you develop when living with girls. The friendships I made there in the latter days of the Vietnam War and the tumultuous Sixties are still vibrant today.

We gathered several times during the course of those golden 48 hours, once at a classmate's home (Thanks Ruth – you are still rockin'), once at the college for a luncheon, and once at a restaurant for dinner out, some of us with spouses, some without.

As I drove back today to northern Virginia from Raleigh, I had a lot of time to think. So I thought, - I need to do my lesson plans, decide which pile of laundry to do first, and try not to think about my appointment tomorrow to get a crown. Meanwhile, the one feeling that I couldn't sweep away was a sense of lightheartedness. It was as if all the worries, and heartaches, aches and pains, losses and burdens of the past 40 years were swept away…had never happened. For 48 hours, I was once again an innocent 19-year-old girl – My first sweetheart hadn't yet hurt me, I hadn't yet made the D in Old English, my parents were still alive and taking care of me. I hadn't yet gone through the pain of childbirth and the pangs of setting my three children free. All these burdens were mysteriously and temporarily lifted from my shoulders.

Curiously, I seemed to see the same reaction in all the girls I saw seated at our Class of 70 tables. I say "girls" but, of course, anyone who saw us would call us "old women." We had all changed physically in some fashion. Most of us had white or graying hair; some chose to cover it up – I know, I know…it's a losing battle but I'm still fighting it. To listen to us talk, you heard descriptions of the typical ailments common to all who are lucky enough to get older. We creak, we have arthritis, and we're slower. Our waistlines have expanded in direct correlation to our years on this planet.

Around our table at Meredith were women who had experienced the gamut of what life had to offer – marriage (some of us more than once!), the birth of our children, the death of our parents, sadly for some the death of a child or a spouse. Some had children who are physically challenged in some way so that they are still giving primary care (Jean – I'm in awe of you – you are such a strong person.) - All of us were women who had experienced successes in life and a few failures. We changed the way the world looked at women - We owned car dealerships, managed companies, became executives at corporations, became lawyers, advocated social change, taught generations of schoolchildren, and most importantly, managed homes and raised children.

Our class, known throughout our history as the class who didn't have time to write notes to the alumnae magazine, or show up for class reunions, finally found time – there were some 40 or 50 of us present this year. Finally, with our children raised, and our parents either deceased or stable for the moment, at last there was time for us. So we came and we laughed and we hugged and we came away from it realizing that what we had at our little girls' school was something very precious, something that not many people can say they have ever experienced. There is a bond among us, a band that wraps around us like a cord of iron, so that no matter where we go or how far away from 1970 we travel, we will always be Meredith girls.

PJ spoke eloquently of the great relief it was to unburden herself among us with no need to put up a brave front; Many of us spoke of our faith in God, something that would not have come up in our younger days; it was as though we finally realized that we were not immortal and that some thought must be given to who we are and what we leave behind.

We spoke of past hurts and present pains, of the joys of grandchildren or the freedom of retirement. We hugged each other, seemingly unaware that our waistlines had expanded over the years, or our faces had become careworn and lined or our hair streaked with gray (or completely white in some cases!)

None of that mattered because for 48 golden hours we were 19 again, carefree, young and trying to decide which door to open first. We were wearing white dresses and carrying a daisy chain on our shoulders. We were sitting cross-legged on dorm floors, our hair in curlers, opening a box of home-baked goodies from Mom (or the Nonie Gravett circle from our church – remember that, Cindy?) Oh, what a glorious two days they were.

When the final event broke up last night, we were reluctant to tear ourselves away from each other. We kept posing for one more picture, telling one more hilarious tale, each one beginning with "remember when...?" I was the very last one to leave, my car filled with boxes of memories to be stored in my basement for another time, my heart filled with emotion over the depth of feeling I have for these women. At my age, I know there is a possibility I will never see some of them again in life. And yet this weekend, and forty years ago and all the time in between, they have made such an impact on me – changed me for the better.

I have not made much of a ripple in my 70 years of life. I have hardly traveled beyond the small circle of a few southeastern states and never held positions of influence or power on the job. I have never made a great deal of money. But God has blessed me with a circle of friends from Meredith College who still see me as they did 40 years ago. They still love and support me and wish only the best for me as I do for them. I may not have much in the way of material wealth, but in my friendships from Meredith, I am richer than Croesus.

MAMA

nce upon a time, a long time ago on a farm in Kentucky, a tiny baby girl was born to a tall, handsome farmer and his wife. The girl was the sixth of seven girls born to this couple and her mother would die when the little girl was only four. To a farmer who needed sons to help on the farm, another girl must have been a bit of a disappointment. But these two were my Grandparents and the baby was my Mother. If my Granddaddy was sad about having all girls, I never knew it.

Theodosia as a baby

Her name was Theodosia, an old fashioned name if ever there was one. She was named for her Uncle Theodore and she hated that name as long as she lived. My Daddy always called her Doty (that's the way she spelled it) and that's the name she preferred, but I think Daddy liked calling her Theodosia, too. I like the name. It sounds romantic and from another era, as was my mother.

She only held a paying job for a couple of weeks in her life and hated it. Her calling was to be my father's wife and the mother of us four girls. For a woman who had no living mother to model herself after, she did a wonderful job of being a mother to us. An outstanding Southern cook, she could fry chicken so light and golden that it almost floated to your plate. She was an excellent seamstress and made most of the clothes for my sisters and me. I imagine that was a real help financially because my Father, a Baptist minister, never made a lot of money. I have many memories of seeing her leaning over her old Singer, her mouth full of pins, and a Simplicity pattern on the sewing table beside her. She always dressed Jerry and me alike (twins) so when she'd make one dress, she'd always have to turn around and make another one just like it. Many years, on the night before Easter, she was up well past midnight putting the finishing touches on our Easter dresses.

We always had new dresses for Easter with plenty of starched crinolines underneath and new polished leather shoes. One year mine had an ankle strap which I loved. We always had corsages at Easter - orchids for Mama and rosebuds or carnations for us girls. Daddy always had a red rosebud tucked in the buttonhole of his lapel.

Almost the whole time my own children were growing up, we went out for Sunday dinner; but that almost never happened with my mother. We'd return from Sunday services to the succulent smell of a beef roast with potatoes and carrots, green beans which she'd canned, fresh tomatoes from Daddy's garden and a bowl of strawberry shortcake. I never gave it a thought back then how much effort it took to provide for us the way she did.

My Mother was the last of the Southern ladies. She wore hats to church, was always a stay at home mom, never had a girls' night out as far as I knew and never needed one. She simply loved being my Daddy's wife and our mother. She taught Sunday School, volunteered at our schools, gave us piano lessons (which in my case, never took!) taught us how to sew and cook (which, in my case, never took!) reminded us to hold in our stomachs, speak in a measured tone, do our homework, and remember who we were.

She was a sweet, quiet presence, a kind of satellite around the Jupiter of my dad. She rarely gave advice, discussed politics or expressed opinions. It was something Southern women of her generation just didn't do. What she did do was to listen to us. Night after night I stood by her side drying dishes and pouring out my heart to her over some boy I was "in love with" or some trouble I was having with my history project. She never really solved the problems for me but, in being present all the time, in letting me talk through my problems, she allowed me to solve them and develop the confidence that I needed to carry on. Her personal history was something of a mystery because she was reluctant to talk about herself. She wanted Daddy to be center stage or she wanted to watch her children and grandchildren. She was an amazing cook and homemaker who made the old home place a safe haven all the years of my life. As we both grew older, we became closer and shared lots of interests. We watched "Days of Our Lives" together, we went shopping at Belk's, or she tried, albeit unsuccessfully, to teach me to cook. Whenever I left Daddy and her with a hug and went home to my own family, I left refreshed and strengthened to face the situation there. At age 76, she suffered a massive stroke which left her paralyzed on her right side and unable to speak for the rest of her life. Our daddy died from a heart attack right after that - on his way to see her in the rehab unit, he struck an 18 wheeler truck and died instantly. She lived another 10 years that way in my twin sister's home - Jerry dressed her, bathed her and gave her a life of activity few women in her condition could hope for. At the end when she had to go into a nursing home, Jerry brought her coffee in the mornings on our mother's china teacups poured out of our mother's silver coffee pot. Jerry was God's final grace gift to Mama.

When this Mother's Day rolls around, I'll be thinking of my mother as always, not with sadness, but with gratitude for the simple, uncomplicated, patient and lovely life she led. And I'll wear a white rose in her memory as she always did for her mother on Mother's Day.

NO ROOM FOR A PUMP ORGAN

y sister Jerry just called me - said she was downsizing and wondered if any of my children or I wanted our old pump organ. None of her children wanted it, she said, and she hated to junk it. I was immediately overcome by a feeling of such sadness that tears came to my eyes.

My Daddy was a great one for bringing home old furniture and fixing it up, polishing it, restoring it and making it look beautiful. My sisters and I all have pieces in our homes that he brought into our childhood home back in the fifties - marble topped dressers, music stands, washstands. Paul and I have a beautiful grandfather clock that he brought home one time. All of these pieces he bought for almost nothing and lovingly brought back to life. I can see him now in our garage rubbing them down with steel wool or a cloth or applying stain with a brush. He took somebody's castoffs and made them magnificent again. Now all these years later, they have the patina of age and pride of place in our homes.

But the pump organ was always a little different. It was out of time before he even brought it home. A tall, kind of awkward Victorian wooden organ, it had shelves on which you could place candlesticks. You lifted the music stand for a little cubbyhole where you could store your hymnal and a few pieces of sheet music. There were two foot pedals that you had to pump to fill the bellows with air in order to create the sound. Above the ivory keys of the keyboard were round stops you pulled or pushed in to make the various tones.

To be frank, Mama hated it. It was old timey from the minute Daddy unloaded it from the truck. She wouldn't even bring it into the house. So it went into our playhouse where we played at church and practiced our piano lessons on it - at least Jerry did. Mostly I just listened and sang along, holding my doll baby and wearing dress-up clothes.

Now that I'm all grown up, I know why Daddy brought it home. It must have reminded him of the little country church where he'd grown up, the church I attended as a young married woman. There at Middle Swamp Baptist Church, he'd given his life to God surrounded by his father and mother, brothers and sisters. The church is there still in the middle of farm fields. It burned down early in this century but the community loved it so much they rebuilt it exactly as it was before the fire. I go there at least once a year for the old family reunions and I can almost see my daddy as a young boy sitting on a pew.

But as Jerry said, people worship differently now. Instead of pump organs, there are sound systems and projection screens and almost no one sings from a hymnal. They follow along as words and beautiful pictures are projected high above them on a screen. There are orchestra instruments now - flutes, violins, oboes, cellos, saxophones, trumpets and French horns to accompany the great choirs in our churches.

So I imagine no one will want to take the old organ. Even I can't - as sentimental as I am; I know there's no room for it in our home. And so a little more of my connection with the past, with my Daddy, will pass away.

I am a realist. I know that our lives move too fast to stop long enough to sit at a pump organ and pedal to make a chord. It's too simple; the sound it produces is no longer appealing to our ears. But just for a moment, just for a few tender moments, it would be sweet to sit by my Daddy's side and hear Jerry play the old pump organ again.

I HATE THIS DATE

I hate this date. I have hated it for the past twenty-seven years. Twenty-seven years ago, I was a housewife with three children – Tom – 15, Katherine - 8 and Caroline – 5. I was at home caring for Caroline who was sick with strep when I got one of the worst phone calls of my life. A nurse from a hospital in Rocky Mount called to let me know my daddy had been in an automobile accident.

"Let me put the doctor on," she said.

Then some faceless doctor got on the line and proceeded to tell me that they'd gotten my name from a card in Daddy's wallet. I was the only family member they could reach. He proceeded to tell me a long string of things that had happened which basically boiled down to this –my daddy had possibly had a heart attack and plowed into an eighteen wheeler truck. I had to ask him if my daddy was all right. Only then did he tell me, "He didn't make it." I then had to call my sisters and my daddy's siblings and relay the awful news. I will never forget the heart-rending wail of my sister Louise who was at work as a social worker when I told her, "Our daddy died."

My sisters and I had just been through a horrendous five month period during which our mother had suffered a massive stroke and was completely paralyzed on one side. My sister Martha Jean had predicted something bad was about to happen to Mama right before her stroke, but in my dismissive way, I refused to believe it. Mama would live another ten years after the stroke but never utter another word. My sister Jerry and I had been taking weekly turns sitting with her as we tried to help her in her rehabilitation. It happened to be Jerry's week when Daddy died, so she had the awful task of relaying to our mother the news that her husband of over fifty years was dead. We weren't even sure she understood us, so profoundly was she handicapped by the stroke.

We learned a few days later when we held Daddy's funeral that the love she felt could break through her speechlessness. She hadn't even come home in the five months since her stroke but we were determined, even against her medical team's wishes that our mother would be at our daddy's funeral. And somehow, with all four of us girls pulling together, we got her there.

As we rolled her into the church to see Daddy for the first time in the beautiful yet terrible mahogany coffin, she had no reaction…at first. Then we turned her to the side that had not been affected by the stroke and she saw him in his awful state – I just cannot forget her terrible moan. That was literally the first time we knew she understood what had happened to our daddy.

We struggled for quite a while after that. Eventually, Jerry became our mother's permanent caregiver in her home. God bless Jerry and Larry always for that. They gave Mama as meaningful a life as possible given the circumstances. Mama died January of 2000 from another stroke, but her death was more of a release from all the years when her body had imprisoned her.

The pressure was too much for my husband at that time. He left soon after that. I wish him well. My four sisters and I grew closer after the terrible year. We were all we had left, except for some wonderful memories. So all the other days of the year except for June 3rd, I think about those – the way my daddy could tell a joke; how he loved a big garden; the feel of a big bear hug from him when times were tight, as he used to say; the way he gave everybody a nickname; the way he led our family spiritually.

It was a hard time for me and, because of that, I will never, ever like June 3. But oh, what a wonderful Daddy I had for 77 years. That's enough.

I HEARD MY MOTHER'S VOICE

Last night I heard my mother speak again. She came to me in a dream as she does occasionally. My mother's voice was stilled forever by a massive stroke twenty-seven years ago and, overnight, her sweet, reserved Southern tones became a memory. She lived for another ten years after the stroke but never spoke again.

My youngest child Caroline, now 31, has no memory of her but one - she remembers sitting in her Nana's lap and rubbing Nana's thumb while sucking on her own finger - her comfort position. My middle child Katherine remembers Mama telling Daddy not to slip the grandchildren Fig Newtons or thin slices of country ham right before dinner. My oldest child Tom, always a quiet, sober sort, never was much of a talker himself, so he's kept his memories of her to himself.

But I remember what Mama told me of the time she kept Tom as a baby while I taught school. They took walks together - Tom toddling to pick up apples that fell from the trees in my parents' backyard on the farm - apples that she later turned into an applesauce so pink and sweet it was like nectar from Heaven. She used to hold Tom in her lap in the same old recliner I have in my basement while she watched "Days of Our Lives." She and Daddy took Tom with them to Rountree & Riddick, the little country grocery store nearby for a "Co-cola."

I still have a few grainy tape recordings of her urging a reluctant two-year old Tom to talk and "tell Mama what we did today." Her voice is Southern and tender and loving. As a young woman, I worked hard to make mine different from hers. I wanted to be smart and sassy and funny. There was never any of that in my mother's voice. Most days I go along never remembering how sweet and tender and quiet was my mother's voice. But every once in a while, she comes to me in a welcome dream, and then I remember. Oh, how I remember.

MY DAY AT THE SPA, OR "A MULE IN HORSE HARNESS"

y wonderful husband Paul gave me a day at the spa for my Christmas present one year. What with one thing and another, I just wasn't able to go all winter and spring. So I finally decided to go one day after school (I was a teacher.) It was quite an experience. I got there in the morning and changed into a thick robe emblazoned with the Elizabeth Arden insignia and was guided to the "relaxation room," a large rectangular room surrounded by deeply cushioned banquettes. The lighting was low, very low, with maybe a couple of 25 watt bulbs in gigantic chandeliers and two or three of those fake candles that run on batteries but look like flames. Curiously, there were tables of thick women's magazines in the center. No

way could you read in that light, but I guess you could fan yourself if the robes got too hot.

Anyhow, soon the first stage of the day began when Petya, a Bulgarian woman whose tiny stature masked the strength in her hands, called me to the massage room. She introduced herself and gave me a bone crushing handshake. She instructed me to get on the table face down. You have to put your face in this hole and let your arms flop down. In the background soft flute music is playing. Apparently birds are in the room too because you hear them chirping every once in a while. Anyway, she then proceeded to pile lots of heavy warm things all over me. You can't tell what it is because the light is so low in this room too, but I think they were rocks she'd gotten out of the river. Anyway, then she greased me up and through some mystical movements, turned all my bones and muscles to complete jelly. Oh my gosh – that little girl had the strongest hands I have ever seen. If I had worked that hard for fifty minutes, I'd have been exhausted. She wasn't even breathing hard, though. In fact, she might have even gone to sleep, because I definitely heard snoring one time in that room and I know it couldn't have been me. I don't snore. You could ask Paul.

Next was the facial – I wasn't as wild about this – the "facialist" was a big intimidating woman named Aziza who, unlike Petya, spoke loudly and had a tendency to put her hands over my nose, then tell me to take a deep breath – uh, kinda hard, Aziza, when your hand's over my nose. Anyway, she then turned on a steam machine and pointed it toward my face for, like, thirty minutes and greased me up again. I was already pretty slick from the massage. It's a wonder I didn't slide off the table. Then she took a socket wrench and began pressing it down on my face – hard!

Aziza: "Whiteheads."

Me: "OWWWWWWWW!"

After that it was time for her to do a little face painting. I think she said this was a "mask," only she spelled it "masque" so she could charge more. After that she took some wet towels out of the microwave and proceeded to wrap them on my face where they stayed until the epidermis had burned off, I guess. Then she wiped all the mess off and declared me "finished."

At this point Aziza took me to the "relaxation room" where I got lunch, a salad and bread and butter. I was pretty hungry after all that relaxing, so I polished it off pretty quickly and tried to read in the dim light. Soon they called me to the nail area where I got first, a pedicure, and then a manicure. Best part of that was the massage chair. Heated. Rolling. Massage. 'Nuff said.

The final stage was "make-up application." A girl dressed all in black who appeared to be about 13 then proceeded to sit me in a chair and roll out about forty brushes on a black towel. She took one look at me, sized me up for the old lady that I am and went for the extra quick version. I'm sure she was thinking "What's the use?" So she pulled out a few tubes of stuff, a couple of colored pencils and applied them with a heavy hand. For the final flourish, she brushed on a slick coat of WHITE lip gloss. Then with a TA-DA look on her face she handed me the large square mirror.

Me: "Thanks. Looks nice.

Me (in my head): "Lord, I really do look like a greased pig."

I did buy a bottle of nail polish. That looked really nice although as Que, the nail technician said, "Your nails too short to work with."

Anyhow, I came home, took one more look at myself in the mirror, and took a shower to get all the grease and make-up off. I had wanted to seem like the kind of girl who has regular spa treatments with exciting events to go to afterwards. But all I could think of was what Mammy said to Scarlett and Rhett in *Gone with the Wind* when they came home from their honeymoon. She said they could "give ourselves airs and get ourselves all rigged up like we were race horses but we were just mules in horse harness and we didn't fool anybody."

A LOVE LETTER TO AMERICA

ear America,

I have loved you for over half a century now and I thought it was about time I told you so in a love letter. I've spent almost every waking moment within your loving arms except for a couple of weeks when Paul and I traveled to Europe so it's hard for me to imagine being anywhere else on your birthday. In fact, when I married Paul twenty-four years ago, one of the delights I discovered was that I'd be living in the Washington, DC area.

Today after twenty-four years of living here in your capital, I still thrill to the sight of the monuments Americans have erected to you so proudly. Crossing the bridge by the Tidal Basin, I still get a frisson of pride when I see the grand Lincoln Memorial looming ahead. And the Washington Monument, the White House, the Jefferson Memorial, the imposing buildings of the Smithsonian scattered around the Mall bring such a feeling of pride in me that I am half embarrassed to admit it.

Then I reflect that Washington is only a tiny part of your glories. For, America, you are so much more than your capital. You are the farm country of North Carolina where I used to live. You are the salt-of-the-earth people who befriended me then and helped me settle on a twenty-five acre Gates County peanut farm. You are the tall buildings of Chicago and New York, magnificent evidence of our engineering prowess and belief in the future. You are the rocky shores of Maine and California and the sandy beaches of Carolina and Georgia and Florida. You are the wheat fields of Kansas and the cattle grazing on Texas acres.

I love you America for the simple idea on which you were born – that I'm as good and important as anyone else on the face of the earth; that Freedom is a non-negotiable concept and that we, your children, will do whatever it takes to ensure that Freedom prospers around the world. I love you, America, for the idea that "We the People" are the holders of the reins of power, not some king or queen whose only qualification is that he or she was born into a certain family. I love that you take as your Presidents men (and someday women) of all races, creeds, religions, and backgrounds. Our leaders have come from the marbled halls of great wealth and tiny, hand-hewn log cabins and, in your sight and in the sight of God, they are all equal.

And that's another thing, America - you have not forgotten that you are a nation blessed by God. You've even gone so far as to write the words "In God We Trust" on your currency. But in the all-encompassing freedom that you give us, your citizens are free to worship God or not in whatever way we choose with no interference from you whatsoever.

I love you for your people, America – for those selfless souls who dedicate themselves to ensuring your survival down the centuries. I honor the memories of those who paid the ultimate sacrifice in wars through the years – the men who, with no thought for their own safety, landed on Omaha Beach on D-Day, or faced rifle and artillery fire at Cemetery Ridge at Gettysburg or Khe Sanh during the Vietnam War.

I love you for the way you respond to tragedies around the world – hurricanes, floods, mudslides, earthquakes or devastating oil spills on our gulf shores. America, you are the first to respond always, even to countries who have not always been our friend. I love you because even after terrorists struck our shores with such force on September 11, 2001, you stood tall. You didn't cower or back down. You pledged to shelter us all and this you have done with your great and powerful arms.

Finally, America, I love you now with a small sense of sacrifice that so many others have felt before. My son-in-law Ben, a young Navy

Lieutenant, is deployed while we wait at home praying for his safe return. I love you America, for the sense of patriotism that you instill in young men and women like Ben and our daughter Caroline so that they give up the comforts of home and family to ensure that Freedom lives around the world.

You are a great idea, America, a great nation. I feel truly blessed by God to live within your bounds. So each morning when, with my hand over my heart, I pledge allegiance to your flag – I mean what I say –

I pledge Allegiance to the flag

Of the United States of America

And to the Republic for which it stands,

One nation under God, indivisible,

With Liberty and Justice for all.

Thank you, America. I love you.

TOYS FROM MY CHILDHOOD

Look at any picture of me, age 9 – clearly it was the face of a child who had nothin' goin' on. Back then, at age 9, I lived for my toys and in my imagination. Inside there, I could be or do anything I wanted. I was reading a book on old toys from "back in the day" and decided to make a list of toys I used to own (or covet.) Did you ever have any of these?

- Always wanted a FLEXIBLE FLYER SLED but lived in the Deep South (Hello? Snow in Savannah?) So it didn't make much sense.

- Always wanted a LIONEL TRAIN. An old friend of my daddy's, Zeb Whelchel, had no children. He was a Gulf Oil dealer and he and his wife lived alone in a grand home. In the basement he had a train layout for his 0-27 scale model trains. I thought they were magic. But it was the fifties and I was a girl – 'nuff said.

- CRAYOLA CRAYONS. I always had plenty of these; although the biggest set I ever had was the 24 or 36 pack set. My friend Terri had the 64-count box with the sharpener on the side. I was a little bit jealous; I'm not gonna lie. I loved coloring in coloring books. Had stacks of them.

- Played with my cousin's ERECTOR SET – didn't do too much for me.

- Had a wonderful set of LINCOLN LOGS. It was kind of a small set, though, so I just kept building the same thing over and over. We also had a couple of other building sets – BLOCK CITY and AMERICAN BRICKS. Google 'em. They were kind of the forerunner to Legos.

- RADIO FLYER RED WAGON – Originally bought for my older sisters. It became the workhorse for Jerry and me. It was, by turns, an ambulance, a space ship, a covered wagon, or a car. Turned on its side, it sheltered me from attack by the Nazis. Definitely a great toy.

- BOARD GAMES – I loved them. – Some that I had included Monopoly, of course, Scrabble, Park 'N' Shop, The Barbie game (I always ended up with Poindexter), The Game of Life

(I always wanted a car full of kids,) Clue (Daddy bought it from Sherman the German, who ran a second hand shop. It was missing the little metal pieces - wrench, candlestick, etc. but we played it anyway.) I always wanted Go to the Head of the Class, Cootie, and an Operation game – I think my friend Terri had them. Jealous!

- VIEWMASTER – Had a black plastic one with slides of the Grand Canyon and other scenic sites in America. My favorites though were slides of fairy tales like Little Red Riding Hood. We even had one that told of the birth of Christ. I thought someone had actually photographed the real baby Jesus.

- Always wanted a SLINKY. My Aunt Cassie had one (she had no children) and it was the only interesting thing in her house to play with, except for her Victrola up in the attic which we weren't allowed to touch. We used to make the Slinky walk down the attic stairs. (We used to sneak up to the attic and just stare at the Victrola - a crank on a record player?)

- Had a MR. POTATO HEAD. You used a real potato and stuck plastic eyes, ears, noses, etc. into the potato to make a face. I seem to recall it had felt eyelashes and little hats too.

- I think I had one can of PLAY-DOH.

- I had one of the first BARBIES. She had dark hair in a ponytail. I still have her with the box and some of her original clothes. Probably worth some $$$ but I'm not selling.

- Always wanted SILLY PUTTY. I couldn't figure out how it could pick up images from a comic book.

- Always wanted a MAGIC 8 BALL – again, Terri had one. Did I get one for my children? "You may rely on it."

- Had a WHAM-O SLIP N SLIDE. I think we used it once and it tore up the grass so it "got lost!"

- Jerry and I had to share a blue HULA HOOP. Daddy brought it back to us one time from a trip he was on. It was during the hula hoop craze. We were so ecstatic. But I mean, c'mon Daddy, hula hoops couldn't have been that expensive. Couldn't you have brought back two?

- Loved PICK-UP STICKS and MARBLES. Jerry and I played on the carpet in our front hall.

- Finally, my blue COLUMBIA BIKE. It was never a bike, though…it was my trusty steed, the horse I never had.

INEY'S COIN PURSE

I had to go to the bank today to put the title to Paul's car in our safe deposit box. While there, as is my custom, I took a minute to look through the contents of the box. There's not much of any real value there, just some photos of household contents for insurance purposes, our wills, a few old coins my daddy collected, and the titles to our cars. But in the little bag with the coins, I happened to pull out a tiny coin purse, about two inches square with a little brass snap closure. It was made of the softest brown leather imaginable but the leather was faded and cracked. The purse belonged to Inetta Hunter and that's who this is about.

I knew Iney, for that's what we called her, as the cook who worked for my grandmother. Iney was probably in her sixties when, as a child,

I knew her best. She was an African American woman who lived in my grandmother's house, an old farmhouse up a long lane in North Carolina. I found out many years later to my surprise that Iney's grandmother had been a slave when I found the following obituary for her mother online:

THE GATES COUNTY INDEX Wed., Sept. 15, 1943.

"Woman Born in Slavery Dies"

Sophie HUNTER, 92-year-old Negro house maid who has worked for a number of people in and around Sunbury, died on Sept. 5 from the infirmities of old age. Her parents, Isaac and Amy ROUNTREE, were slaves of Solomon ROUNTREE of Gates County. Sophie served as maid to one of Mr. ROUNTREE's daughters and she stayed with her mistress until slavery was abolished. Sophie served as midwife for both white and Negro mothers in this section for many years and was respected by people of both races. In 1863 Sophie, then 14, married Tom HUNTER and to them were born 17 children, four of which are still living. James Crowder HUNTER and Inetta HUNTER never married and were living with their mother at the time of her death."

I remember when I was quite a young child that Iney and her brother Crowder lived in a small house near the highway at the head of the lane leading to Grandmama's house. Crowder was an invalid and Iney took care of both her brother and my grandmother. When Crowder died, Iney moved into a room in my grandmother's house and lived with her until her death in the late sixties.

Iney wore rimless glasses that always seemed to be falling down on her nose. She walked slowly and wore shoes that were run down at the heels. Often the backs of her shoes were broken down so that Iney could just slip into them. She, of course, never wore anything but dresses and I never saw her without a faded cotton apron unless she was going to New

Middle Swamp Baptist Church at which time she put on an old flat black hat with a net that covered her eyes.

Iney Hunter

My strongest memories of her were in the kitchen. I would get up, a sleepy child of eight or nine, and wander down to my grandmother's kitchen to see Iney frying eggs or turning bacon in a cast iron skillet. I still have the little wooden handled fork she used to turn that bacon and I think of her every time I use it. I also remember her replenishing the big platters of homegrown vegetables that my grandmother served us when we came to visit her for weeks each summer. She'd sit in the kitchen to eat while we ate in the big dining room.

At night, there being no television to watch, we'd sit on the front screened porch and watch the cars go by on the highway. When the bugs got too bad, we came inside and the adults told stories of long ago and people I never knew. Iney sat in a straightbacked wooden chair by the oil stove and listened. If the story was a funny one, she'd laugh and nod her head. More often than not, though, we children would watch to see how long it took Iney to fall asleep sitting straight up in her chair. It never occurred to us then that she might be bone tired from all her labors.

I remember very well we were visiting my grandmother on the morning of the tenth birthday of my twin sister Jerry and me. We came down for breakfast and my mother was in the kitchen helping out. When we came in, Mama said "Happy birthday!" Iney looked at us and smiled. "You ain't got no more babies, Mrs. Morris," she said. I was so proud. At last! Someone recognized me for the adult that I was!

To my lasting shame, however, that's about all I know of Iney – how hard she worked. I never thought to engage her in conversation. To think what she could have told me about her family history. Here was the grand-child of a slave - surely her mother must have told her stories and these stories were in my grasp but I never thought to ask. I wonder now, did she ever have a sweetheart? Did she ever long to go to school? I'll never know because I didn't ask.

Long after my grandmother died, I went into her old farmhouse looking for memories. In Iney's room was an old hinged wooden shotgun shell box – inside it were a few pennies in the leather coin purse, an old medal on a faded brown ribbon, the kitchen fork and a picture of Iney as a young woman. I took them home with me and think of her when I see them.

She died a year or so before my grandmother and, as she had no living family of her own left, our family buried her. I have thought of her from time to time since then. She probably never traveled much beyond eastern North Carolina. She had no children or possessions of any value. My grandmother seemed to be her only companion after Crowder's death. She worked long and hard all of her life yet I never heard her complain. I never thought to ask her anything other than to make me a sandwich or bring the butter. I assumed she was happy in her life. I know better now.

I know it's just the way it was if you grew up in the South of that time to have someone like Iney in your life, but that doesn't mean that it was right. I wish I could have given her the respect she deserved while she was still alive to receive it. I'd like to do that now.

BEACH THOUGHTS

I spent last week on the North Carolina Outer Banks, a place where I've been vacationing for over 60 years. Time spent there has an almost magical quality and I try each year to reach the same touchstones, visit the same places, eat at the same restaurants, and do the same things I have done in years past. One of the things I like to do is search for one perfect shell to bring back as a souvenir. The shells I find are never very big and it seems to get harder each year to find one that hasn't been broken by the waves, but this year I found two – a pink and white scallop shell on my first day and a black scallop shell on my last day, each about an inch in diameter and each one perfect.

I started going to the beaches of Nags Head, Kitty Hawk or Kill Devil Hills in the fifties with my parents and sisters. My father, a minister, usually held a revival in some nearby church in late August and used the honorarium he received to pay for a week's stay in some tiny un-air-conditioned, sandy-floored cottage along the beach. I remember watching Daddy and my grandmother pier fishing with shrimp, or seine fishing with one of his friends or brothers. Watching him do this always brought to mind the story of Jesus telling His disciples to "cast your net on the other side."

We didn't eat out in restaurants often but when we did, it was memorable –seafood dinners at the Oasis Restaurant with its barefoot college coeds in sailor shirts bringing baskets of heavenly lace cornbread, or breakfast on the Nags Head Fishing pier deck, the sound of the waves crashing just beneath our table on the sands below.

I usually got one new toy to play with – a plastic toy car (I remember a blue convertible I loved) or a shiny metal sand pail and bucket. Days were spent on the shore with my mother in her rubber bathing cap and stretch nylon bathing suit with "modesty apron." I never recall her playing in the sand with us as I did with my children; rather she spent her few hours on the beach looking worried, and calling after us to "look out for the undertow."

When I became a teen, my sister and I became obsessed with getting the perfect tan and poured copious amounts of baby oil all over us in the mistaken belief that it would help us to a golden brown safely. We also used a product called Sea and Ski and if I ever find that lotion again, I'm going to buy a case of it. The smell of Sea and Ski was the very essence of summer itself. Nights on the beach were spent tenderly rubbing Noxema on our blistered skin in preparation for doing it all again the next day. After all, that cute boy from the cottage next door might be there tomorrow.

When Paul and I married, we took our children to the Outer Banks again and I introduced them to the delights of a week at the seashore. We stayed a few years in the tonier grand palaces on the northern beaches of Corolla and Duck but they never felt quite the same. So we returned to the southern beaches again where so many memories still lived. There were the Grey Ladies, the old cottages in Nags Head that I loved so; there were the little stores like the Trading Post or Winks where Mama and Daddy bought fishing lures, suntan oil, the August issue of Seventeen Magazine and quarts of milk for our cereal.

This week I returned again to the Outer Banks, this time as a grand-mother. We played in the water, soaked up the sun, ate lunches of tomato sandwiches and Cheese Waffies and read novel after novel. Tom and Julie brought our granddaughter Leighton to the cottage Paul and I rented. She toddled and babbled and splashed in the buckets of water I brought up to her, time after time, under the umbrella. She walked around the cottage with a box on her head and waited for us to laugh at her. She learned to say "Pabo" for Paul but would not say "Nana" under any circumstances. One morning, though, she waddled next to me and leaned her little face against mine to give me some love, unasked, unprompted. It was the highlight of my week. And everyone saw it.

After they left, the house was quiet, too quiet, so I took the low folding chair Paul had bought me and went down to the beach. Paul, never much of a beach person, stayed inside with his laptop. I positioned my chair just at the shoreline and stretched out. The gentle waves came lapping at my feet and occasionally covered my legs. In between each wave, I let my hands dangle over the side in sand the color and texture of cashmere. Rarely have I ever felt such peace.

Returning to the same spot each year could be seen by some as boring, lacking in creativity. But for me, it's sweetness itself, a way to commune once again with my parents long gone, and the teenage Janet, also only a memory. Now I'm the one in the oversized bathing suit (thankfully, though, no rubber bathing cap!) And having our children and grandchild with us at the Outer Banks is a stepping stone to the future as we create memories with them.

Life is so very good and so very short. Like the waves that pound relentlessly onto the sandy shore, the years keep rolling by. It's good, once a year then, to stop the routine and feel the soft sand under my flip flops, smell the Sea and Ski and watch a nineteen month old baby experience the whole thing for the first time. Yes, life is very good.

FINDING BLESSINGS ON A COUNTRY ROAD

On Saturday night Paul and I attended the wedding of two perfectly lovely young people, Arthur and Holly. Arthur is the identical twin brother of my son-in-law Ben and, like Ben, he is a Navy Ensign. Holly and Arthur are going to be stationed in Florida. As I sat in the pretty Lutheran church and watched the two of them repeat their vows, I said a silent prayer that life would be good to them, that their love would flourish through the years ahead of them filled with deployments, disappointments, joys and sorrows.

Holly and Arthur's parents looked on with a mixture of pride and a little sadness at the next step their children were taking. But I couldn't help feeling happiness in seeing the bride and groom. Holly and Arthur were both raised to be charming, friendly, mannerly, intelligent young people and it showed on their special night. Whenever I spoke to them during the course of the evening, they stopped whatever they were doing to give me their complete attention. They (as well as their parents) seemed determined that all of their guests, including me, should know of their gratitude for all of life's blessings. It seemed as if they were including me in that list of good things God had given them on that particular night. How rare it is to find young men and women today who have that gift of gratitude, charm, kindness and goodness about them. Because of their parents and because of who they are, Holly and Arthur will have a wonderful life, wherever life leads them. God bless them always.

On Sunday, I traveled a completely different road, literally. I got a message from my dear friend Ellen who told me of the passing of another old and dear friend Leon in Gates County where I used to live. Leon's wife Emeline (whom he always called "Miss Emeline" in that sweet old Southern way) has been my friend since I moved to Gates County in 1974. Leon was a farmer and a pillar of the community so the tiny church where I used to be a member, Middle Swamp Baptist Church, was filled to overflowing on perhaps the hottest day of the year, well over 100 degrees. Middle Swamp Baptist is the oldest church in the county, having been formed in 1806. The building, a lovely white frame structure with magnificent stained glass windows, burned to the ground a couple of years ago, but such was the love of the community for the church that it was rebuilt almost exactly the way it looked before. Even today when I sit in the sanctuary, I can convince myself that it is the very same structure where my grandparents and great grandparents worshipped. It was in that newly constructed building where hundreds of friends gathered Sunday to say goodbye to Leon. He'd been a friend to so many people, including my own family. Leon and my daddy were great coon-hunting buddies. In his retirement years, Daddy could often be found at Leon's peanut shelter, drinking a "Co-cola" and swapping coon-hunting tales. Leon loved children and even took my own son Tom under his wing when Tom was a toddler, giving him tractor rides and even a small red International tractor of his own.

After the funeral, the mourners gathered in the church reception hall for refreshments as is the custom in the country. The ladies of the church set out plate after plate of ham biscuits, sugared pecans, peanuts, tiny cakes, and other delicacies. A line to speak to members of the family wound around the hall. Emeline looked exhausted and wilted as did her three children but all were gracious in their grief, greeting guests and thanking them for coming. I made my way to speak to them, then headed for a cup of tea, but could hardly take a step for being greeted by former students of mine. These were kids I taught thirty years ago, now in their forties and fifties, some of them grandparents like me. Each of them seemed glad to reacquaint themselves with their old English teacher of many years ago. I was amazed at their kindness. Only in a small farming community like Gates County could a person still matter to those she'd left behind thirty years ago. How I love that place.

After the funeral, my sister Jerry, her husband Larry and I went to our family cemetery to place pots of flowers on our Mother and Daddy's grave. It was so quiet there, the air so still and hot that it was hard to draw a breath. But there was a sense of peace that I always feel in that place. I drove quiet country roads then to spend the night with another sister (Martha Jean who'd lost her own husband only three months before). As I got in bed later, my head was filled with the myriad images I'd seen that weekend – a wedding of two hopeful young people, a community gathering to bid farewell to a dear friend, and a host of old friends who embraced me warmly.

I think that's what I'm learning old age will be like – watching younger people start out in life, saying farewell to those I lose and occasionally having joyful meetings with old and cherished friends. As a twenty year old, I would not have desired such a weekend. Today, I know that all of those things, even saying goodbye at the passing of my friend Leon, are blessings from God. There are not many people who have been as fortunate as I to know them all. On the quiet of a country road, I found peace and the scope to remember those blessings.

THE BLESSINGS OF BEING BORN IN THE SOUTH

B y a lucky toss of the genetic dice, I was born in the South, in Gaffney, South Carolina, to be specific, and raised in Savannah, Georgia. What a gift that has been to me for all of my life. Because I am from the South, I know the names of my grandparents, great grandparents, great great grandparents and on back quite a ways beyond that on both sides. To Southerners, "Who are your people?" is a question that's not meant to be nosy. We just like making connections so we know our family history.

Southern girls also have the good fortune to have the right phrase to use in that long drawn-out drawl of ours. "Bless her/his heart" – an expression of infinite uses – is a phrase we use, honey dropping from our lips, when Grandma's rheumatism is acting up or your BFF's son was kicked out of college, or your daughter got left at the altar. If there is a corresponding Yankee expression, I don't know it. Then of course there is the ever useful "y'all," the shortened term for you all. The plural, of course, is "all y'all."

Another blessing of living in the South is the lovely way we raise our children to say "yes sir" or "no sir," "yes ma'am or no ma'am" to anyone who is even a little older than they are. This has nothing to do with color or caste. It's just to show that we revere age in the South. Now that I am the old one in most groups, I appreciate it even more. And in the South, ceremonies are important – weddings and funerals, for example. Weddings for our daughters are grand affairs that mark the joining of two families with God's blessing. We have grand parties after the ceremony orchestrated down to the final dance. And we send off our departed loved ones with great decorum. We pull over to the side of the road to let the hearse pass. We shake our head and "tut tut" when we hear of a loved one's passing. We take casseroles or pies or a plate of deviled eggs to the home of the deceased. And we hug. There's nothing like a hug when you're sad.

But so much of living in the South revolves around happy things too – like dancing the Shag, or Spring break at the beach, silver patterns, barbecue and college football. It means azaleas blooming sometimes into December and pleasant winter days where coats are not needed and a sweater is enough. Living below the Mason Dixon line has brought sunshine and warmth into my life and though we Southerners tend to be a little quirky at times – We're always "fixin'" to do something or parading down the street with green in our hair on St. Patrick's Day – being Southern has been a blessing to me and for that I am grateful.

15 REASONS I'M A DINOSAUR

I have noticed as I get older that I like more and more things that are kind of, shall we say, "dated." I'm not sure why but I've just never been much of a trendy person. Paul calls me "hidebound." I prefer to think of myself as a classic. Here are some of the things I still like, long after everyone else has moved on.

- HAIR SPRAY - I "set" my hair every morning after styling with a little swoosh of Aqua Net. It doesn't make it look any better or last any longer (I have very fine hair) but it makes me feel like I've tried.

- APRONS - I wear one every time I set foot in my kitchen. (I also use rubber gloves when I wash dishes.) I remember my mother wearing aprons to prepare those wonderful home-cooked meals of hers. I wear one to put my Lean Cuisine into the microwave. Still it makes me feel like I'm trying to cook.

- A NEW EASTER OUTFIT - (And who calls them outfits anymore?) Ever since I was a little girl, I've gotten a new dress, shoes and pocketbook for Easter Sunday. And of course I always get new underwear to go with it. When I was a little girl, we'd get big dresses with wide crinolines to go under them, the bigger the better. I remember Louise and Martha Jean actually used to have real hoop skirts, like Scarlett O'Hara. I always wanted them but by the time I was of the right age, they were no longer in fashion. We also used to get new hats at Easter. I got new ones until I was about 22. Then nobody wore hats anymore.

- A CORSAGE ON MOTHER'S DAY - Daddy used to grow roses in our back yard. He'd always cut a red rose for each of us girls and a white rose for our mother to wear. (You wore a white rose if your mother was deceased.) I still do it in memory of my mom but now I use a silk flower because I'm too trifling to grow roses.

- OLD BOOKS - I always prefer to read books that were on my high school English teacher's reading list - Mrs. Beulah Harper knew what she was talking about. You just can't beat *Jane Eyre* for real romance.

- HYMNS ON SUNDAY - Paul likes to listen to classical music as we drive to church (actually he just likes to listen to the purr of the engine) but if I'm driving, I put on one of my CDs of hymns. And of course I always like the old ones best. "Amazing Grace" just seems to put me in the mood to worship.

- CALLING A CHURCH A CHURCH, NOT A "WORSHIP CENTER" - just seems right

- HAND CRANKED HOMEMADE ICE CREAM - I believe it tastes better than that made in an electric crank machine.

- NEWBORN BABIES BELONG AT HOME AT LEAST FOR THE FIRST 5 OR 6 WEEKS. I see people out today with babies that can't be more than a few days old. Just think of all the germs out there.

- BOARD GAMES – I LOVE MONOPOLY OR SCRABBLE - so much more fun than a video game

- PUTTING YOUR HAND OVER YOUR HEART WHEN THE NATIONAL ANTHEM IS PLAYED - Most people just seem to stand at football games now and many don't stop talking!

- SAYING "SIR" OR "MA'AM" TO YOUR ELDERS - Up here in northern Virginia, it seems to be frowned upon by the parents of my students. I think it conveys respect and cordiality and I like it when I hear it.

- HANDWORK - I like quilting or sewing although I have less and less time to do any. It's a very peaceful activity.

- SAYING GRACE AT MEALS - I even do it at McDonald's. That proves how important it is to me because I am ALWAYS hungry and don't want to delay eating for a minute - I could get hit by a bus.

- DRESSING UP FOR CHURCH AND CHRISTMAS DIN-
  NER AND OTHER OCCASIONS - seems like a lot of people
  just want to stick with jeans and a tee shirt anymore no matter where they go. I could probably go on and on but you get
  the idea. I think I am finally coming to the conclusion that I
  am a dinosaur...and I'm ok with that.

DIGGING PEANUTS

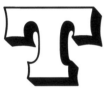he mornings here in northern Virginia these last few
days have been crisp, with an almost unbelievable clar-
ity to the sky. And yet, by the time the sun is up, I am
already at work so I hardly get to enjoy them. It's hard to
imagine my life moving any faster. And I'm dancing as fast as I can to stay
up. But, oh, to wake up one more time, some bright, brisk autumn dawn
on a farm in the country.

My family lived for eight years on a small farm in Gates County in
eastern North Carolina where corn, soybeans and peanuts were our crops.
I didn't know then how brief our tenure would be in the country. But I was
a lot younger then and I thought time was forever.

Years later, though, a cool morning brings that period in my life back
instantly. It's 1981 again and rays of sun poke insistently through the eastern windows of my big farm kitchen. With bacon sizzling in a pan on the
stove and eggs in a basket to be scrambled, I dig sweaters from the bottom
of a dresser drawer and encourage Tom to get ready for the school bus.

The weatherboarding of my 150-year old farmhouse is loose in spots,
but occasional drafts fail to dispel the cozy atmosphere of the kitchen. A
rocking chair sits by the old oil heater where a kettle simmers. In summer,

I shell beans in the rocker on rainy days. In winter, my first grader Tom sits there to read to me as I prepare supper.

Outside on this particular autumn morning so many years ago, there is an intangible excitement in the air. There's no time for rocking. We're digging peanuts today!

Breakfast is quickly dispensed with and tooth brushing forgotten as the diggers come rumbling into the driveway, headed for our fields. We crowd the back windows of the kitchen while I button the last button and comb the last wayward strand of my little boy's hair. Beyond the pecan grove behind our kitchen, dust fills the air as Jimmy digs our buried treasure.

Jimmy, a neighbor in his late fifties who walks with a limp and lives with his mother, farms with us on thirds (We pay for one third of the cost of seed and fertilizer and realize one third of the profit.) Years later, in a happy surprise, he'll marry a delightful widow from out of the county, providing grist for the gossip mill for weeks. But on this morning, it's just Jimmy and his helper, a teenaged boy who lives up the road, turning over row after row of peanuts.

Tom reluctantly plods down the long lane to meet his yellow school bus. I watch from the back porch as he stoops to scratch in the dirt. Is he pretending to dig peanuts in the driveway? Soon the bus arrives and Tom is gone. I head around back of the house for a look. Jimmy's nearly finished this field already. A pungent aroma fills the air, unlike any other - freshly dug peanuts.

Stepping into the field, I pull a few peanuts loose. They're huge, a bumper crop this year. Dollar signs fill my head as I plan how to spend all that money! I can see Christmas toys and new shoes and maybe even a coat of paint for the kitchen. Several days of nervous thermometer watching follow. A frost would do us in. But our luck holds and soon Jimmy's back to harvest the peanuts for us.

It's another morning and the combine and trailers line our yard, each one waiting to be loaded. Later on, I fill a couple of grocery sacks with peanuts. I'll roast a few tonight. I pull my sweater tighter around me and scurry back to the house. A smile crosses my face. It's been another successful harvest, another good year on the farm.

The sounds of traffic snap me out of my reverie and I'm back in the city, back in the present. My children are all grown and married. I'm older and, I hope, a little wiser. Life is good here, too - just different. I still miss my farm, but I try to think instead of just how much richer my life is because of my few years in the country.

THOUGHTS ON FALLING LEAVES

I've always had an acute awareness of the passage of time, even as a child. I remember very well one morning sitting in the kitchen when I was about eight or nine years old. It was an unusually chilly morning for Savannah and I was huddled next to the stove while Mama put a barrette in my hair to get me ready for school. My mind wandered as a child's will do and I was soon musing. "I wonder if I'll remember anything about this day when I'm an old woman." Well, I'm now an old woman and I don't remember a single thing about that day except for that brief moment in the kitchen. I think that's a pretty fair example of one of the latest buzz words in education – "metacognition" – thinking about thinking!

I was thinking about that morning this afternoon while resting in my hammock. Today is one of those perfect fall days that happen occasionally when the sun is high enough in the sky to bring some warmth but there's just a hint of a breeze – enough to let you know that this kind of weather is only temporary. Something much harsher is just around the corner.

I was lying in my hammock, looking up into the blue Virginia sky and watching leaves of every hue as they spiraled down to the deck and the ground below. It occurred to me that I have been a witness to the falling leaves for 70 autumns now. Who could ever believe it? I am now a grandmother, surely in the autumn of my own life and yet the days of my past are as vivid and alive to me as though they happened yesterday.

I remember walking with my Daddy in the woods around Merchants Millpond when they belonged to him. He told me about following his father's mule and plow in the fields nearby when he was a lad, as he called himself. Now those woods are part of Merchants Millpond State Park in Gates County, North Carolina and my father lies buried in the old family cemetery nearby. I remember sitting next to my mother in church when I was a little girl and watching her make a baby doll out of her folded handkerchief to keep me quiet. (What lady even carries a handkerchief anymore?) As I watched her, I wondered silently about her crooked little fingers but never, not once, asked her why they were that way, in all the 85 years I had her. Now she, too, rests beside my father.

I don't believe most people are aware of how quickly time passes, of how soon we are gone from this earth, leaving only a faded memory that becomes dimmer with the passage of time. I would like to have one super power – just one. I'd like to be able to go back and spend more time with my parents and grandparents and all those people I have loved and lost. But the leaves keep falling.

MY FATHER'S LOVE

In a wooden house on a farm in rural Gates County, NC 104 years ago, my grandmother Beulah Morris labored and delivered her sixth son, my father, Frank Elliott Morris. 1914 was a time when transportation was by horse and carriage and there were no televisions, Ipads, or cell phones. Although he was raised in a time that seems foreign to my 21st century lifestyle, I have always felt very close to him, maybe even more so now that he is gone.

My father was a tall man with beautiful blue eyes, dark hair and a nearly constant smile. He was a minister of large Baptist churches in Gaffney, SC and Savannah, GA when I was growing up, so on most days during the week, he wore suits and ties. But on Saturdays, he occasionally took me fishing in his small green, wooden motorboat on the Ogeechee River. On those days, he wore a pair of worn corduroy pants with a plaid flannel shirt and a ball cap. It was on those fishing trips that we had some of our best talks. He'd show me how to bait a fish hook or help me reel in a white perch and I'd tell him about my latest boyfriend trouble. Before the trip was over, we'd have an ice chest full of fish and I'd have no more worries.

My father loved to tell stories, many of which were about his own childhood. One of my favorites concerned his love of peanuts. His father, my grandfather Walter, grew peanuts on his farm. Each year Granddaddy would set aside a certain amount of the peanuts he raised as seed for the next year's crop. These he put into large burlap bags which were stitched closed with heavy twine and stored in one of his barns. One winter, when he was a little boy, Daddy decided to wiggle his finger into the seam and try to sneak out a peanut or two. When it worked, he began to come back every day and try the same thing. Eventually his finger had opened the seam of the bag large enough so that he could get his whole fist into the bag. By the time the winter was over, Daddy and his brothers and sisters had eaten half a bag of seed peanuts, a serious offense. With so many seed peanuts gone, there would be fewer seeds to plant for the next year's crop. When his father began to scold him, Daddy said he just smiled and said, "But, Papa, I was hungry." His father gave him a hug and Daddy evaded serious punishment.

In his retirement years, Daddy and Mama had a farm in Gates County and always had a large garden of about a quarter acre in size. He raised many beautiful vegetables of all sorts and shared them willingly with friends and family. He and my mother were famous for the delicious foods they served at our family dinners – butter beans, fresh Silver Queen corn, sliced tomatoes, cantaloupes and watermelons, Kentucky Wonder snap beans, Irish potatoes, and okra – all raised and picked from his own garden.

Daddy always wanted to teach me how to work in the garden, a task I didn't particularly enjoy as a teenager. One day he told me he wanted me to plow his garden. The difficult part of this plan was that he used a mule to plow the rows of his garden and I had never plowed behind a mule before. The mule, named Sally, realized instantly that I knew nothing about plowing, so she decided right away not to cooperate.

I took the reins and the plow handles in my hands and clucked to her to "get up." Deciding she did not want to work that day, Sally immediately took off at full speed toward her stall in the barn, pulling the plow with me hanging onto the handles for dear life. She jumped the fence but the plow and I went through a little lower, breaking boards as we went. Finally I had sense enough to let go of the plow handles and turned to look at the fence with its broken boards swinging in the wind. Just beyond the fence, my father was hurrying toward me.

"Oh, no," I thought, "Daddy's going to kill me."

He reached down with his big hands and picked me up off the ground, a worried look in his eyes. He hugged me in his big bear hug and, seeing I was ok, he chuckled a bit at my distress. Then he went out to tie up the mule and repair the fence.

Now that my father is no longer with me, I think about him and the wonderful lessons he taught me. The thing I have realized most is that many of his best lessons were never spoken. My father lived his lessons – with gentleness, hard work and a loving and forgiving heart. He lived his faith in God and taught those he knew of God's love by his example. Though I can no longer talk to him, I still learn from my father's love.

HAPPY BIRTHDAY TO TOM – A NOTE OF APPRECIATION

I've officially been a mother for forty-two years now. Today is the forty-second anniversary of the birth of my first-born child, my son Tom. It would be hard to overstate just how much the birth of one's first child changes you. In so many ways my life BT (before Tom) was bland, unrewarding and, of course, somewhat easier! AT (After Tom) my life was full of so many wonderful, vibrant things - colors, toys, nursery rhymes, the quiet cooing as he nuzzled into my neck, soft little baby toes and most wonderful of all, the smell of his fine baby hair, a fragrance more enchanting than anything that Chanel could bottle.

I spent hours just looking at him – the way his mouth formed little "O's" and his large dark brown eyes looked placidly at his surroundings, the perfection of his skin, as soft as a lamb. Soon, however, he became a toddler, running from me to explore the world around him. Before I knew it, it was time for him to enter school and he never looked back. An able student, Tom excelled at whatever he studied in grammar school, junior high and high school where he became a National Merit Semi-Finalist.

In the midst of Tom's junior year my life fell apart with the death of my father, my mother's stroke and the ending of my first marriage. Through it all, Tom was a rock, supporting me through each difficult time in a way that was far more mature than his years. I have a permanently etched memory of the 16 year old Tom drying his sisters' hair after shampooing them while I struggled to help my sister take care of our invalid mother. Through it all, he never complained - not once.

He earned a scholarship to North Carolina State University and earned a degree in Mechanical Engineering, a good fit for him because as a child he was always making the most intricate constructions with his Lego set. Always a quiet and easy-going child, Tom became the typical strong, silent type. He found a job as an engineer and settled down in marriage with Julie, a kindhearted firecracker of a blonde who is the most perfect companion for Tom. Together they have given me another great joy - our granddaughters Leighton and Naomi and our grandson Mason. On this special day, I thank God for another of his many perfect blessings to me - my son Tom.

HERE COMES NOLAN
"TRAILING CLOUDS OF GLORY"

"Our birth is but a sleep and a forgetting...Not in entire forgetfulness, And not in utter nakedness, but trailing clouds of glory do we come From God, who is our home....")

kept thinking about this line from Wordsworth's "Ode: Intimations of Immortality" that moment two days ago when I held little Nolan, my second grandchild, in my arms for the very first time. He was just a couple of hours old. Leighton, my first grandchild, was already more than a day old when I got to hold her for the very first time two years ago. And I had my own three children by C-section, and was medicated so thoroughly that I was either asleep or made to lie flat because of the kind of anesthesia I'd had. So I didn't really get to examine them right away.

But with Nolan, I was healthy, and wide awake. And there he was, just three hours out of Heaven, his little halo still practically visible. Looking at his tiny perfect face, his little fingers curled around mine, I was overcome with emotion. That first day, his eyes were closed most of the time I was there, as though he were still safely tucked away. "Those lights are too bright," he must have thought. "And that noise is too loud. Stop talking so much. I'm trying to sleep."

But we went back to the hospital the next night and there he was … wide awake and looking up at me with the most beautiful eyes you've ever seen – so alert and intent. What was he thinking? No sound he made until it was time to eat. Then Shon, my son-in-law, gathered him up easily in his big arms and carried him to Katherine, still sore and tired from her own C-section, but already becoming a confident mother.

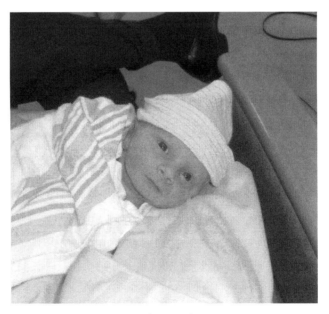

Newborn Nolan

It made me think of the long line of love centered in that one tiny boy. Shon and Katherine fell in love in high school and dated all through college. How many nights Shon drove his Honda over to our house to sit on the couch next to Katherine pretending to do homework or watching a game! At bedtime, I'd have to run him home, never once dreaming he'd one day give me such a precious gift.

Before she even met Shon, I think Katherine prepared to give love to Nolan too. She dressed her dog Reckless in doll clothes and pushed her in a doll buggy; she hauled around her doll Rebecca throughout her childhood and teenage years – who would have ever dreamed that one day she'd have a real baby of her own?

Now Nolan has come to join that other precious child in my life – my other grandchild Leighton. She calls us Nana and Pablo – I guess those are the names we'll be called from now on. Who would ever have dreamed I'd be a grandmother of eight – or that I'd ever be this lucky?

Finally I think of the long line of my family who are represented in Nolan's bloodline. The genes he carries from Katherine and me and my father and mother and my grandparents and great grandparents – all are joined with a similar number of genes from Shon's family. They are what make Nolan what he is and will be.

Thinking of how God has blessed me with such wonderful grandchildren reminds me that my days here on Earth are numbered, and the influence I have is limited. But because of these children, gifts from God, I have seen, as the poet William Wordsworth said, "Intimations of Immortality."

So now…here comes little Nolan, "trailing clouds of glory." Welcome perfect little Nolan. Nana and Pablo already love you. Don't grow up too fast.

MY MOTHER'S MOMENT OF FAME

This is my eighteenth Mother's Day without my mother. Each year before January 10, 2000, I spent Mother's Day with her, having her over to my house for a meal, or taking her out for dinner or, when a child, making her some outlandish gift like a macaroni necklace or a construction paper card. The void she left behind has never been filled in all the years since.

Mama with her newborn twins Jerry (L) and me

My mother was a quiet, gentle Southern lady who never liked to draw attention to herself. In fact, the picture above probably represents the only time my mother acquired any fame. In the summer of 1948, my father, a minister, was off in North Carolina holding a series of revival meetings when he found out that my mother had gone into labor, perhaps a month before she was due. He and his sister Edith got in his car and practically flew back to Gaffney, SC where my mother had entered the Cherokee County Hospital. Daddy told me years later that he drove so fast back to South Carolina that he blew out the engine of his '48 Ford. When he finally arrived at the hospital, he waited in the waiting room as was the custom at that time. Soon, this father of two girls received the news that he was now the father of one more…me! About nine minutes later, he was told that Mama had delivered another girl – my twin! As incredible as it sounds today, Daddy had no idea they were expecting twins although Mama always said she suspected something.

Mama became sort of an instant celebrity then because multiple births were really quite rare in those days. Though she had some household help, I'm sure it was a lot of hard work raising four girls ages 10 and under. My mother had no example to follow for her own mother had died of diabetes when Mama was only four. Nevertheless, no one could ever have found a better homemaker, cook, dressmaker, or mother. In fact, I always thought she worked too hard at being a great mother – so hard that I rarely remember seeing her at rest.

Back in the 1960s though, she began watching "Days of Our Lives" an NBC soap opera that is still limping along on the network. She'd dry the last of the lunch dishes and put them away, then sit in her Lazyboy for an hour to "find out what the Bradys and the Hortons were doing in Salem this week." Afterward, she'd pick up her Bible and read a little to prepare for the Sunday School class she taught each week. In later years she kept my son Tom while I taught school; she'd rock him to sleep in her lap while John and Marlena and Roman or Patch and Kayla entertained her. Even today, I record the show and watch it as I grade papers, an invisible cord still connecting me to my sweet mother.

Mama never became famous for any reason. The only autographs she ever signed were my every 6-weeks' report cards that included the usual "Janet needs more help with number facts" or "Janet is a cheerful presence in my class." Mama never made much of a ripple in life and she rather liked it that way. Daddy was always the star in the family and she was just fine with being behind the curtain waiting with his supper.

But to me, Mama was a star of the brightest magnitude. I can still see her, apron at her waist, moving about the kitchen preparing fried apple pies or roasts of such tenderness that the beef fairly melted in your mouth. She volunteered at my school, she replaced the Blue Horse notebooks that I carelessly lost, and she made my dresses and starched my petticoats to go under them.

Most importantly though, my mother taught me two important things – to love God and to respect myself. That meant church twice on Sunday and once in the middle of the week as well. It also meant to hold myself accountable in all parts of my life – at school, on dates, in my first job wrapping packages at Belk's, or choosing a college. I chafed a bit under her restrictions but now as a mother of three grown children, I realize what a blessed gift she was to me.

This year for the eighteenth year in a row, all I can do is place flowers on my mother's grave. But I am remembering you today with love, Mama. I am who I am because of you.

PARIS MEMORIES

aul and I saw the Woody Allen movie "Midnight in Paris." It was delightful - a very unique story. But the best part was just the scenery itself. Paris is such a beautiful city. I don't claim to be a world traveler. I've only been out of the country for two trips. During Christmas 1999, Paul and I spent a week each in London and Paris. And in spring of 2014 we toured the Normandy beaches in France and met our children Ben and Caroline to tour Paris and Northern Ireland. Other than that, I've been here in the United States. Those two trips were enough to last a lifetime, (although I hope there will be more trips in my future.) Anyhow, seeing all the amazing sites of Paris in the movie reminded me of my trip. If you've ever been to Paris, maybe some of these visual memories will ring a bell with you:

- The lights in the trees and the Ferris wheels set up along the Champs Elysee for the Millenium Celebration

- The doorways and doors of the old apartments, courtyards and shops of the I'le Saint-Louis

- The greenery around every shop window, usually with tiny white lights and large foil bows

- Christmas trees sprayed white

- Sidewalk cafes

- The sound of the choir in the far recesses of Notre Dame Cathedral as they walked toward the congregation singing "Stille Nacht"

- The sight of Notre Dame rising like a ghost in the mists of evening, standing majestically behind the bronze statue of Charlemagne, or greeting me each morning as I walked across the bridge

- Watching people walk home with a baguette in their arms

- A row of geese hanging in the butcher shop window, completely cleaned but with their feet and heads still attached, feathers hanging in a ruff about their necks

- Going to the grocery store each day for a single clementine wrapped in tissue paper

- Being greeted everywhere with "Bonjour, Madame!"

- So many real fur coats!

- The Hall of Mirrors in the Palace of Versailles

- Ice cream from Bertillion

- Opening the window of our hotel room every morning and leaning out to greet the day

- Walking along the Seine in the moonlight and kissing Paul under the streetlamp

HOG KILLING

I have always loved pork of any kind - pork tenderloin, pork chops, sausage, and especially bacon. I think bacon will be served in Heaven. Many people today think that bacon comes from those plastic wrapped packages in the refrigerated cases in their grocery store. But I have very vivid memories of where it really comes from – I participated in hog killings at Mama and Daddy's farm in Gates County, NC.

One cold day in January of 1980, Daddy killed five hogs. The next day, I was at their house all day long cutting up meat. Most of the morning, I was under the shelter of the barn cutting skin off and trimming the fat from the meat for sausage. Daddy, Uncle Tommy, Uncle Thurman, and Ed Walton, were sawing off the hams, shoulders, sides, etc. My twin sister Jerry, Golden Brinson, a woman who went by the name of "Little Bit," and I were at the sausage table. Then we scraped hair from ears and feet. Holding the feet after they'd been soaking in warm water was eerie. They felt just like human hands. Yechhh!!! Then the fat we trimmed was cooked in a kettle over a fire for lard.

When the fat pieces were nice and brown, they were dipped and poured through a new pillowcase to strain the grease. Uncle Desmond used a wooden squeezer to squeeze the grease from the cracklin's (the cooked fat.) By that time, Daddy was back from getting the sausage ground at Gramps and we made it into patties. We also put up the roasts, spare ribs, pork chops, tenderloin, and backbone. Our freezer was full but my back and arms ached! I'll bet not many of my friends have ever had that experience. It's a memory I will always treasure.

A GOOD DAY

Not long ago, I had my annual mammogram. They spotted an "abnormality" and called the next day to schedule me for a retake.

I went in a couple of days later and they found a mass in my left breast and scheduled me for a biopsy. At the biopsy, the radiologist told me, "Either I'm going to put this needle in and withdraw fluid (meaning it's just a cyst) or I won't be able to withdraw anything and I will have to take tissue samples for a further look (meaning it could be cancer.)"

I said, "Look, Doc, yesterday was my birthday. You know what I'd really like for a gift from you?"

He said, "I have an idea."

A few minutes later, he withdrew the needle, and in a moment he held a tiny test tube in front of my eyes, a test tube containing FLUID!

"Happy birthday!" he said and my eyes filled with tears.

A week of worrying and not sleeping were all behind me now. Thank you, God, for medical science, for Paul who was with me all the way, and for a future of possibilities.

I left the office, went grocery shopping for the hurricane that's coming and came out in a downpour. I just took off my shoes and walked barefoot in the rain, pure joy in my heart. All I could think about were all of my friends who wished me well the day before (they took my mind off the upcoming biopsy), all the days ahead with my husband, children and grandchildren, and all the many ways God has blessed me. It's a good day.

SAVANNAH HIGH SCHOOL CLASS OF '66 - OUR 45TH REUNION

y husband says I go to more reunions than anyone he's ever met. It's probably true. I have had a long and very happy life and I like to look back at it from time to time. A weekend a few years ago was a perfect example. In the third of four reunions I had that year alone, I went back to Savannah, GA for the 45th reunion of my high school there.

I didn't actually graduate from Savannah High School. My father was the minister of Savannah's Bull Street Baptist Church and he accepted the pastorate of a church in Virginia just before my senior year. So I actually graduated from Hampton High School, but my heart has always belonged to SHS. Luckily, Savannah people aren't sticklers for details like actual graduation, so my sister Jerry and I were welcomed back as though we were legit.

Coming back to Savannah was an amazing time warp kind of experience that I have written about before. It always shocks me that, while I have moved away and had so many life experiences, both good and bad, Savannah is still there, changed in many ways but in many ways still exactly the same.

The city itself is incredibly beautiful. I forgot how grand it truly is until I returned to my home in Virginia and no longer saw the long, muscular arms of the live oak trees outstretched across broad avenues. I had forgotten the gothic beauty of the grey moss dripping from the tree limbs and framing the magnificent old homes. I had forgotten the simple elegance of those historic district squares carefully laid out so many years ago which slow down the daily traffic as well as the everyday pace of life.

It was a breath of fresh air to hear the Southern accents in the voices of the people around me. Everyone, whether they knew me or not, was gracious and friendly. From classmates at the reunion to the lady who cleaned my room at the hotel or the doorman who held the door for me – all were genuinely kind. So many times I heard from Linda or Ginger or Johnny or Cliff to "Come back, honey, so we can do this again." People in Savannah have not forgotten that life, as hard and awful as it is sometimes, goes down a little easier when sweetened with sugar.

Seeing my old classmates this weekend was a lovely reminder of just what a magical childhood and youth we all had. The Class of '66 grew up before Vietnam, before the racial unrest, and before the Kennedy assassination that, when they did arrive, took away our innocence. But somehow, having that foundation of innocence made us stronger to deal with those things when they finally came our way. And they all did eventually.

At the reunion, we remembered that some of our classmates went to Vietnam; many more than I remembered served our country in various branches of the military at a time when it was not popular to do so. And having grown up in the Deep South, we recalled the struggles we had as the Civil Rights movement touched and changed our lives. We told stories of where we were when we heard that President Kennedy had been shot (Mrs. Harper's room…never to be forgotten mental image of the scratchy sound of the radio report coming over the intercom.)

We toured our old high school, now proudly serving the city as a school for the arts. How grand a building it is, not anything like the modern (and dull) school buildings of today. We looked for some sign anywhere that we had once walked those halls. Here was Mr. Saunders' home room; here was the library where Ginger and Karen and Nancy researched and read. (No computers for us back then.) Here was the gymnasium where Robert and Bill, Charlie and Mike, Harry and Allen and Alan, made their mark (and where notably I went down to ignominious defeat day after day in physical education classes. The gym shorts alone were enough to humiliate me.) Here were the fields surrounding the school where Johnny and John drilled with the ROTC and Henry practiced the high jump.) So many memories surrounded us as we walked the halls – how can over 50 years have gone by so quickly?

Finally, we had long hours of catching up and laughing over old pranks and recalling sweet memories with one after another of our classmates. At the dinner Saturday night, we had a video tribute to our deceased classmates – 48 of them out of a class of over 650. Each missing classmate's photo engendered a hundred memories in the minds of those of us who had gathered. Each photo reminded us of the brevity and uncertainty of life and the importance of staying close.

Now I am home again. The mounds of laundry and chores greeted me the minute we came in the door (as well as a brief but welcome visit with my new grandson!) Almost immediately, my few days back in Savannah among all my old friends felt like a dream. It all passed so quickly. I wanted more time with everyone. I wanted to live closer so we could continue the old patterns that we fell back into almost instantly.

It didn't matter that some of us had thickened a bit around the middle, or had lost a little on top. It didn't matter that some of us had gone grey or attempted to hide the grey. What mattered was the love that we all felt – a tender, sweet, longing for the past and a pride that we had been a part of such an amazing group. For that is what my classmates are now – community leaders, business men and women, parents and grandparents, and genuinely nice people. Some of us had dealt with cancer. Some of us had lost mates through death or divorce and were still standing. Some of us had suffered the unimaginable loss of a child and most of us had lost one or both of our parents. But there we all were again – still standing, still loving our old school and still loving each other.

I'm proud to be a part of the history of SHS. I'm proud to be in that wonderful class of '66. Thank you, reunion committee, for making the weekend so memorable. And thank you Savannah for nurturing all of us. I love you all.

NOLAN'S DEDICATION SERVICE

oday Paul and I attended the dedication service for our new grandson, Nolan Thomas Klegin. It was held at his parents' lovely church, First Baptist of Alexandria. The service was brief and consisted of the pastor introducing Nolan to the congregation followed by a few questions to Nolan's parents, our daughter Katherine and son in law Shon. They were something along the order of, "Will you pledge to bring up your son in a Christian home where love is present?" Of course, their answer was "yes." The pastor then welcomed the large group of family and friends who had come together to support Nolan and his parents on this important day. The pastor shared a life verse for Nolan which his parents had selected:

"For this reason, since the day we heard about you, we have not stopped praying for you. We continually ask God to fill you with the knowledge of His will through all the wisdom and understanding that the spirit gives, so that you may live a life worthy of the Lord and please Him in every way: bearing fruit in every good work, growing in the knowledge of God."

– *COLOSSIANS 1:9-10*

Then he offered a prayer of dedication we all silently shared – a pledge to give Nolan a life of love and service to God. After that, the service continued and Nolan slept through it all!

It was an emotional morning for me as I looked around at the people gathered in that church…my husband, our three children, their spouses, their children, their in-laws and grandparents, their friends – all together because of one emotion – love. I thought of the other members of the family – my parents, grandparents, uncles and aunts, all now residing in Heaven, who surely would have looked down on this day with great joy. How I would have loved to share tiny Nolan with them.

Days like this and emotions like this – where I am conscious of the passing of time - seem to come more frequently for me now. I am no longer the slender college girl I used to be with a lifetime of opportunities beckoning. I have fewer years ahead of me than the number I have already enjoyed. More often than not, as a senior citizen, I am practically invisible to all but Paul, God bless him. Our children have left home and established homes of their own. They find fewer reasons to spend time with their parents because their own lives are so busy.

I know that one day, time will end for me and I am ready for it, whenever it happens. Jesus has promised me eternal life and I am counting on that. But until that day comes, I will clutch days like today to my chest and inhale their sweet fragrance. I will be reminded that a few small molecules from my soul will live on forever because Nolan and our other grandchildren born since I wrote this are alive. And I will rejoice to know that the heritage of faith that I passed on to their parents will live, God willing, in them.

A VISIT FROM THREE ANGELS

ne morning in Sunday school, our wonderful Sunday School teacher and friend John Edwards asked us to tell of times when God knew our innermost prayers even when we were unable to express them ourselves. I was reminded of a time years ago when my mother suffered a massive stroke.

Overnight she changed from a vibrant, active senior citizen on whom we all depended to a helpless, pathetic woman, completely paralyzed on one side of her body and unable to speak. She was in a coma for days, days in which my father, sisters and I kept a sad and tearful vigil in the hospital, waiting for good news. We prayed to hear that it was all a mistake and she was going to be fine, after all. That good news never came.

Day after day, when the pain got to be too much for me, I'd make my way down to the tiny hospital chapel and pour out my heart to God, pleading and negotiating with him to bring our mother back to us. Why had God not granted my fervent prayer, I wondered. My mother was a wonderful woman who with my father had served God all her life. Surely He ought to heal her. Then I'd wipe my tears and go back up to her room to try to encourage my daddy and look for any sign of her healing.

One day, though, it all became too much for me. I went down alone to the chapel and, as usual, approached the large Bible that was opened on a stand at the front of the room. It was opened to Psalm 46, the familiar passage that reads in part,

"God is our refuge and strength, a very present help in trouble. Therefore will we not fear, though the earth be removed and though the mountains be carried into the midst of the sea."

It seemed as though we had just gone through an earthquake, so devastating was my mother's illness. At that moment, it felt as though the very earth beneath my feet had opened up, threatening to swallow me. I was so completely lost in grief that words to God, any words, failed me. I remember very well placing both hands on the two large pages of the Bible and sobbing, great salty tears falling onto the pages beneath my hands. My shoulders heaved, my tears apparently endless.

Suddenly, I felt arms around my shoulders. I turned to see who it was and was met by three large, older African American women. They were dressed as though they were going to church with suits and elaborate hats. "Pardon us," one of them said. "We heard you crying and wondered if you wanted us to pray with you." At that, fresh tears came to my eyes and I tried to explain what my mother was going through and how lost we all were without her. The tears returned and I was unable to say anything else. "Would you mind if we prayed?" one of them said. I nodded my head in approval, unable to speak. I don't remember her words or the words of the other two who prayed after her. I do remember the tender embrace they gave me afterwards and their promise that God was with me, even in that dark hour. Then as silently as they came in, they went away.

I never saw them again. I went back up to my mother's room still sad but knowing that I was not alone in my grief. I'd like to say that my mother recovered from her stroke but that was not to be. She lived another ten years unable to speak or walk. And yet, there were many joys in those years with her. My sister Jerry and brother in law Larry took Mama into their home and cared for her as tenderly as she had cared for us when we were babies. Mama was a sweet and loving patient while enduring the imprisonment that her stroke forced upon her. She even bore the loss of my father who died in a car accident six months after Mama's stroke.

It was a difficult and sad time for our family which we have never forgotten. Yet there were grace gifts from God, one of which was the visit of the three women in the chapel. I've come to think of them as angels, and perhaps they were. They helped me realize then as now that even when I am too grief-stricken to have words to pray, God knows what is in my heart. And He sends angels of mercy to surround us with tender embraces.

ADVICE FROM NANA

I am now, incredibly, a grandmother of eight. If you asked me how old I think I am, I would probably say about 38. But a look in the mirror in the morning before I apply spackle and paint quickly disabuses me of that notion. I am every bit of 70.

I do love being a grandmother and I thank my children for making these scrumptious little people for me to play with. I just thought that by this time, I would be viewed by my children as the wise elder, full of gems of knowledge to be passed down to them. But my children somehow have developed a self confidence that I don't think I ever had at their age. They never ask my advice! And even if that's not true, the rules have changed so much since my babies were little. You can't even put a baby to bed on his tummy now, for Pete's sake. And blanket them? No way. They just sleep in little sleepers.

Car rides are different too. When our children were small, we just tucked them behind our shoulders and let them stand on the seat beside us or sit on the front seat. If I had to stop suddenly? No problem – I'd just swing out my arm and clothesline the little buggers – that would have kept them from an unplanned ejection. Nowadays, you have to have a degree in mechanical engineering to fit a child into a car seat. And getting them out is even worse. There are more buckles and straps than in an Indy race car.

So since I'm no good for helping out with all the current safety stuff, I'll just pass along this little bit of unasked for advice on a topic on which I AM an expert – raising a Southern child!

First, never correct a child for his or her Southern accent. It is a gift from God. The ability to stretch out a one-syllable word like "pie" into at least two syllables and flatten the "I" makes one gifted and talented. Using terms like "fixin' to" or "y'all" is the mark of a well-educated child.

A Southern baby should wear smocked clothes to church or synagogue with no shoes until he starts to walk. If it's cold, use booties his grandmother knitted for him.

A Southern child should be able to tell you who his people are, where they're from and the names of right many of his kin. Southerners are rightfully proud of their family because often, they're all we've got. We lost everything else in the War – You know which war I'm talking about.

Southern children should have some experience on a farm – either their parents' or grandparents' place. Nothing good can come of being raised entirely on concrete. Children need fishing holes, cow patties, dirt roads and ponies to ride.

Southern children should be taken to church regularly – preferably to a country church where there are fans with pictures of Jesus holding a baby lamb.

A child raised in the South should have a home cooked meal made with food he or she has helped grow. If a child can select his own ear of corn and pluck it from the stalk minutes before it goes in the boiling water, his IQ goes up by at least 10 points, I'm certain.

Finally, a well- reared Southern child should spend lots of time with his or her grandparents. It benefits all the parties. As the old saying goes – Grandparents and grandchildren get along so well because they have a common enemy.

TILL NEXT THANKSGIVING DAY

nother Thanksgiving has come and gone. I'm back home now, suitcases and memories to unpack and store for another day. Our family has gathered at Thanksgiving as long as I can remember and it's always the most joyful time of the year for me. For one week, my three sisters and I, along with our children and grandchildren, gather at a central location and put away the outside world. There are no jobs to go to, no bills to pay, no daily commutes to fight – there's just time to enjoy life.

When I was younger, we gathered at our parents' home. They had a farm in Gates County, NC with horses, pigs, goats, chickens, and lots of uncles and aunts nearby. When my parents passed away, it struck us that there was no longer the old home place to go back to. So my sisters and I decided to make a concerted effort to stay together. We devised a plan to have a grand Thanksgiving celebration every other year with one of the four sisters and her children and grandchildren as hosts for the year. We began at each other's homes but as our families grew, we decided to rent a large home at a beach location (usually the Outer Banks in North Carolina) for Thanksgiving week.

This year it was my sister Jerry's turn to host and we met at Kill Devil Hills for an amazing sun-filled week. There were forty of us in one house - a lot of chaos but it was my idea of Heaven – all my family in one place. The host for the year rents the house and plans the activities and Jerry and her family did not disappoint. We had the usual round of games and activities

- the Theodosia Morris Baking Contest (named for our mother who was a great cook,) the Frank Morris Rook Tournament (named for our father who loved that card game,) the biannual 5K race (this year named the Gobbler Gallop) with beautiful maroon tee shirts for everyone. You should have seen all of us running, or in my case plodding, along Beach Road. By the way, I won first place in the Sweeper division.

We had our usual adults only Battle of the Sexes with trivia questions. (Girls ask the guys questions which involve typically female knowledge and vice versa. The answers were occasionally slightly off color and often played off family inside jokes so funny and ridiculous that we cried with laughter. We found out that the men in our family are surprisingly in touch with their feminine side as they defeated us handily.) However, it made for some hilarious moments to hear them struggle with some of the questions. This year for the first time, we had volleyball on the beach. Teams consisted of everyone from grandmothers to preschoolers. Players ranged in height from about 6'5" to about 3'10". Rules were, shall we say, flexible, especially where the preschoolers were involved. It was wonderful exercise and beautiful to see with the Atlantic surf pounding in the background.

Finally, of course, we had the biannual Crips vs. Bloods competition. In our family, sadly, there is no limit to the depths to which we will sink for a joke. So we have named those who were born into our family the Bloods. Those who marry into the family are named the Crips. There is always a wicked competition between the two groups for dominance at various activities. This year's competition was our version of Family Feud. If I recall correctly, I think the Bloods won that with no effort at all.

All too soon, of course, it was time to pack up and come home. As each family left the house, I shed fresh tears. My face was a blotchy mess by the time I finally arrived home. But I'll carry with me enough memories to last until the next time we're all together. I'll remember the sight of my grandchildren playing with their cousins. I'll cherish the time with my sisters. I'll love the thought of all my nieces and nephews and all my children now grown to honorable man- and womanhood, married and raising families of their own. I think I'll remember most of all the Thankful Tree that Jerry placed in the dining room. All week long we wrote things we were thankful for and attached them to autumn leaves, then placed them on the tree. After our Thanksgiving Day meal, Jerry read them one by one. The little ones had written in their childish scrawl "I'm thankful for giraffes," or "I'm thankful for Mommy and Daddy." The older folks wrote things like "I'm thankful for memories of days gone by." We remembered our loved ones whose empty chairs at the table would never be filled. We remembered my son in law Ben who is deployed with the US Navy right now. (Thanks to Skype we were able to visit with him half a world away.) But two thankful notes in particular brought a catch to our throats and a realization of how God had richly blessed us. One dear family member who had struggled with his own personal demons for a while wrote, "I'm thankful for a second chance at redemption." And our son and his wife wrote, "We're thankful for Mickey and Jennifer (a nephew and his wife who have twins) for helping us know how to raise our twins!" – It was their way of announcing the blessed event(s!) to the family.

So after a week at the beach surrounded by my favorite people in the world, I'm stronger and happier and very tired. The dark days of winter will come soon. I'll be overwhelmed once again with work and aches and pains. But thanks to this past week, I am blessed with a renewed realization that God has smiled with sweet benediction on me. I'm thankful for the heritage that our family shares. I'm thankful for dear loved ones – the old and the newborn and for the promise of the ones to come. The kitchen is empty, the dishes all washed and put away. The families are gone to their homes along the eastern seaboard – from Georgia to Pennsylvania. But in my heart, I'll treasure forever the memories we made this week.

THE COTTAGE

ummers in my childhood meant trips to Kentucky and North Carolina to visit my grandparents. During these visits, my daddy would hold revivals in local churches. Following the revivals, we'd spend a week in a rented cottage on the Outer Banks of North Carolina. I know we must have had vacation weeks in other places, but for the life of me, I can't remember any others. So summer and a week in a beach cottage have always been synonymous to me.

For years we'd rent tiny cottages with two or three bedrooms and one bathroom, and a kitchen with odd smelling utensils and plates. The salt in the shakers was always stuck together because of the humidity. The pots and pans were of the cheapest variety and, of course, there was no such thing as a dishwasher - that task belonged to my sisters or me. Yet even in such minimal surroundings, my mother prepared meals of the most delectable quality - eggs and bacon with sliced peaches and tomatoes for breakfast, tomato sandwiches on white Sunbeam bread with iced tea for lunch and seafood dinners of preposterous portions for supper - fried perch, boiled potatoes, hush puppies, butter beans, tomato pudding, and fresh ears of corn. We didn't have dessert every night but when we did, they were amazing - peach cobblers, fried apple pies, or hand cranked ice cream. My mother was a magician.

The houses we rented were barebones cottages with very little decoration - I remember a couple of years we stayed in a cottage owned by my Uncle Corbell. It's still standing near the Black Pelican Restaurant but nowadays has been raised on pillars to protect it from the ravages of the

Atlantic Ocean. I remember the tiny bathroom had a little wall decoration made of red cedar painted with a hillbilly headed to an outhouse. There was a nickel glued to it under which were written the words, "$.05 per use." At first I thought we had to pay to use the bathroom!

Finally, though, Mama and Daddy bought a little waterfront cottage on the Albemarle Sound, just across the bridge from the beaches of the Outer Banks. They bought it from my Aunt Ella's sister Christine and her husband whom everyone called Pike. It was a tiny house built of cement blocks with two bedrooms and a bathroom, a kitchen and living room and a front porch. That was it. Yet for the years that our family owned it, it was Heaven.

The bathroom had a shower with the most rudimentary plumbing facilities and a wooden slat floor and a toilet that regularly got stopped up. On the ledge of the shower stall were giant plastic bottles of no-name varieties of shampoo and suntan lotion. On the top of the toilet tank was a large blue glass jar of Noxema cream which we slathered on our noses and shoulders at night to recover from our sunburns. The bedrooms were big enough only for a double bed and a crib or twin bed and an old dresser. The living room had an old couch and chair and end tables from the forties or fifties. The end tables held old Glamour and Mademoiselle Magazines from the 1950s which intrigued me. I dreamed lazily of being a winner of the Mademoiselle Guest Editor competition, an event always featured in the August issues. There were paperback novels of ancient vintage left over from Christine's ownership which I devoured, as the family bookworm. I had no interest in learning to cook as my sisters Martha Jean and Jerry did. They could often be found working in the kitchen with Mama. The kitchen in the cottage had an apartment sized stove, a sink, and about five feet of counter space, all told. There was a toaster which was about a hundred years old and a hand mixer which worked occasionally. Often my sister Louise would bring her boys there and leave a new "improvement" to the cottage - lamps or other things that were needed but were not there before. The tile floors were always a bit sandy and I recall my mother constantly sweeping.

The screened porch was the place to be if you were a teenaged boy or girl. The grandchildren slept there, talking well into the night, and slipping out to check the crab pots that Daddy hung off the long dock. The dock was an amazing feat that he built himself with the aid of his sons-in-law and grandsons. Though Daddy was a minister, as a child of the Depression, he had many other skills which he honed during his lifetime. He could build or fix almost anything. The dock was the jumping off place for the swimming parties which were the delight of all ten of Mama and Daddy's grandchildren. The water was only four or five feet deep close to the dock so no diving was allowed, but the soft sandy bottom made for a fun place to play. Daddy tied up his boat there and took a few of us fishing in the Albemarle Sound. I never recall having much luck, but Daddy never went out without bringing in a string of fish enough for supper. Mama would fry them up and serve whoever was there, a number which often grew to include several of Daddy's brothers and sisters, who enjoyed the raucous atmosphere of our family.

Outside there was a picnic table where Daddy cleaned his catch, hosing it down in case we cut a watermelon there later. There was no TV, no radio, and certainly no laptops or internet. Yet I never recall having a bad time there. Mama and Daddy owned the cottage until Daddy's passing and Mama's stroke. Then my sisters and I gathered to discuss what to do. We rented the cottage out to others for a while but finally decided reluctantly to sell it. It was the site of so many happy memories, but none of us were in a place in our lives to keep it up.

I went back there a couple of years ago just to see it. It's still standing, newly painted, still no bigger than when our family owned it but the landscaping had been cleared. It didn't look as happy as when our family was there. For a time in our lives, that humble little cottage was the site of many happy, innocent days and nights. I hope whoever owns it now loves it as much as we did.

HOME FOR CHRISTMAS

or many years, when I heard or said the words, "Home for Christmas," I knew immediately what they meant. Home was wherever Mama and Daddy were. When I was a toddler, home was in Gaffney, SC in a brick four-square parsonage where I received gifts like tricycles, and cardboard housekeeping closets with tiny samples of Oxydol detergent and child-sized mops. When we moved to Savannah, I learned to think of Christmas in the tropics. We wore shorty pajamas to unwrap our gifts around the scrawny trees we got at the Winn-Dixie each year. There were six of us still - my mother, father and three sisters and me. Then Louise and Martha Jean married and brought brothers into the family - Shug and Hines and the precious niece and nephews that followed. But each Christmas, we gathered around Mama's table still, its surface laden with delicacies - roasts, hams, pickles, nuts, potatoes, salads, rolls, and cakes and pies.

Our mother was a miracle worker in the kitchen and she worked tirelessly to provide abundance for us. I can still see the tables she set - her snowy white tablecloth with Christmas poinsettias printed all over, the silver goblets at each place setting and her silver service, brought out of the sideboard. She counted each piece after each meal, an odd thing, I thought, because she never did that with the stainless we used every day. Now I know why!

Years passed, we moved to Hampton and my sister Jerry and I married and moved away. Jerry went to Germany with Larry, compliments of Uncle Sam, though I always tried to stay nearby. Finally Daddy retired and

Mama and Daddy moved to their farm, to the old house that my great grandfather had built. Perhaps because those memories are some of the last I have of Mama and Daddy, those Christmas memories are my favorite.

Having moved quite a bit in my lifetime, I am hard pressed to pin down which of my old houses feels most like home. But I guess if I had to choose, I'd say it is the old Morris home place, a term which in itself conveys the living and love that existed for so many years within its old walls.

The house, sitting on the edge of what is now Merchant's Millpond State Park in Gates County, NC, was built before the War Between the States by my great grandfather Ephraim Morris on land given to him by his father in law. Ephraim and his wife Sally Mary raised eight children there, one of whom was my grandfather Walter Morris. One of Walter's nine children, Daddy's brother Gladstone, lived there for several years, and then moved with his wife to a nearby house. Upon the deaths of my grandparents, my father Frank bought the house and accompanying 90-some acres from his siblings as a gentleman's farm, intending someday to retire there.

Daddy and Mama did indeed retire there but not before giving the old house a makeover. Never a grand house, it had a bedroom, dining room, kitchen and living room on the first floor, plus two bedrooms on the second floor. A bathroom was tucked onto a back porch sometime before 1950. As Daddy's retirement drew closer, he and Mama polished and painted the old girl so that it was barely recognizable - new kitchen, two more baths, new fireplace in the family room, master bedroom on the first floor and a new library wing.

Mama and Daddy moved in right after he retired, but they allowed me to live there for a year while I was restoring an old house of my own nearby. Still, it never really felt like home until Mama and Daddy moved in. Then what Christmases we had there! I can still see Mama in the kitchen preparing turkeys and country hams which she sliced and placed on her silver platter. Vast bowls of vegetables from Daddy's garden, cut glass dishes of Mama's homemade pickles, and cakes and pies of every description covered almost every inch of her table. The table was covered with her Christmas tablecloth and set with her wedding china and silver flatware. In my mind's eye, I can still see Mama, her red apron tied around her waist, giving instructions to whichever of her daughters happened to be around. Daddy was usually at the counter with his electric knife, slicing ham so thin you could see through it and slipping bites to hungry grandchildren.

Most of my sisters and I gathered there with our families for a few days before and after Christmas. If the weather was crisp and cold and the moon was bright a few days before the great day, Daddy would load the back of his pickup truck with a dog box full of baying coon hounds and an old rifle or two. Then he and a couple of his strapping grandsons would head off into the woods in search of raccoons. Next morning, I'd see Daddy out in the barn lot, skinning a raccoon carcass strung up from the barn eaves. He'd smile at me with that dimple in his cheek and say, "A little Christmas money for your Mama!" Then he and the grandsons would head off to Edenton to sell the skins and meat.

Christmas dinner was usually around 6:00 PM and there was an adult table and a children's table. Usually Daddy's three Gates County brothers, Gladstone, Desmond and Thurman, and their wives would come in just before dinner. Daddy, of course, would insist they join us, and Mama would squeeze in a few more place settings. Gladstone, Desmond and Thurman and their wives were childless and, I think, didn't know what to make of all the noise and commotion that came along with a family as big as ours, but I like to think they were seeking to warm themselves in the reflected glow of our big family. They stayed until all the little ones had opened their packages and dragged themselves, complaining, to their beds.

The Morris home place about 1900

The remodeled Morris home place in 1989

Some years it was so cold on Christmas that Daddy would build a roaring fire on the hearth next to Mama's recliner. Other years, it was so hot we'd have to open the back door to release the steam of the dishes Mama was cooking on the stove. After dinner came the chaos - the tearing of paper, the tangle of ribbons, exclamations of delight over gifts received, the laughter of little ones, their hearts singing over some new toy or doll! It was the essence of an American Christmas.

After all the gifts had been opened, Mama would sweep the house of wrappings and ribbons. I remember one year, she cleaned so thoroughly that she threw away the cord that came with someone's new electrical appliance. Ever after, we had to sort through the trash carefully. Then I'd take the paper out to the old oil barrel in the barn lot and set fire to it. In the quiet of Christmas night, watching the sparks rise to meet the stars, I used to marvel at how big the sky was and how many stars I could see out in the country.

But, of course, those days came to an end and so many of those dear loved ones are now gone. The children we gathered to us then are grown now with children of their own. My parents both rest beneath the sod of the old family cemetery next to the house. All the aunts and uncles and even Shug and Hines are gone. The house and land were bought by the state park system some years ago and they deemed the old house "surplus." So the house and all the outbuildings were razed. Park officials don't realize how many memories still float around that old place and how many of my family of ages past lived and loved there.

If that were all I had to hold onto of Christmas, it would be bleak, indeed. But Home for Christmas means something much more to me now - it means my Heavenly home. And the older I get, the closer my Heavenly home seems, where Daddy and Mama and all those dear loved ones are gathered today. Because of Christmas and the Child who was born in that stable so many years ago, Mama and Daddy live on. Because God took on human form and lived on this earth as you and I, we have the bright promise of reunion with our loved ones. I thank God for the birth of this tiny Child, Jesus Christ, Emmanuel, God with Us. My wish for each of you is that you can go home for Christmas too. God bless you all.

MAMA AND HER SISTERS

ama was the fifth of six living sisters to be born to my grandparents and her relationship to her sisters never faltered through eighty decades of living. After the massive stroke that ultimately felled her, Mama was visited by several of her elderly sisters. They traveled by plane from Kentucky to see her in the rehabilitation center in North Carolina where she stayed for a few months. We all still carried the hope then that Mama would return to "normal." But that was not to be. Mama stayed paralyzed and unable to speak for the rest of her life. So our family developed a new normal.

After her release from the rehab center, Mama came to live with my sister and brother in law, Jerry and Larry. Occasionally she'd come to visit me for a week or so, but for the most part, Jerry was her daily caregiver, a backbreaking job which Jerry (and Larry) performed selflessly. They provided a life for Mama which would have been unthinkable otherwise. Jerry, a hard dog to keep under the porch if ever there was one, took Mama in her car to church, to shop, and traveling around the state for her job.

One week, though, in 1992, a year and a half after her stroke, I decided to take Mama back to Kentucky to see her sisters. Mama had never flown much before her stroke so it was a real leap of faith to take her in her condition. So, wanting to help however I could, I bought a couple of seats in coach and hoped for the best. It was not an easy trip with all of Mama's necessary items that I had to carry. But onboard were some angels – flight attendants who bumped Mama and me up to first class seats and made my flight as delightful as could be.

The Buffalo gals – L-R Cassie, Helen, Theodosia, Kelly Mae, Frances and Daisy

Once in Kentucky, we stayed in Versailles, KY with my cousin Nancy Helen and her husband Peter, more angels who made Mama's stay as easy as possible. Mama's sisters traveled to spend a day with Mama. In the way that only Kentucky grandmothers can do, they all brought fabulous foods to share. The sisters were solicitous of Mama and did what they could to make her feel welcome. A year into Mama's new life, I was still kind of unsure of how to take care of my mother. But the sisters, the Buffalo gals I called them as they grew up along the banks of Buffalo Creek, talked to Mama as though she were still the same. They patted and held her hand, told her stories of people she knew from her childhood and nudged me to help her in some way.

It was one of the last times they were all together, the six Dever girls, and they all seemed to know it. In 1995, the oldest sister Frances passed away at age 90. We brought Mama to the funeral and one of the sisters, probably Helen, suggested that they all hold hands as they usually did when they were together. Aunt Cassie reached inside the coffin and held for a moment the stilled hand of Aunt Frances while the "girls" prayed the Lord's Prayer. It was a moment I will never forget about the love among sisters. Though Mama had been dealt a bad hand with her health, she was surrounded for the rest of her life with the love of many loved ones, not the least of which were her five sisters Frances, Daisy, Cassie, Helen, and Kelly Mae.

BEULAH JANE SMITH MORRIS

Lately, I've been scanning pictures of my ancestors – members of my daddy's family – from northeastern North Carolina. Many of the pictures were of male members of the family but there is one whose face has not appeared – until now – my paternal grandmother, Beulah Jane Smith Morris.

I called her Grandmama but my older sisters called her Grandmother, I believe. Daddy called her Mama, as did my own mother in her rather quiet unassuming way. There was absolutely nothing quiet or unassuming about Grandmama, though.

Never a great beauty, she was quite short, only about 5'4" or so and her figure was always on the dumpy side for as long as I knew her. She always wore her hair in two braided knots at the nape of her neck. I never paid much attention to her hair until one night during my childhood when she spent the night at our home. I sat on her bed and watched as she took the pins out of her hair and unwound the knots, then loosened the braids. Her hair reached down to her waist! Who knew all that hair was in there?

Grandmama always wore black lace-up shoes with stocky heels about an inch and a half in height. Now I occasionally see beautiful young girls wearing such shoes and I can't help thinking of my old grandmother and the shoes she wore. In all the years I knew her (and she passed away when I was 18) I never knew her to wear anything but a dress, usually of some dark nondescript cotton for housework or nylon for church. Around the house she was never without a faded calico apron, much like the one in the picture. In fact, this is one of my favorite pictures of my grandmother because she is actually smiling.

Beulah Jane Smith Morris

Grandmama was not a great smiler. She always had too much work to do to spend time amusing us children, but we never felt anything but love from her. She admonished us for not eating enough at her table (I was a picky eater!) but always fixed the most delicious cheese toast for us for breakfast (melted hoop cheese on white bread – HEAVEN ON EARTH!) And to drink at breakfast, she gave us cups of coffee cut by half with cream and spoonfuls of sugar, never listening to our mother's "No!"

We visited her at her old farmhouse down a long country lane where there was not much to do except run our toy cars in the sandy dirt around her front door and shell butterbeans or break up snap beans. In the afternoons, she'd pull me to her side and say, "Here, Janet, get that pan and come sit with me in the swing. Let's fix these beans for dinner. There was no telling her "No," as I occasionally tried to do with my mother. There in the swing, she'd lift a paper sack full of beans, pour some into my pan and before you knew it, we'd have the beans shelled or snapped. If I was quiet and good, she'd tell me about her childhood. She told me, for example, that she didn't remember her own father much except that he'd been good to her. She told me her hair had been styled in long ringlets when she was a girl and she remembered her father playing with her ringlets as he held her. What a nice memory, I thought.

After our work was done, she'd always bring out a cold bottle of Dr. Pepper for us. The bottles used to have 10-2-4 printed on them, and my grandmother was of the opinion that those were the prescribed hours you had to drink a Dr. Pepper. I never drink one now, without remembering her.

Grandmama was an excellent cook and always had her big meal of the day at noontime. There were usually platters of salty country ham and fried chicken or Dan doodle (you don't want to know!), big bowls of Irish potatoes swimming in butter, tiny butterbeans afloat in pot liquor and thick slabs of red tomatoes. I always wanted something sweet afterwards and Grandmama didn't disappoint. She was an accomplished baker and usually had a cake or pie of some sort on her table. After dinner, she'd throw a clean white tablecloth over the leftovers to keep the flies away and that would be our supper.

There was almost no television reception and her TV was ancient and tiny anyway, so after supper, we sat on the screened porch and talked. Occasionally a car would turn in her long dusty lane, and there'd be much speculation about who was in the car. I'd lean my head against my mother in the glider and soon sleep would overtake me. My grandmother would say, "Theodosia, you better get those girls into bed." And my mother would do what she said, for no one failed to mind Miss Beulah.

Mama took us to the bathroom where we'd take a quick tub bath. There was no hot water so water had to be boiled in the kitchen then hauled all the way to the bathroom and poured in the tub. As a result, half the water in the tub was frigid while the other half was scalding. Our baths didn't take long, needless to say. We shimmied into our pajamas and ran up the stairs, diving into the feather mattress atop an old mahogany bed. That bed with its tall carved headboard and footboard nearly as tall, now resides in my guestroom and I think of my grandmother every time I see it.

There was no bathroom upstairs so Mama would have to carry a lidded enamel pot upstairs to use in case of emergency. More times than I care to recall, Jerry or I never made it to the pot in time. But if my grandmother ever fussed at us, I don't remember it.

Finally it was time for lights out. We knelt on the rough wooden floor and said our prayers beside the bed, then sank into the depths of the feather mattress and bolster. To cut off the light, I just pulled a string. Grandmama had tied a cotton string to the hanging bulb in the center of the room and attached the end of the string to a nail by the bed.

Deep sleep overtook me and I didn't wake up until the light broke through the thin, cheap curtains at the window. I could smell the sausage and eggs wafting up from the kitchen and I knew if I hurried down, Grandmama would have a piece of cheese toast waiting for me.

DUSTY'S SADDLE

I t was the fall of 1989 - Saturday, October 22 to be precise. I got up at 6:00 AM to help my Daddy set up for the auction sale of his and Mama's farm implements and furniture. The weather that day was dreadful - blustery and cold all day. It was weather to match my mood, I thought. By the end of the day, I had a terrible headache and was depressed to see the accumulation of years of their things being sold off at giveaway prices. Daddy was 75 and Mama was 74 at that time. Both felt that they were no longer able to maintain the farm which they had owned for decades and to which they had moved after Daddy's retirement from the ministry. So they sold the farm, land which had been in the Morris family for over one hundred years, and moved to the small town of Ahoskie nearby, closer, they told me, to their doctors and a hospital.

To say I was unhappy is a great understatement. The day has become something of a blur, lost in the mists of time, except for the memories I wrote down in my journal. But I do remember bidding $25.00 for Dusty's saddle. Dusty was Daddy's faithful little pony. Hitched up by my daddy, he gave countless rides to all the grandchildren. He plowed Daddy's huge garden and he was Daddy's little companion. When the saddle was held up for auction, a catch came in my throat. The saddle was old and worn out, but I couldn't bear to see it go, so I held up my hand to bid and broke into tears. Daddy stopped the auction at that point and took the saddle off the block, handing it to me.

"If it means that much to you, Janet, I want you to have it," he said tenderly.

I hugged the saddle to me and wiped away tears. The day was not all sad and there were funny moments. When the auction resumed, the auctioneer began auctioning off a .22 rifle in five dollar increments. I heard $5, $10, $15. Then I heard little Katherine, who was then six years old, bid $20.00! I quickly clamped my hand over her mouth and negated her bid. Everybody laughed and she ran away and hid.

The next day, we helped Mama and Daddy move a truckload of things to their new house. I remember thinking the new house seemed nothing like home to me.

Nearly thirty years have come and gone in a flash. The farm I loved so much is now a part of the Merchants' Millpond State Park in Gates County, NC. Mama and Daddy are buried in the Morris family cemetery at the edge of the state park. The home they moved to in Ahoskie has been condemned and probably torn down because of flooding in the area. Katherine has grown up, married, borne three children and buried one of her own. The charmed spell of the glory days on the farm has passed from our lives, as all good things must.

Yet Dusty's little saddle remains as a reminder of happier times when I was younger and all things were possible. It sits now atop a stool in my office. Sometimes I rest my feet on it as I watch TV and remember all the little children who rode it so many years ago. It waits for one of my children - Tom, or Katherine, or Caroline to claim it now.

THINKING ABOUT MAMA

As Mother's Day Weekend approaches, I have been thinking a lot about my mother. Her name, as old fashioned as she was, was Theodosia Ellen Dever Morris.

She was tall, beautiful and quiet in a dignified way. She was born and raised in Kentucky and to the last day of her life, she thought of herself as a Kentucky girl. Every year, when I hear *My Old Kentucky Home* played at the Kentucky Derby, I get a lump in my throat as I remember old times.

My mother spent over fifty years as the wife of a minister, my father. My dad was the family "star" and I remember lots of big moments with him. But with my mother, I remember quiet moments – her soft and wrinkled hands crocheting receiving blankets for my babies; standing beside her at the sink drying dishes while she washed and I talked about my troubles; working beside her as we cut off corn for the freezer; sitting at her dinner table faced with an amazing array of foods – country ham, butter beans, corn off the cob, tomato pudding, sliced tomatoes, biscuits, gelatin salad, apple fritters (she called them apple jacks) – my mouth waters even now.

She never seemed to tire. And yet now after she has gone, I can see that her poor body finally wore out after years of hard work and giving to others, especially her family. She passed away in 2000 after suffering for ten years from the effects of a massive stroke. And yet she taught me even when the stroke removed her ability to speak. Stricken with a crippling paralysis, she maintained a dignity and quiet patience through that decade that spoke volumes about her reliance on God in her time of trial. What a lesson! What a mother!

This weekend I could only put flowers on her grave. If you still have your mother on earth, I hope you'll go to her this week and wrap your arms around her and tell her how much you love her. How I miss my mother tonight. A gentle gift from God, a reminder of His mercy, my mother was ever my teacher, the sweet and tender housekeeper who each night swept the mischief from my heart. She was the best friend God ever gave me and I was lucky to have her.

Mama

HOW DADDY CAME TO BE A MINISTER

y father, Frank Elliott Morris, was born the sixth of nine children in a frame house on a country lane in Gates County, NC just three years before the United States entered World War I. Just as he was graduating from high school, the country was entering the Great Depression, yet his

parents somehow found a way to send him off to college and then to the seminary. I can imagine it was difficult to get the money for his tuition, especially because they had already sent two of Daddy's brothers to college and law school.

Daddy's oldest brother Chester went to law school and ultimately became a judge, a path which Daddy said he had always planned to follow until life and the will of God got in the way. Daddy's first job during college was at a fast foods place known as Red and Dick's in Portsmouth, VA where he sold Virginia ham sandwiches. After that he worked in the summers at his cousin's Portsmouth service station. That's where he decided to give his life to the Lord.

Daddy

Later he worked at Ocean View Beach in the bathhouse and took up tickets at the Pavilion where dances were held. There, guys were always trying to get him to dance with the pretty girls who were there. It must have been very tempting for a handsome young man. But by that time, Daddy had decided to become a minister and attend the seminary. So he started a prayer meeting in one of the little rooms near the roller coaster.

This all sounds pretty tame by today's standards. But I believe God was planning a life of real service for Daddy and the events of his early life were merely laying the foundation for what he would do in the coming years. Daddy was never a rich man. The most he ever made in salary was about $13,000 per year. Yet I believe my Daddy was a very important man. Through over sixty years as a minister, he pointed the way to God for thousands of people. He married many hundreds of couples. He held the hands of sick people in hospitals. He helped many men and women who were caught in the grips of addiction to come to sobriety. He spoke words of comfort at the funerals of servicemen who were lost during the Second World War, the Korean War and the Viet Nam war. He grieved with parishioners when Death entered the room. In 1991 Daddy died. The man who had been my own spiritual leader for so long now left us without anyone to speak words of comfort to us at his passing. Now that he is gone, I want the world to know what a wonderful man he was.

HOW MAMA MET HER GRANDCHILDREN

ama had four daughters and ten grandchildren. After the birth of each one of her grandchildren, she came to her daughters' homes for several days to help out around the house, usually giving the babies their first baths, washing mountains of diapers (no Pampers back then!) cooking delectable meals for her sons-in-law and getting some up close and personal time with her new grandchild. She kept this up for twenty-three years

starting with the birth of her first grandchild, Johnny, in 1963 until the birth of her last, Caroline, in 1986.

She never once complained, although Daddy whined a bit about losing his girl for a few days. He was never much good without her. But she delighted in each of her grandchildren, crocheting crib blankets for each one. She taught their mothers how to diaper a baby without sticking them with diaper pins. She stocked our freezers with homemade vegetable soup and her famous spaghetti sauce to eat after she had gone home. She cleaned our homes and washed our dishes and laundry.

Finally in 2000, after a massive stroke, her body gave out and we laid her to rest beside Daddy in the little family cemetery in the country. We had her funeral in Middle Swamp Baptist Church, the tiny church where so many of my ancestors had worshipped, been baptized and finally had been given back to God. On that solemn day, all ten of her grandchildren were Mama's pallbearers. The six boys, Johnny, Skip, Frank, Mickey, Chip and Tom, carried her coffin. They were all so tall and handsome dressed in black suits and wearing somber expressions. The four girls, Jean, Ellen, Katherine and Caroline, followed behind the coffin, each carrying a long-stemmed white rose. All four girls were so tall and slim and pretty, wearing slender column dresses. They looked beautiful in their grief. It was heart-rending, really, to see them carrying the one who had carried them all at their birth.

With the loss of Mama, I felt for a time like an orphan, which I guess I am still. It was dreadful to lose her quiet presence in my life and I still think I want to call her every weekend the way I used to. Many people are sure that their mothers were wonderful. But for the nearly 85 years that I had her, I know I had the best mother of all.

SLACKER INVENTIONS

'm thankful for Slacker Inventions. I know it's important to express my gratitude for the big things and people in my life…but it's about the small things, too. Here's a list of what I mean:

- DRIVE-THROUGHS – Fast food, banking, pharmacies as well as anything else where I don't have to exit my car. Believe it or not, I'm not always dressed in my Sunday best. Thank you, Mr. or Ms. Drive-through Inventor, for making it possible for me to ~ahem~ "cook dinner" for the man of the house and me without getting out of my pink pajama bottoms.

- FROZEN MEALS – I know, I know. Laugh if you must. But not all of us are gourmet cooks. And, actually, before I went back to teaching, I almost never served these. But now that the children are grown and on their own, and when I held down a fulltime job, it became difficult to conjure up a reason to spend another few hours in the kitchen at night after eight hours at school. Plus, Paul is OK with that.

- HAMMOCKS – You're out in the fresh air looking up through the trees at the sky; you're horizontal; plus I attach a little rope to the deck railing so I can pull it occasionally for movement – that's exercise. What's not to love?

- GOOGLE/WIKIPEDIA – As an English teacher, I know I should promote the use of other research tools, but when I want information, I usually just want it FAST – these give it to me. Of course, the fact that 13 year old John Q. Public from Keokuk, Iowa can "update" Wiki concerns me a little, but not a whole lot. For quick and dirty info, these two are the bomb.

- REMOTE CONTROLS – The older I get, the more I appreciate them. Of course the TV goes without saying. And Paul and I never argue about these. He has one for his TV; I have one for mine. We also have them for the garage door and for all those Christmas candles that Colonial Williamsburg has decreed that all Virginians must have in their windows. We have one for the Christmas tree too. No more crawling around on the floor.

- MALLS – Blow out your credit card in one spot and you only have to park once

- YOU TUBE –Where else can I see old videos of Topo Gigio and my grandchildren (Time to post some more, kids.)

- FACEBOOK – No need to wonder whether or not my old friends are still kicking. We've reconnected here. Yay!

- INDOOR PLUMBING – Charmin three ply or a couple of pages from the Sears catalogue with the chance of splinters – you decide.

Yes, I know – I'm pretty triflin' as my daddy used to say. But hey, life is tough. Nothing wrong with making it a little easy on yourself, I say. So thank you to all of the nameless, faceless people who have made my life so much easier. I'd salute you but I've got to go to McDonald's – Paul is hungry.

DADDY THE OUTDOORSMAN

y father, Frank Elliott Morris, was a happy man. He was tall, about 6' 1", the tallest of his siblings, and had, until late in his life, very dark hair. His eyes were a robin's egg blue, a color I now see in my granddaughter Naomi. He had a delightful dimple in his cheek which presented itself whenever he smiled - that was almost all the time.

Daddy liked people - talking to them and getting to know them, and he was liked by almost everyone. This was a characteristic that embarrassed me mightily when I was a teen. It seemed that Daddy would strike up a conversation with anyone, anytime. He would crack a joke with the lady in the grocery store check-out line or ask the fellow next to him in the airport who his people were, a Southern phrase if ever there was one.

His skin was medium but tanned very easily. He carried an almost year-round tan because of his love of the outdoors. In the summer he could be found in a boat somewhere, most every Saturday with a line in the water. Daddy was a great and patient fisherman, pulling in fish after fish while I sat on the seat next to him gloomily waiting for the bite that never came.

Uncle Desmond and Daddy after a successful fishing trip

When we lived in Savannah, Daddy enjoyed bird hunting, bringing home bags of quail for Mama to fry to a delicate tenderness. After he retired to his farm in North Carolina, he went back to a favorite form of hunting which he had enjoyed with his father and brothers as a young boy - 'coon hunting. The swamps around his farm were full of the little critters and Daddy enjoyed going out in the middle of the night to tree a raccoon.

This was a hobby that brought about another enjoyable pursuit - Daddy enjoyed raising 'coon dogs. Kept in a pen near the pasture behind Mama and Daddy's house, the dogs were some of Daddy's greatest pets. He named them all with names that would be easy to call - usually one or two-syllable names. My nephew Johnny Adams, who was a frequent co-conspirator on these late night jaunts, recalled the names of some of the dogs - Blackie was his first, a black and tan. Then there was Smokey, Joe, Boss and finally his best beloved Trailer, a blue tick hound. I remember when Trailer gave birth to puppies - She was such a good mother. I remember walking back in the barn lot on cold mornings after one of Daddy's late night coon hunts to see him skinning coons, their carcasses hanging from the barn rafters. He sold the meat, and the fur which he called his "Christmas money." My nephew Johnny said Daddy used to say that skinning a coon was the same as cleaning catfish, "like pulling a cat out of his pajamas."

Johnny, Daddy's first grandchild, was the son Daddy always wanted and after raising four girls, he enjoyed time with him and his other grandsons immensely. But there was also a special love between Daddy and his granddaughters. Ever the Southern gentleman, he put them, as he did our mother and his daughters, on a pedestal. Daddy had a wonderful laugh and an amazing sense of humor that allowed him always, even in the darkest moments, to be positive about life. I like remembering my daddy and am looking forward to seeing him again.

HOW DADDY MADE ME FEEL SPECIAL

 s the father of four girls and the pastor of a very large church, Daddy often found it difficult to make time for his family. But he did, nevertheless. He once took my five year old twin sister Jerry on a trip of several hours to visit his parents at Christmas. She remembers that special time with him with great fondness. I had one on one time with Daddy, too. I remember waking up quietly on vacations so I could have a morning fishing trip with him alone. I was never a great fishing buddy but I loved having him all to myself. We'd go to the bait shop where I got to look at the bloodworms and crickets that he'd buy. Then he'd fill a cooler with ice, Cokes in green glass bottles, cans of Vienna sausages and packs of Nabs for our lunch. By the time lunch was over, the cooler was full of fish, mostly caught by Daddy

but occasionally a few caught by me (with Daddy's help - "Here, Janet, hold this fishing pole," he'd say, knowing full well that he had already got a fish on the line for me.)

Left to right: Jerry and Daddy leaving on a Christmas trip to North Carolina; Janet and Daddy at Mt. Mitchell State Park, NC ca. 1957

Daddy had a knack for making me feel very special and loved. One night while I was a student at Meredith College, I got a call from the Dean of Students' office. "Janet, you have a visitor." It was after dark, probably eight or nine o'clock. I couldn't think who it might be - maybe a boy? Men couldn't go up on our dorm hall (we were very well protected back then) so I hurried down to see who it was. Imagine my surprise to see my daddy there, dressed in corduroy pants and a plaid shirt with his cap in his hand. He gave me a huge bear hug and told me to go with him out to his truck. He'd been to Gaffney, SC of course, the center of his universe, and was on his way back to Mama. He had brought back a truckload of goodies, as was his usual way, and wanted to stop by and drop off a few of them with me. So he gave me a bag of peaches, some chocolate Heath bars, some butterscotch candies, and the prize - a "new" secondhand watch from E.H. Jones Jewelers in Gaffney.

I hugged him again, thrilled more to see my daddy than the loot, and told him I'd sign out and we could go off campus to get some dessert or something. But he didn't have time. He had to get back on the road. He always wanted to be on the move, especially if Mama was at the end of the road. So he gave me another hug and handed me a $5 bill with the admonition "Don't spend it all in one place." Then he got in his truck and drove away. I stood in the dorm parking lot watching the taillights of his truck as they faded away into the night. It occurred to me then that it hadn't been a long enough visit for me with Daddy. That's the way I still feel about his life. I didn't have enough time with him and I miss him still.

Daddy and me

A LUMP OF COAL

very year at Christmas, I hear the expression "you'll get a lump of coal in your stocking." But I've only known one person who ever actually got coal in his stocking – my daddy. On the day he first told me this, I couldn't believe it. My father, the Baptist minister, my spiritual leader for as long as he lived, was naughty enough once to receive coal for Christmas! He never talked about his childhood much except to say that they didn't have much. As he was the sixth of nine children (seven boys and two girls, all healthy and spirited) in a Depression-era farm family, I can imagine it was easy for him to get lost in the mix.

Daddy told me about sneaking out to the barn when he was a child where his father's seed peanuts were stored for the next year's planting, wiggle his finger into the burlap bag and grab a handful of peanuts for a snack. Eventually, half a bag of seed peanuts was gone, as his father discovered, a big loss for a farmer. Perhaps that was the year he got the coal.

Or maybe it was the time he and his cousin R.G., not only his cousin but his best friend, harassed R.G.'s younger brother Clifford. Daddy and R.G. fancied themselves all grown up and didn't want a younger brother/ cousin tagging along. So they ditched him and went fishing. Could that have brought the coal?

I have one of Daddy's old schoolbooks, titled Literature and Life, copyright date 1922. It was well used by many of Daddy's brothers and sisters as well as other classmates, for their names are scribbled throughout the book. Daddy's name seems to be written quite a lot alongside drawings of a clock face, and the words "Sunbury, NC," the little village near where he lived. I can imagine him sitting in a classroom at Sunbury School watching the hands on the clock on the wall as they crawled toward freedom. There are girls' names scribbled in the margins of the books, too. I was told once by one of Daddy's classmates, that he was quite popular with the ladies in high school. A line of verse he scribbled in the back of the book offers a look at where his mind was during school hours: "Don't forget me little darling, when from me you are far away. But remember little darling, that we may meet again someday." Could that be a reason he received a lump of coal?

Daddy told me that after high school and before college, he worked in a dance hall in Ocean View, VA taking up tickets. In that summer, he heard the call of God to become a minister and his life's course was set from there on. After college, he entered the seminary and served God for the rest of his 78 years. I like to think of my daddy, the little boy who was mischievous enough to get coal in his stocking but obedient enough to God's call when he grew up to be one of God's shepherds here on earth. May it be so for all of us – May we turn our coal into diamonds.

HOW MAMA AND DADDY FELL IN LOVE

In the summer of 1934, my Daddy, Frank Elliott Morris, a college student, was working for his cousin Paul Saunders in a Portsmouth Gulf service station when he finally decided to give in to the call to the ministry that he had been feeling for nearly a year. Sometime later his brother Desmond, a student at Louisville's Southern Baptist Seminary, made arrangements for Daddy to join him there. After taking some classes, Daddy was asked to preach at what was my mother's home church.

My mother, Theodosia Ellen Dever, known as "Doty," was the fifth of six tall, beautiful daughters born to a Kentucky farmer. Her mother died when Mama was just four years old and her stern but loving father raised his girls more or less on his own. After our parents' death, my sisters and I discovered a cache of love letters they had written to one another during their courtship and for several years after their marriage whenever they were apart. The letters were charming, using the slang of the day. Weather seemed to have figured prominently in their lives, more so than in ours today. For example, once in a while the mailman didn't come because it had rained so hard or snow had melted so that the creek was up! It was fascinating to see just how different courtship was in the 1930s from today. And going somewhere unchaperoned was just not done.

My Uncle Desmond introduced Daddy to Mama at church one Sunday. Mama was dating another boy at the time and the letters hinted at this fellow. It's easy to see why Mama soon fell in love with our daddy instead - he was a handsome, charming, good natured young guy. They began dating slowly while initially maintaining relationships with others. I can imagine that Daddy introduced himself with some reserve to my formidable grandfather and charmed Mama's five sisters with his dimpled smile and happy personality. They went to church meetings and on double dates with Uncle Desmond and his wife, riding in the rumble seat of Uncle Desmond's car to places like Mammoth Cave, Kentucky. The letters, so many of them, told the story of their love. But there was so much in these letters that was left unsaid. They'd frequently toss off little asides which left me wanting to know more. And they seemed to delight in teasing each other with hints of news they'd reveal when they saw each other next.

*Mama and Daddy about the time they were dating
or early in their marriage ca. 1936*

Though the letters left out so much, what they did show me was how much they liked and depended on each other. They revealed Mama's quiet, lady-like reserve, and Daddy's jovial, tenderhearted personality. I can still hear Daddy, at age 65, telling someone that he married a girl from Kentucky where the women were fast and the horses were pretty, an obvious twist on the original statement! And the letters after they were married I found to be especially tender. How Daddy missed Mama when they were apart! Mama and Daddy were married nearly 55 years at the time of my Daddy's death. Mama closed one of her letters to Daddy like this - "In closing, I want to say that I still love you and there will always be a place in my heart for you." I'm glad they are together now.

Mama and Daddy in Savannah ca. 1960

Daddy was with Mama until the very end, after her tragic stroke.

"GOD ALWAYS BATS LAST"

ot so very long ago in Mothertime, our daughter Katherine Yearwood Klegin was a teenage girl playing on her high school's basketball team. Shon Klegin was an unsuspecting teenage boy sitting quietly in the stands at her game, unaware that she had asked me to take his picture. Before he knew what was happening, both Shon and Katherine were falling for each other. Paul and I watched as they marched in the marching band at their school. We cheered Shon in his high school baseball games and Katherine in her basketball games. We went to their band concerts where they dressed in formal wear, Shon with his saxophone and Katherine with her piccolo and flute.

We wondered if their high school romance would last when they went to different schools, but of course it did, and over sixteen years later, they remain in love, now married and the parents of three little boys, one of whom lives in Heaven.

Yesterday, Paul and I attended Easter Sunday services with Katherine and Shon and their sons Nolan and Hudson. They attend First Baptist Church of Alexandria, VA. It was the first time I had been in the church since the funeral of Katherine and Shon's eleven month old baby Camden. I wondered how I would handle it and decided to take my cue from Shon and Katherine.

I needn't have worried, though. They are two of the strongest people I know. After losing their baby in 2015 to complications following surgery to repair several heart defects, they held his funeral in the very sanctuary where we were now worshipping. But, instead of grieving and giving up on their faith in God, their faith only became stronger. Since Camden's passing, Katherine and Shon have begun playing in their church's orchestra each Sunday.

Yesterday, as they do almost every Sunday, they sit in chairs placed just a few feet from where their son's casket lay. They walk down the aisle where they carried their son's casket to the hearse after the funeral when not enough pall bearers could be found. They look at the podium from their seats in the orchestra where, so recently, they took their infant sons, Camden and Hudson, to be dedicated to God in the Baptist tradition.

Yesterday's sermon, given by their Pastor Don Davidson was taken from the text of 1st Thessalonians 4:13-14. It reads,

"Brothers and sisters, we do not want you to be uninformed about those who sleep in death, so that you do not grieve like the rest of mankind, who have no hope. For we believe that Jesus died and rose again and so we believe that God will bring with Jesus those who have fallen asleep in him."

And I realized anew that Katherine and Shon have embraced this text. Though they miss Camden terribly, they do not grieve as those who are without hope.

So yesterday, they were there in their orchestra seats, dressed in their Sunday best, playing to the glory of God. Our hearts soared as we listened to their rendition of the old hymn "Were You There?" I marvel at their resilience and their courage as they continue to serve God. I'm thankful on this Easter Monday for a God who loves us and understands what it is like to watch a Son die. And I rejoice with Katherine and Shon in the sure and certain knowledge that Death is not the end of things because, as Pastor Davidson said yesterday, "God always bats last."

COMIC BOOKS

I know, I know...I was an English teacher so I should be promoting good literature. But I firmly believe that one of the things that developed in me a love of reading, besides Miss McCall, the children's librarian at the Savannah Public Library, and my daddy and mama who bought books for me, and Mrs. Beulah Harper, who insisted that I read the classics - besides all those people, I owe my love of reading to...wait for it...comic books, or as we used to call them, funny books.

Comic books cost 10 cents when I was a child so it was pretty easy to acquire a nice collection. They were printed on the cheapest paper possible with the brightest colors of ink - perfect to attract the eyes of a child. Comic books have become quite collectible now with early editions of Superman and Wonder Woman comics going for many thousands of dollars. While I enjoyed those two a lot, my personal preference was, sadly, for the very varieties that were destined never to be worth the paper they were printed on.

My sister Jerry and I and our buddy Terri could spend hours reading and rereading each other's copies of such classics as Katy Keene and Millie the Model. Ever heard of them? Probably not. They always had a page devoted to paper dolls with the starring character modeling clothes that had been designed and submitted by readers like me. I once submitted a drawing of a fashion design to Katy. I'm still waiting for it to be published. It's hard to find these comic books in comics stores because they were always cut up for the paper dolls.

I also liked Archie comics - with Jughead and Betty and Veronica. I probably became an English teacher to disprove the Miss Grundy stereotype. Miss Grundy was Archie's old maid schoolteacher who wore her grey hair in a bun and had a permanent frown etched on her face. I always wanted Archie to end up with Betty, by the way. Veronica was a spoiled brat.

Another favorite was the Uncle Scrooge comic books, probably for the scene where Uncle Scrooge slides down a mountain of coins in his vault. Those nasty Beagle Boys were always after his money, although I always wondered why the police couldn't see they were the bad guys. They always wore their masks!

The Sunday comics in the newspapers were another favorite of mine - I used to hunker over the heating vent in the front hall on winter days and read Dixie Dugan, The Phantom, Casper the Friendly Ghost, Popeye, Mutt and Jeff or, for obvious reasons, The Jackson Twins. I so very much wanted Jerry and me to be the Jackson Twins.

Finally, lest you think me a complete lunkhead, let me remind you that some of my very favorites were the Classics Illustrated comics. It's where I got my first taste of Robinson Crusoe, Treasure Island, or The Three Musketeers.

So whenever you see a child reading a comic book, don't automatically think negatively. For many children, comic books are gateways to the classics. Just ask this English teacher!

DADDY TELLS A TALE

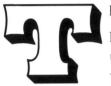his summer (in August for your gift planning purposes!) I turned 70, an impossible thing to comprehend unless you stop to think that I have eight grandchildren. Yet here I am - a senior citizen. I thought of this because I saw a photo recently of my daddy on his 69th birthday. I thought he was old then! March 27th, is the anniversary of my sweet daddy's birth. He lived to the age of 77 when a car accident and heartbreak over Mama's poor health after her stroke took him away from us.

But I try not to think of that terrible day much anymore and focus on all the happy times I had with him and there were so many. He could brighten any gathering just by being there. He had a million stories to tell, all of them hilarious or heartwarming. For example, I have laughed every time I drive over a certain spot in Gates County, NC where he grew up, because of the story he told about it. He said there was an old fellow who was learning to drive at that stretch of road just when automobiles began to be widely seen. He had his daughter Martha with him in the old Tin Lizzie he drove and felt he was going so fast that he couldn't take his eyes off the road to look down at the speedometer. Fearing he was about to crash, he yelled to his daughter [and here, Daddy changed his voice to sound like a scared old man,] "How fast am I doin', Marthy?" [Then he switched his voice again to sound like a young girl's.] "You're settin' on twenty, Daddy." We laughed out loud EVERY TIME he told that old nugget, just to think of some old fellow who thought driving at 20 MPH was speeding!

I wish I had all of his stories catalogued but, of course, I don't. No one could because they were boundless. I like to think of him sitting in Heaven on his birthday, a fishing pole in his hand with Mama by his side and maybe his little great grandson Camden in his lap telling more tales. Who knows what Heaven will really be like, but I know it will be a great reunion when I can hear my Daddy tell his stories again.

SLATS

esterday we went to Home Depot to get a few board feet of lumber for slats on one of our guest beds. (One of the original slats was just a fraction too short and kept falling out.) This was a bed which I inherited from my parents. It's an old mahogany tall bed, and weighs about a thousand pounds. Back in the 1930s, my Daddy bought it second hand and gave it to his mother and daddy. Daddy always had a soft spot in his heart for his parents and, though he lived far away from them most of his life because of the churches he pastored, he took every opportunity to go see them. He loved bringing gifts to them, usually peaches, but this was something special. The bed came with a mahogany marble top dresser and mirror, now lost to time. When I was a little girl, I slept in this bed with my twin sister, Jerry. At that time, in the 1950s, it was fitted out with a feather mattress and, as I recall, about a half dozen quilts. There was something called a bolster rather than two pillows for our heads - it looked like a very long pillow stuffed with goose feathers and covered in ticking.

The bed resided in one of two upstairs bedrooms of my grandparents' house, a 200 year old house in Gates County, NC. known as the Daniel Williams family house (for an earlier owner.) The house no longer stands except in my memory and there it looms large for the memories it held. There was only a single light bulb overhead in that room, but Grandmama had attached a string to the bulb and tied the other end to a tack on the wall near the bed. So when we got in bed, we just gave a simple tug on the string and it was lights out.

Daddy got the bed back after his parents passed away, and when I was a young married woman, he gave it to me. At one time or another, all three of my children slept in it when they were little. Because it has a tall footboard, it was perfect for them. A few times, after the girls got married, they came home for a visit and slept in it with their husbands. That must have been a tight fit, though - kind of a corner to corner situation.

I was thinking about that old bed a lot tonight as Paul and I enjoyed a fire while we watched a couple of TV shows. It's all of a sudden gotten pretty cold here (going down into the twenties tonight) so the fire felt good. He brought in some firewood before dinner, I fixed a salad and he warmed up some of his famous chili which we had in the freezer.

He pointed to an old, rough board and said "That's the slat." He had sawed up the old slat into firewood size and put it on top of the fire where the rough pine board crackled and spit loudly. In a way it made me sad to think of all the times people I love had slept on that old board, but I certainly want the bed to be sturdy. I was looking at the fire encircling the old board when Paul turned to me and, reading my mind as he frequently does, said, "Don't worry, there are still three more under the mattress." You've just got to love a man who understands why I feel sentimental about a hundred year old board.

A LOVE STORY

aul and I have known each other since our senior year in high school. He was my first steady boyfriend. But we kind of lost our way for a few years until life and circumstances brought us together again some thirty years later. When we married in 1994, it was the beginning of some of the most wonderful years of my life. I love Paul for who he is. I like it that he still wears suits and ties to work and when he gets home, he just loosens the tie a little. Dressing down means wearing khakis and a starched shirt. I like it that his word means something. When he says he'll be there, he is. He's kind of like my very own Atticus Finch. He was there for all of our children - paying for their entire college education plus all that went before, giving them solid, well-thought-out advice, helping them with carpentry projects, providing cars for the children to drive, giving Tom his rehearsal dinner, walking the girls down the aisle in the weddings he paid for, and now becoming a grandfather to their children. He never once asked to be a father but he became one willingly. He gave me the freedom to explore my dreams and gave me the time and tools to do just that.

In 1965, Daddy accepted a call to become the pastor of a church in Newport News, VA. We had been living in Savannah, GA and I was to graduate from Savannah High School in one year. To say I was disappointed is an understatement. But we moved and very soon afterwards, several teenaged kids (including Paul) showed up on the porch of the new parsonage to meet my sister Jerry and me. ("Scoping out the fresh talent" as Paul has often said.)

Anyway, Paul, whose parents were members of the church my dad now pastored, and I became good friends and dated regularly. We went steady and I even wore his senior class ring. But at the end of the summer before college, I gave it back to him as we were attending different colleges and I didn't want to attempt a long distance relationship. So during college, he and I both dated others and occasionally got back together.

After college, I met the man who would become my first husband and we were married. Meanwhile, Paul entered law school at the College of William and Mary and was married to another law student. Neither marriage would go the distance, though they each lasted a couple of decades. [No one could call Paul or me quitters!] And my marriage produced three wonderful children – Tom, Katherine and Caroline.

When our marriages didn't work out, my sister Jerry, who had maintained contact with Paul through the years, invited us both to Larry's and her home for a Fourth of July barbecue in 1993. Shortly afterwards, Paul told me, "Whenever you're ready to start dating, I'd like to see you."

A few months later in October, we agreed to meet at the annual NC State Fair with Jerry and Larry. We had such a wonderful time that we began that long distance relationship I hadn't wanted earlier. I was a single mom living in Raleigh and working as a marketing rep for an engineering firm and Paul was an attorney living and working in Washington, DC.

He began coming to Raleigh on weekends to visit and before too long he asked me to marry him. As Harry said in the movie "When Harry Met Sally," "When you realize you want to spend the rest of your life with somebody, you want the rest of your life to start as soon as possible."

We were married in October of 1994 and overnight, Paul became the father of three children, which also meant he took on all the burdens, debt and care of having three children. But as he told me often when we were dating, he wanted the whole package – me and the three kids, ages 18, 11, and 8. In the 24 years we've been married, he has provided a better life for all of us than we could ever have imagined. He attended every single one of the girls' band concerts and football games and every single one of their basketball games, often leaving his law office downtown to hurry to make the games or concerts, then rushing back to his office to finish his work.

Though he doesn't often express romantic sentiments to me, Paul has been by my side and supported me through every good and bad thing that has ever happened. When my mother needed care because of her stroke and when she died, Paul was there. When our son and daughter in law lost two babies to miscarriage, he was there. When our daughter and son in law lost little Camden, their 11 month old baby, after open heart surgery, he was there. When our youngest daughter was left alone while her husband was deployed with the Navy or when they lived across the country, Paul took me to see them.

All of the children have come to depend upon him for wise counsel on business, legal and tax matters. They have enjoyed spending time with him doing woodworking projects or dining out together. And they have shared eight amazing grandchildren with him. The grandchildren call him Pablo and he loves it.

I wish I could have had a marriage that lasted like Mama and Daddy's or Paul's parents Glenroy and Maria. But if I hadn't married Paul, there would never have been a Shon, or Julie or Ben or those eight amazing grandchildren – Leighton, Nolan, Naomi, Mason, Will, Hudson, Camden and Henry. I lost Paul once, but I'll never lose him again. As the saying goes, this marriage isn't my first but it will definitely be my last – I love you, Paul, forever. Finding love the second time around is a tough proposition for anyone. I struck gold.

WASHING DISHES

I have a very nice dishwasher - a Bosch - which costs more than it should. It's very quiet and energy efficient. I just load the dishes in it and it does all the hard work for me. I don't even have to rinse the dishes ahead of time. But I often wish I could go back to the years when I was in college and would come home for the weekend.

Mama would stand at the sink, put her soft hands in the soapy water and wash the dishes after one of her amazing meals. I'd take one of her carefully pressed linen dish towels from the kitchen drawer, dry the dishes and put them away. But the best part was that I had Mama all to myself. Daddy was off doing dad stuff and my three sisters were either married or somewhere else. So Mama and I talked.

She told me, in her quiet way, about her childhood, about her father, about growing up in Kentucky without a mother. (Mama's mother died when Mama was four years old.) We talked about my boyfriends, my career plans, or shopping trips we planned. It's when my mother began to be my best friend. It's been many years since I saw her last. After so many years, I suppose I shouldn't feel lonely for her. But she was a blessing and I thank God for her memory. I miss her.

SHOPPING – GRRRRR

s any woman of a certain age knows, it can be a difficult thing to find suitable clothing to wear, especially if you are, shall we say, generously proportioned. Yesterday was Paul's bridge day (where he plays bridge and eats junk food all day with his buddies,) so I took myself to the mall just to see what was out there. As you can imagine - not much! Nothing has sleeves anymore. Either dress manufacturers assume that all women have Michelle Obama arms, or that it is permanently 80 degrees, or, (and this is my personal belief) it's a conspiracy to make you buy a sweater or jacket to cover up. More items sold = more profit.

So, since Paul wasn't home yet, I thought, what if I could make something? I used to sew, having been taught by my mother who was a magnificent seamstress and numerous underpaid Home Ec. teachers through the years. So I went to our local JoAnn Fabric store to see what was what.

Fabric stores have lately become "craft stores" because apparently there are not many home sewers anymore. So in the large space previously devoted to bolt after bolt of fabric, now you are more likely to see adult coloring books and pencils, hot glue guns and Styrofoam. Still there was a small island in the middle of the store - a large table with a few chairs and the giant pattern books I remembered. There they all were - Butterick, Simplicity, McCalls and Vogue, along with newer ones like Burda and New Look.

A warm feeling washed over me as I pulled the first book from the stack - Simplicity, my old standby. To my surprise the woman modeling the clothes on the cover was covered in tattoos. Literally - both arms sleeved in colorful tattoos of flowers and birds. This does not bode well for me. Hmmm - not like the old days, I thought, but I soldiered on. I looked through all of the books, turning page after page in search of a service-able dress pattern that had the following requirements: short or mid-length sleeves, a collar, a rather relaxed waistline (I am a senior citizen after all,) and a style which didn't look like the granny which, admittedly, I am.

What I found inside each of the books, instead of the dress pattern I was looking for, was - Vintage! Each of the pattern companies has now begun offering patterns from their archives. Each has the actual artwork from the original pattern along with the date of its first issue - 1942! 1912! 1965! The most distressing thing was that I saw many of the patterns my mother had made for me now advertised as vintage! Yes - you, too, can look like a girl from the sixties with this mod dress pattern.

Finally, after an hour of searching, I found ONE pattern that fit the bill - McCalls 7080. You can Google it. I pulled it from the drawer, and then went in search of fabric. I thought - a simple solid in a quiet shade with a contrasting collar. But there was NOTHING except fabrics for crafting - calicos for quilting, upholstery fabrics for slipcovers, sequined and studded fabrics for Cosplay (a kind of costume dressing up that I'm WAY too old for.)

So, finally admitting defeat, I put the pattern back in the drawer and left the store. Maybe I'll just keep wearing my old clothes a while longer.

~Sigh~

FRIENDSHIPS

In 70 years, a person can accumulate a lot of friends, some of whom are with you for decades, and some of whom are with you for the moment. Many of my friends are on Facebook and, for that I am grateful because it has enabled me to reconnect with you. Some of my friends I see almost daily because we live or work together. Others are lost in the mists of time – unreachable but unforgotten. And there are a few friends I have through the medium of Facebook whom I've never met but feel I know so well. It would be almost impossible to call all of you by name because I would surely leave out someone important.

My very first friend Nancy lived next door to the parsonage where I spent my first five years. We had tea parties outside in our own little playhouses constructed of her mother's old lace curtains draped over tree branches. Then there were my childhood friends from Savannah – Eleanor, Terri, and Beth with Jerry and I formed clubs (The Bones Club, The Pat Boone Fan Club!) and shared our pangs of middle school yearnings and heartaches. I have reconnected with friends from my elementary, middle and high school days - an amazing thing.

My college friends were my first adult friends and they saw me through the throes of my first real romances and breakups. They threw me in the fountain when I got engaged and let me cry on their shoulders when my boyfriend and I broke up. They played powder puff football with me, coached me through Algebra 101 and helped me get over my homesickness.

I found friendships on the job with co-workers who both taught me how to teach again after a 25-year layoff and commiserated with me in the trenches. I have church friends who have helped me to grow spiritually and taught me so much about God's love. I have my country friends I made during those glorious days when I had a farm in Gates County. I'll never forget one friend bringing me bushel baskets full of potatoes, butter beans and tomatoes on the day I moved into my farmhouse. I have some friends I haven't even met yet but you encourage me daily with your comments to me online.

I'll never forget how my friends cried with me when my first marriage ended, and when my parents and my grandson passed away – the notes they wrote me, the flowers they sent, the visits they made. Some of my friends are even distant family members I don't get to see nearly enough. You see what I mean? I just can't name all of you. That's how richly I am blessed with friends in my life. On this day, I'm thankful for all of you, dear friends.

EIGHTY YEARS LATER

 n September 10, 1936, my Mama woke up in a white clapboard farmhouse on a farm outside the tiny village of Gravel Switch, Kentucky. It was her wedding day and she was preparing to marry a handsome, tall preacher from North Carolina. She was 21 and her groom was 22. They'd met when the preacher, my father-to-be, was introduced to Mama by his brother who pastored her church at the time.

Mama and Daddy were married for 54 years, 8 months and 24 days until Daddy passed away in a car accident. But in those 54 years, they lived in five states where they served God in Baptist churches all across the South (Kentucky, North Carolina, Virginia, South Carolina and Georgia,) raised four daughters, became grandparents to ten children who adored them, and made the lives of countless people better for knowing them.

No pictures remain from their wedding, although Mama often described the day to her daughters, telling us of the small ceremony in the parlor of the home of a Rev. Gabbert in Lebanon, Kentucky, a few miles from Mama's home. That year of 1936 was a brief interval between the deprivation of the Great Depression and the start of the Second World War. There was no grand white wedding gown for her, the fifth of six daughters of a widower farmer. But Mama often described to us her wedding attire - a burgundy two piece suit with mink tails around the collar. Every time she remembered the suit, she lamented the fact that she hadn't saved it, at least the mink tails.

For a honeymoon, Daddy took her to Mammoth Cave in Kentucky and then to North Carolina to meet his parents. Mama had grown up on a neat farm in Kentucky surrounded by green fields of cattle and corn, so the 200-year-old farmhouse in the swept sand yard of her in-laws must have been a bit of a shock. My Uncle Corbell ran the Virginia Dare Hotel, a luxury hotel in Elizabeth City, NC and, in a typical gesture, he gave them the honeymoon suite for their stay.

After both Mama and Daddy died, my sisters and I discovered a cache of love letters between them, letters we had always known about but were never allowed to read. Mama was a private person, not given to sharing emotions openly in stark contrast to our Daddy who was an open book. The love revealed in those letters brought to life the young couple who became our parents. We were blessed to have them as our North Star through all the years of our growing up. They guided us, encouraged us, disciplined us when necessary and always loved us. On this day, so many years after the fact, I am grateful to God that Mama and Daddy began their life together.

A THANK YOU NOTE TO MAMA

I receive lots of wonderful messages from friends and family on each birthday. I have connected with so many people from my past and I'd really like to thank you all for remembering me each year. But there's one person I would really to thank. Unfortunately, I can't. It's my mother and she is in Heaven.

Recently I turned 70, an unimaginable number, especially when I remember that my daddy was only 78 when he passed away. I am O.L.D. Yet, my memories of my parents remain strong even though it has been many years since I last saw my mother and even more since I last saw my daddy. Still, I remember them with such love.

I think that birthdays should really be celebrated by the mothers instead of the children, because they are the ones who do all the work. I've been thinking of that day so many years ago when my mother was at home in the brick parsonage in Gaffney, SC. Daddy was in North Carolina conducting a series of revival meetings as Baptist ministers do. Mama was at home taking care of my two older sisters, Louise and Martha Jean who were ten and eight at the time.

I can just imagine how afraid Mama must have been when the labor pains started. I imagine she worried that she would not get to the hospital in time without Daddy there to drive her. I imagine she worried about who would take care of my sisters in her absence. I imagine she was in a lot of pain because in the primordial days around the time of my birth, prenatal care was quite different from what's available now. In addition, as

Mama told me many times, her doctor never knew she was having twins, although she always said she knew there were two of us in there.

The due date for my sister Jerry and me was a month away making our expected arrival sometime in late September, so Daddy felt that he had plenty of time to be back for the delivery. Hence the revival in North Carolina. But as we know now, twins frequently arrive ahead of schedule, so on the morning of August 24, 1948, things began to happen very fast for Mama.

Thank God we had a wonderful neighbor next door in the person of Belva Clarkson, the mother of my first friend Nancy Clarkson Fowler. Mama either called her on the phone or sent one of my sisters over to the Clarksons with a cry for help. Mrs. Clarkson immediately took things in hand and drove Mama to the Cherokee County General Hospital, leaving, I assume, my sisters in the care of Mrs. Clarkson's mother in law who lived behind the Clarkson's.

At 2:00 PM, I made my entrance into the world weighing in at 5lbs 5 oz. Nine minutes later, Jerry followed weighing a puny 5 lbs. In the meantime, Mrs. Clarkson had called Daddy at Mama's request and told him to get home. He left North Carolina immediately with his sister, my Aunt Edith. I never knew if he got home before we arrived or not, but Daddy always told us that he burned out the motor of his brand new Ford getting to Gaffney for our birth.

I'll bet he was a little disappointed when he realized that he had two more girls to add to his harem. Daddy was always a man's man – loved fishing and hunting – so I know he would have loved to have a son to go along with him. (Girls didn't do that in those days.) That's probably why Jerry got her boy's name and spelling. And I think he was surprised to find that Mama had given birth to twin girls. Double whammy!

Nevertheless, Daddy never once in all the time I knew him said he wished they'd had boys. In fact, he was pretty proud of being the only rooster in the barnyard, though I'm sure we four girls gave him fits when we were teens. So, anyway, thank you to all of my friends and family who send me birthday wishes each year. They mean everything to me. And thank you to Mama in Heaven for all your hard work. I hope I've made you proud.

JUST ONE NAME

 ately, I've been looking at all the old memorabilia in my basement and barn, trying to straighten some of it, toss some of it, and relive old times. Today's treasure from the "Archives" comes from a time I would rather forget, but I just can't. Our mother had had a massive stroke and was in a rehabilitation center. Shortly after she entered the facility, our father was killed in a car accident while on his way to see Mama. To say my sisters and I were devastated is an understatement. We hardly knew what to do.

Mama could no longer speak, was paralyzed completely on one side and had no way of taking care of herself. Daddy was gone. We now had to learn to speak the language of Medicare, Medicaid, Assisted Living and many other foreign terms. Jerry and I took turns going to see Mama each week as the rehab center was in Durham, near our homes in Raleigh. Martha Jean and Louise came when they could, since they lived much farther away. Ultimately Mama came to live with Jerry and her family fulltime but for quite a while she was in the Greenery Rehab Center as therapists worked with her in a futile attempt to help her regain her abilities.

Somehow during these awful days, God gave us strength and angels of mercy who encouraged us. I've talked about the three angels who comforted me in the hospital (African American church ladies garbed in beautiful suits and giant hats.) They saw me weeping in the chapel, came over and surrounded me with their arms and prayed mighty prayers of comfort, though they didn't know Mama or me.

But in the Greenery, we received another angel in the form of Mama's roommate. I can't remember her name but she was as plain as our mama was beautiful. Her body was twisted and misshapen with rheumatoid arthritis, so she spent her days in bed. She almost never had any visitors that I can recall, yet she was as cheerful as could be. She talked to us as though we had come to visit her; and strangely enough, it was a comfort to hear her voice as our own mother was now so very silent. She seemed to take our mother under her wing and let the rehab center nurses know when Mama needed something. She let us know, too, if Mama had been neglected in some way.

Just one Name

I wondered how she could remain so cheerful when she had been reduced to such a state. One day when I was visiting Mama, her roommate handed me the piece of needlepoint in the picture. She had put the name "Jesus" in blue yarn, the letters spaced unevenly, on a narrow piece of canvas.

"Here, honey, this is for you," she said, and put it into my hands. "I just keep writing His name and it helps me somehow."

I soon learned that she gave those little rectangles of embroidery to everyone she met- nurses, orderlies, and complete strangers. Needlepoint after needlepoint - all with one name on them - "Jesus." It was her way of sharing her faith from a bed from which she would never rise.

Our mama has been gone for many years. That sweet lady who gave me the needlepoint has probably been gone even longer. Yet I still have the gift she gave me and it still strengthens me when my faith falters. Just one name - JESUS.

OUTER BANKS MEMORIES

I just returned from a few days at the Outer Banks, a place where I have vacationed for nearly 65 years, first with my parents, then with my children and now with our grandchildren. Nags Head, Kill Devil Hills, and Kitty Hawk – all have changed dramatically since I went there for the first time in the fifties. On the bypass road, where there used to be only gnarled, windswept trees leading to the dunes of Jockey's Ridge, now are chain restaurants and beach shops by the dozens, each louder and more kitschy than the next. The beach road, where there used to be long stretches of seagrass waving in sandy hills, now consists of restaurants of every description and cottage after cottage.

The houses one sees now should hardly be called cottages – they are more like three-story mansions. Painted in bright pastels or garish primary colors, the houses loom over the road, as grand as they are out of place. A few of them even have palm trees, unseemly and just wrong, planted in landscaped beds which bear no resemblance to the unpolished look I remember.

The old Nags Head-type cottages Mama and Daddy rented back then were unpainted wood-shingled style with wrap-around porches. Many of the porches had lean-out benches and hammocks where we whiled away the rigidly-observed one-hour wait after lunch before going back in the water. Around every porch was a clothesline where we hung our bathing suits overnight to dry. The next day, we'd put them on again, the sand from the previous day still clinging to the seams. Many of these houses were owned by the same family for decades. I used to love seeing the names and locations of the owners posted proudly on signs outside the house facing the beach road. You'd see "Mrs. S.J. Outland, Scotland Neck, NC" or "Carroll Winslow, Suffolk, VA." It was neat to see who owned these structures and made the Outer Banks feel like a family.

There was absolutely no air conditioning and few fans in these cottages. In fact, one of the first things Daddy did upon entering whatever cottage we rented was to go around and open every single window and lift the wood batten shutters held open with a stick. The beds were either twin or full-sized, with mattresses that were more lumpy than firm. The bed coverlets were worn and faded seersucker or muslin. The towels were thin and rough. The bathrooms invariably had no tub, just a shower, with wooden slats to stand on.

We almost never went out to a restaurant for a meal, because, of course, there were so few restaurants to choose from. Daddy would go out on the pier all morning and cast his fishing line into the Atlantic Ocean; sometimes he would meet one of his brothers, Desmond, or Tommy or Chester, and drag a seine net at the ocean's edge. By lunch time, Daddy would have a cooler full of fish and our supper menu was set.

I was never entertained on the beach by my parents. In fact, more often than not, I was left to my own devices with no parental supervision. Jerry and I just knew to show up for lunch and dinner and help with the dishes afterward. Poor Mama! She had to cook three meals a day with battered old utensils and tin cook pots that smelled funny.

Once every few years or so, we'd go to see "The Lost Colony," North Carolina's famed outdoor drama. But mostly, we just played in the sand with our metal buckets and shovels, or our plastic cars. We built sand castles with moats that filled with ocean water. The next day our sand castles would be gone, washed away by the high tide. So we'd start again, building another castle, digging another moat to surround it and pressing shells into the castle for decoration. And the next morning that castle would be gone too.

The memory of those days came to me this week as I watched my grandchildren play in the sands of the Outer Banks. The days when I played in the sand seem like just yesterday. Turn around and I was a teenager listening to "Under the Boardwalk" and looking for cute guys. Turn around again and I was a young mother, shepherding my three children over to the beach. Now, I am the old Nana, watching as my children take their own children down to the water to wash off the sand and look for sea glass or shells.

The beach always seemed like a lower part of Heaven to me when I was a child and it still does, but now I realize I have fewer summers ahead of me than behind me and it's a sobering thought. The memories I hold from days gone by are more precious than gold. And each time I return to the Outer Banks, the ghosts of my father and mother, my uncles and aunts, all long gone, rise before me like a dream, as Daddy used to say. I look at the few cottages still there that I remember; I see the few old places still extant from the old days – Winks, the Avalon pier, the Black Pelican (the restaurant located in the old lifesaving station in Kitty Hawk) and remember the ones that are gone – the Galleon whose clothes I coveted, the Oasis Restaurant with its lace cornbread and barefoot college girl waitresses (I so wanted to be one,) the Casino where I first learned to shoot pool and dance the Shag, Newman's Shell Shop, and Dowdy's Amusement Park, where I took my children to ride the Tilt-a-Whirl.

I see the few flat-top cottages that are left in Southern Shores. Relics of the post-war years, they were the very picture of modernity when we looked at them across the sound from the sound-front cottage Mama and Daddy bought in the seventies from Christine, Daddy's brother Corbell's sister-in-law. My children learned to swim in the shallow waters of the sound and my daddy, their grandfather whom they called Dandy, took his grandchildren out for fishing trips in his motor boat.

Now those days are lost and gone forever, just as are all of my family older than my sisters and me. Someday maybe my children will remember these days as golden days, just as I remember the days of my childhood. When they do, if they do, I hope they remember me with the same love and longing with which I remember my own mother and father and the August days on the sands of long ago.

DADDY

 ll of us who loved our daddies feel lucky to have had them, especially on Father's Day. But Daddy has been in Heaven for many years now and the people who remember him are few in number. Even my youngest daughter Caroline was only five when he passed, so her memories are minimal. But Daddy was a great and wonderful man and I wish all of you who didn't know him could have had the privilege.

He was a minister, yes, but not one of those stuffy, holier-than-thou types. He was almost never without a smile on his face. He loved a good joke or story, especially when the joke was on him. He wore a suit and tie Sunday through Friday. But on Saturdays you could find him in a pair of cords and an old flannel shirt. He'd be fishing in the Ogeechee River or bird hunting with a little rifle he'd gotten from Webster's or from one of his brothers. Then later he could fry up a mess of bream like nobody's business.

Daddy was very tenderhearted about his Mama and Papa. He left the family farm when he was just a teenager and went off to college, but the farm never really left him. From time to time throughout his life, he owned a few acres and had a few head of livestock - goats to keep the weeds down, chickens (always chickens for he loved fresh eggs for breakfast) turkeys, geese, and a few ponies. His favorite pony was Dusty. I still have Dusty's saddle in my office. It's resting on a footstool and I smile every time

I put my feet up on its smooth tan leather. I think of how many of Daddy's grandchildren rode on Dusty's back with Daddy leading them around the yard. In his later years, Daddy had 'coon dogs, for he loved to go out into the woods of his native Gates County with some of his younger friends to tree raccoons, a sport he'd loved in his youth. His favorite 'coon dog was Trailer, who gave him a litter or two of fine pups.

Daddy loved his four girls and was morose every time he had to give one of us away to our new husbands. But he soon came to see the value of our being married as these boys became his unpaid labor - helping him around the farm, or putting up a new dock at his beach cottage. And having sons-in-law meant that he got the most wonderful thing - grandchildren - ten of them, four girls and six boys - all of whom thought he hung the moon. His grandchildren called him Dandy, a corruption of Granddaddy by his eldest grandchild Johnny. The name suited him to a tee.

Daddy's one true love, though, was Mama. Her name was Theodosia, a name she hated, so Daddy called her Doty and he was as in love with her at the end of his life as he must have been when they first met. We lost our Daddy in a car accident when he was on his way to see Mama, who'd had a stroke and was hospitalized. Those six grandsons of his bore his coffin to the family cemetery where I'd walked with him so often to visit his parents' graves. Daddy has been gone for over twenty-five years and not a day goes by that I don't thank God that he was mine. I was lucky to be his girl.

SUMMER DAYS

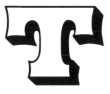he older I get, the greater is my appreciation for summer. I recall happy summer days of my childhood visiting my grandparents in Kentucky and North Carolina. Uncle Thurman would drive up to Grandmama Beulah's

house in Gates, NC with a monstrous green watermelon in the back of his pick-up truck. All of us cousins would gather around the flat roof of the well house while he took a butcher knife from Grandmama's kitchen and cut thick, juicy slices for each of us. Some of us would sprinkle salt on our slices but I liked mine plain. We'd bury our faces in the pink flesh, taking an occasional time out to spit the black seeds in competition with our cousins. What a mess we were when we'd finally eaten all the way to the rind, but who cared? The day was warm and we were satiated and surrounded by loving family – Daddy and Mama were still alive and took care of all our needs. Our grandmamma would bring us wet cloths to wipe our dripping chins and head immediately back to the kitchen where her maid Iney was preparing lunch.

When we visited Kentucky, my grandmother Marie would outfit my sister and me with tin buckets and march us up the Kentucky knobs to milk the cows or pick blackberries (always with the admonition to look out for snakes.) We'd come back to the house where Buddy or Billy would be turning the crank on the ice cream freezer. Peach ice cream made from the peaches my daddy had brought from Gaffney was soon to be enjoyed under the spreading trees of the front yard.

Each summer we also spent a week on the Outer Banks in a cottage that was invariably too small for us – two adults and four girls. So I spent as little time as necessary in the house and as much time as possible on the sandy beach. We got a new toy car each summer and made roads and sand castles by the water's edge. Time moved on and the toy cars changed to transistor radios and diaries. Still the summers were magical times and I remember them with delight for those days were carefree and timeless. There is a J.M. Barrie quote that says "God gave us memory so that we might have roses in December." I think of this often when the days are chilled and my fingers ache with the cold. I'm grateful for the memory of sweet summer days.

THE CARS IN MY LIFE

I've never been much interested in cars, unlike Paul. I see them as merely a way to get from point A to point B. Thankfully, most of the cars I've owned have been dependable, though rather uninteresting from a car enthusiast's point of view. My first car, for example, was a 1970 Pontiac LeMans named Laverne. When I first saw her, she had 12,000 miles on her. When I bought her, the mileage had been rolled back to 2,000. (Unscrupulous dealer trick.) Her ceiling liner dropped (problem solved with a handy stapler!), and my daddy replaced the torn blue vinyl top with a snappy white one. But I drove her for a decade and cried the day she left me.

Laverne was followed by a succession of ordinary looking vehicles including –The Artful Dodger (a Dodge Dart given to me by my uncle after Laverne died (only an English major would name a car after a Dickens character,) Fred Ford (a lime green station wagon I didn't keep long,) The Blackbird (the first in a series of Toyotas) and finally Pearl, my current Toyota Highlander. Paul bought her for me a couple of years ago to satisfy his need for a four wheel drive vehicle now that we live in the sticks. I had a pickup truck once, a blue Ford F-150 named Old Blue which I inherited from my Daddy and drove until Tom took it over to go to college.

As I said, I don't much care about what the car looks like though I do tend to stick to black, white or blue for the colors. I just want them to be reliable. The only car I've ever had that I couldn't depend upon was an underpowered Honda Civic. Paul hated driving it because he said it was like driving a sewing machine; so of course, we named it the Sewing

Machine. It had the unhappy habit of dying right in the middle of a street somewhere far away from help. Katherine inherited it when I got a new car and drove it fearlessly. She carried a portable generator of some kind in the car with her when she drove the Sewing Machine to school. When it failed to start, she simply hauled out the Jumper 1000 (we often gave it different numbers - the Jumper 527, the Jumper 8186, etc.) jumpstarted the car and was on her way again. I was never so bold, so when I have a dependable car as I do now, I am grateful.

WHAT DADDY MISSED

y father has been gone for over a quarter of a century. Even as I write this, I am stunned at the length of time that has passed since I have seen his face. He left this earth June 3, 1991 in a terrible car accident and I cried for weeks afterward. I still do cry occasionally today and long to call him and feel his big bear hug. He was a true anchor in whatever storms I was weathering at the time.

In all those years since his passing, he's missed my girls and son growing to adulthood, their college graduations, the wonderful people they married and the eight terrific grandchildren they have given birth to. He missed getting to know Paul as a son-in-law. What fun they would have had together. He missed knowing Camden. What I would have given to have him to lean on during that year of Camden's illness and passing. He would have been a rock. Yet it would have brought tears to my Daddy's eyes to lose that child, for his children and grandchildren were everything to him.

"Give the kid the best there is," he often said gleefully as he piled a steak or another piece of cake on our children's plates. We would shake our heads realizing he was an unstoppable force.

Each anniversary of his passing still brings a tear to my eye. But as a Christian, I take great comfort in knowing that his soul is in Heaven and he is enjoying a wonderful reunion with all of our loved ones who have gone before. He is probably having long talks with the Master as they walk along the streets of gold. I like thinking that he has even met little Camden as he and Mama welcomed him at the Pearly Gates along with St. Peter.

The time until I will be reunited with Daddy, Mama and Camden is now surely shorter than the decades-long span since I last saw my Daddy. I hope one day to be reunited with them all in a big family reunion in Heaven. I have no idea what glories I'll see in Heaven. My mortal mind is too small to imagine how beautiful it will be. But I know it will be wonderful, and I know that I will never have to say goodbye to anyone ever again, for the Bible passage in Revelations 21:4 tells me -

"He will wipe away every tear from their eyes, and death shall be no more, neither shall there be mourning, nor crying, nor pain anymore, for the former things have passed away."

Until that day, I am trying to be the best I can be (and failing miserably a lot of the time) but still trying. And I am no longer focusing on that terrible day so many years ago. I am looking forward with delight to the day sometime in the future when I'll be reunited with Daddy and all the others again.

MY SOUTHERN MAMA

outherners never really cut the cord that ties us somehow to the woman who is at once our greatest enemy and our greatest ally. That was my mother. Mama never put up with whining or "attitude." Growing up in the Kentucky knobs (small hills,) she had no patience with anything which smacked of condescension or pretension. After listening to our crying for five to ten minutes, her standard response was "Dry up or I'll give you something to cry about." That something was occasionally a switch cut from the forsythia bush in the back yard. (Stripped of their leaves, they make outstanding delivery systems of punishment.) More often, though, Mama grabbed the yardstick she used for her sewing. In the midst of her switching my legs with one or the other, I frequently made the unfortunate mistake of laughing at her as her face turned a shade of red not usually seen. This made her whip me again all the harder.

But I wouldn't have you think my mother was unkind. She was the best mother I could have asked for. And I learned quite a few lessons from her (and not just from her yardstick or switch.) Here are some of them:

Living in Savannah, the streets often flooded after a big rain. We liked to take off our shoes and wade in the water. Mama was flatly against this as it would give us worms. (Don't ask me how.)

Hickeys on your neck immediately branded you as easy. As preacher's daughters, we had to be more circumspect than other girls. This included her admonition not to park in cars with boys. Therein lies trouble, she let us know. "Guard your treasure," she admonished me. "Remember who you are." She and Daddy were suspicious of all boys who came to the door to date us. And God help them if they ever tried just honking the horn.

She was never a helicopter parent. Having been raised by her older sisters after the death of her mother when Mama was just four, she, nevertheless, loved without being cloying. We girls were incredibly healthy, thanks probably to Mama's insistence that we "cover up so you don't catch your death of cold." I remember a few sick days, though, when she tucked me into the navy blue blanket I now have and brought me a tray of tomato soup with a cold Coca- Cola. Then she left me alone in the den to watch "I Love Lucy" until my sisters came home from school.

Mama and Daddy took us to church every time the door was open. That meant Sunday School, preaching, Training Union and preaching on

Sundays, family night dinner, GAs and prayer meeting on Wednesdays, Vacation Bible School and revival meetings throughout the year. When we were too little to listen to the message, she'd entertain us by drawing on the bulletin or making twin babies in a hammock out of the cotton handkerchief she carried in her pocketbook.

Mama was not afraid of hard work. Those who have lived in Savannah know about the roaches that cohabit with humans, no matter how clean the household. These nasty insects are huge, brown varmints that occasionally take wing and fly, especially when the lights are out. I was terrified of them as a child, but my mother, nothing daunted, went after them with her broom or her Keds-clad foot. I hated hearing her crush them under her toe and hated more seeing the nasty mess their murder left behind. But she simply wiped it up and moved on to the next item on her list.

She could also wring the necks of chickens, pluck their feathers, cut them up and fry them to a golden-brown, mouthwatering tenderness, a technique I never learned. She made chicken and dumplings and apple jacks that were so light they could float to your plate. I remember coming home from school and seeing her so happy while she was in the kitchen that she would dance the Charleston to make us laugh. What made her so happy, I wonder?

She certainly had plenty to do as the wife of a minister of a large church. An excellent seamstress, she made most of the clothes of her four girls and herself. Every Easter, all of us got new outfits from head to toe - dresses, petticoats, white shoes and socks, bonnets and white cotton gloves. When we were old enough, she bought us princess heels, training bras and garter belts with stockings for our spindly legs. The first make-up we were allowed to wear was Tangee lipstick, an orange shade that turned a different shade on each person. I watched her jealously as she applied Maybelline mascara with a tiny brush she'd rub across a cake of mascara in a tiny red plastic box. She always finished off her look with a dab of Coty dusting powder and a swipe of Revlon Cherries in the Snow lipstick.

Through the years, we girls learned by observation that you should never let yourself go after marriage. Mama did all her housework in the morning, and then took a bath after lunch to be "put together" when Daddy came home from work. Until she had the stroke that ultimately felled her, Mama never had a grey hair in her head, thanks to Kelly, her hairdresser and the contents of a bottle of Roux Fanci-full "Spun Sand." Mama was strictly old school, believing that the husband was the head of the house. But Daddy knew she was the real power behind the throne, or, as he often said of her, "When she crows, it's day."

Mama was almost always quiet, yet she taught us so much. Many mornings, I woke up to the wonderful sound of her singing "Good morning merry sunshine, how did you wake so soon? You frightened all the stars away, and chased away the moon." What a magical childhood I had! God blessed me with a mother far better than I deserved and I want always to honor her memory.

REMEMBERING A FIRE

I had my annual mammogram today, an annoyance for sure but a necessary one. It was the second procedure of the day. Earlier this morning, I'd had an echocardiogram, something that I have every so often because of a heart abnormality. I'm waiting to hear about that one but expect it will reveal no problems just as the mammogram did. In the course of the procedure, the mammographer took a look at my chest and said, "What happened there?"

My heart skipped a beat and then I realized she was pointing to a scar I have had since age four. It was the Christmas season in 1952 and my sisters and I were "playing church." My Daddy was at church as he usually was. My mother was in the next room sewing, probably something for one of us four girls.

My sisters and I were singing Christmas carols in a bedroom and we were holding lit candles, probably without permission. That day, I was wearing a dress with ruffles down the bodice. You can imagine what happened next. The candle caught the ruffles on my dress on fire and the dress caught my skin on fire.

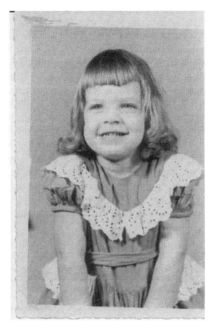

Me wearing the dress in which I was burned

My mother heard my screams, came running into the room and rolled me in a throw rug which was on the floor, no doubt saving my life. I remember going to Dr. Bill Brumbach, our family physician, for many treatments but escaped with no damage except for the raised scars, known as hypertrophic burn scars.

Some years later, probably when I was about eight or nine, our family had moved away from Gaffney, SC where the burn occurred. We came back to visit in Gaffney about that time and had dinner with Dr. Brumbach and his family. I remember there were one or two boys at the table, boys who were older than me by a couple of years. Daddy, not realizing that I was beginning to think about the boy-girl dynamic, pulled my dress off my shoulder to show Dr. Brumbach how well my scar had healed. I was mortified that the boys might have seen more of my chest than I wanted. That is truly the only pain I recall from the entire incident.

I never think of this event anymore, but today's mammogram reminded me of that day. I am grateful for my mother who acted quickly enough to roll me in the rug. In saving my life, she also ensured the lives of my three children and the eight grandchildren I was blessed with. I have come to believe that our days on this earth are numbered and that God alone knows that number. I hope that, in saving my life, God and my mother were pleased with the way I have used it.

FOLLOWING THE COFFIN

 n February 4, 2016, my family gathered to lay to rest my mother-in-law Maria Belvin who had graced the earth for 95 years. This funeral followed by only a little over five months the funeral for my tiny grandson Camden Andrew Klegin, eleven months, who died following heart surgery. The day was gloomy, cold, windy and raining heavily, a stark contrast to the warm sunny August day of Camden's funeral. Maria's funeral was rather sparsely attended as a middle of the week funeral for an elderly person, most of whose contemporaries have already passed on, must be.

Yet both funerals had something in common - In both, family and friends gathered to support us, to remember happy times, to laugh at some bit of silliness, and to shed an occasional tear. It's a rare thing nowadays to have the whole family together, but on these awful days when we gather to lay our loved ones to rest, it is a comfort to be surrounded by those who love us best.

I was brought to tears to see so many of the younger generation in our family take a stop from their busy lives to honor the life and memory of this woman whose life had been so different from theirs. Two of Maria's grandchildren Ross and Emma, read passages of Scripture during the funeral, their voices brave and strong. The pallbearers were Maria's son-in-law Mike, three grandsons Jeff, Ross and Tom, and two grandsons-in-law Shon and Ben. Ben had just served in the same role less than a month before for his maternal grandmother. And just five months before, Tom and Ben had been pallbearers along with Shon and Katherine, who carried their own son's tiny casket to his grave. To see the sober expressions on all their faces as they tenderly and gently bore these two beautiful, wooden boxes to their destination was to see bravery and love in action. I was reminded of the day sixteen years ago when my own mother was laid to rest, her casket born by her six tall, handsome grandsons, and followed by her four beautiful granddaughters, each carrying a long-stemmed white rose.

In the pews around me at the funeral were the girls who also loved Maria. There was Cookie, Maria's daughter who bore the heaviest burden of caring for her mother in the last few years. There was Jackie, another daughter-in-law who has born the same burden for her own mother in recent days. And there were the granddaughters - Jennifer, Katherine, Caroline, and Julie, carrying (and pacifying) some of the babies, amazing great-grandchildren who had livened up the past few days.

Funerals are terrible, life-altering things that no one looks forward to. Our lives are forevermore different. We cry; we laugh; we remember. But mostly we are together, bearing one another's burden. I am glad to see that our children and grandchildren recognize the sanctity of these moments and take time to honor the memories of lives well-lived, no matter how long or brief.

GRANDMAMA'S IRONING BOARD

ave you ever noticed that a tiny change can sometimes make such a difference? I have used my ironing board for 48 years. For all but a couple of those years, it has been missing one or more of the rubber tips on the legs. This made the board not quite stable, but I was careful and never had an accident. I mentioned in an offhanded way to Paul the other day that I'd like to have new rubber tips for the legs and ...Abracadabra Amazon Prime... I had new rubber tips for my ironing board. It's now so steady and sturdy; it makes me wonder what took me so long. Well, here's the answer...I am a sentimental girl.

This ironing board belonged to my grandmother who died in 1966. When she died, my mother put the board in the farmhouse she and Daddy bought for their retirement home. Anyway, Mama used the ironing board very infrequently since she had a much newer one at home. When I married in 1971, she gave me Grandmama's old ironing board and I have used it ever since. I have carried it with me to homes in Hampton, VA; Gates County, NC; Raleigh, NC; Fairfax Station, VA and now to Lovettsville, VA.

It was a Mary Proctor hi-lo adjustable ironing board, a very nice one for its time. In fact, I just saw one on eBay being offered for $135.00. I know my grandmother paid nowhere near that price for it. But somehow it gives me a nice feeling to know that when I'm ironing (which is one of my favorite chores) I'm doing so on the same board that both my mother and my grandmother used for so long. And now, thanks to Paul, it's even more enjoyable to use. My children will probably toss it in the dumpster when I'm gone, but I hope they don't. It's a family heirloom!

GRANDMAMA'S PANTRY

y friend and work colleague Byron Cotten asked me recently if I had a three-sided pantry when I was growing up. We were talking about the good old days as we geezers do and Byron was telling me about his family home. Well, Byron, my folks never had a three-sided pantry (at least one that I can remember) but my grandmother surely did.

Grandmama lived in a drafty old house known in Gates County as the Daniel Williams house. It was built in the 1820s. My grandparents moved there when my grandfather bought the farmland surrounding it. But Grandmama never liked it. She was leaving a new home to move to a home that was probably a hundred years old at the time. The house sat in what was known as a swept yard, meaning it was just soft white sand that was swept or raked occasionally but which grew no grass. However, as my sister Jerry and I can attest, it made for an excellent play area for our toy cars.

The house was unheated except for oil stoves in the front rooms and a wood stove in the kitchen. I remember roaring fires in the dining room fireplace as we ate meals at the long table there. Between the dining room and the kitchen was the three sided pantry that Byron mentioned. It was a dark, narrow room, unlit except for a lightbulb in the ceiling to which a long string was attached. The walls of the pantry were lined with rough shelves on which my grandmother placed the foods she canned or bought at the general store in Drum Hill, NC. Whenever I had to go into the kitchen, I ran through the pantry at breakneck speed fearing whatever might be hiding in the dark corners.

My daddy and I often talked about restoring that old house and each time, I brought up opening the pantry to the kitchen to bring in more light. Daddy kind of liked the idea of having a separate pantry, calling it a "butler's pantry," a ridiculous name given that there was NEVER a butler anywhere near there.

Grandmama never had any money to speak of, her only income coming from the farm crops whenever the boll weevils and tobacco hornworms didn't destroy the profits. But the food that she brought to the table from that humble pantry was fit for a king. Nothing that comes from my well equipped kitchen even comes close.

DADDY TALKS ABOUT HIS CHILDHOOD

 y daddy was a great storyteller. A Baptist minister for over 50 years, Daddy was such a popular preacher because he punctuated his sermons with stories that were heartwarming and occasionally hilarious. People could really relate to the tales he told and often he drew people to his Christian faith simply by the force of his personality, a God-given talent for sure.

But I always wanted him to tell me stories about himself and his childhood. For some reason, he never wanted to talk much about himself. I think maybe that was because he grew up during the Great Depression, the sixth of nine children in his family. Times were hard back then and I think maybe he wanted to move on from that part of his life.

But being the pest that I am, I forced him one time to answer some questions about his upbringing. Here are some of the things he wrote down for me:

"I was born in the Umphlett house (in Gates County, NC) where my family lived until I was about 9. Then we moved to a house in Sunbury which burned down when I was in the 9th grade." [My grandmother told me that in that fire, Daddy raced back into the burning house to save her sewing machine. She was scared to death that he wouldn't make it out alive, but his first thought was of others even then.]

Daddy continued, "I started school at Middle Swamp in the school-house that later became Mrs. Blanche Mathews' house. Our school only lasted till 11th grade and then you graduated." [I have been told that as a teenager, Daddy was quite popular with the girls.]

He had a pretty unassuming beginning for a man who grew up to become pastor of churches with several thousand members. I think it shows that God can take any of us, no matter if we are born in a mansion or in a poor farmhouse on a dirt road, and use us for His glory.

For many years after his retirement, Daddy and Mama lived in the old Morris home place in Gates County, NC. [In fact I lived in that house for a year while I restored my farmhouse a few miles away.] They restored the house (which had been built by his grandfather,) added a couple of rooms, central heat and air, and made it into the place I think of as home. Several of us in the family came to live there with them when times were hard. Daddy loved to sit on the front porch just after the lawn had been cut (usually by a visiting grandson or me) and ponder all that had taken place in that house through the years. Here are more of Daddy's words about his history:

"My grandparents Ephraim and Sally always lived in the house where I now live. I don't remember coming here much as a child. My grand-mother died when I was a child and Grandpappy [I love that Daddy called his grandfather Grandpappy - It's so old-timey.] *came to live with my parents then (at the Bennie Brinkley house near Sunbury.)* [His grandfather was blind and couldn't live on his own.] *Papa was a*

farmer and cut timber and sold it. I don't remember Mama ever work-ing in the fields, much less outside the home.

"*An island in Merchant's Millpond [now a state park on the Morris home place land] named Hog Island was so named because of my grandfather. Grandpappy had a hog to get loose and swim to the island and find pigs there. ['Find pigs' was Daddy's charming euphemism for giving birth to pigs while on the island.] Grandpappy built a pen there and began feeding them. Later he caught them and since then it has been known as Hog Island. Now campers from the state park camp out there.*

"*Concerning decisions about money in our family, we never had any money so we never had to worry about how to spend it. Nowadays people feel they must have millions to be happy. I do remember one time when Mama sold something behind Papa's back. Papa had an old black and tan coon dog named Remus. A man made Papa an offer on it which Papa refused. Later the man came back when Papa wasn't around and bought him from Mama. I reckon she thought they needed the money. Anyway, it made Papa mad. The man later offered to return the dog but Papa refused it. Then when the dog was tried, [as a hunting dog] he was found to be no good!*

"*We always ate every meal together. Papa and Mama were at each end of the table. There was a bench on the backside of the table, next to the wall where four or five of us young 'uns would get to the table the best we could. Mama used to send to the store for a can of salmon fish. It cost about 15 cents but she could make the best fish stew out of that with some potatoes and onions. Mama was a genius when it came to taking a little bit of food and making a meal out of it.*

"*Most of our religious training was at home. We'd have prayers at the table and Bible reading. There was not much church training back then. We went to Sunday School every Sunday. Preaching was every other Sunday.*

"There was not much playing when I was a boy. Children didn't have to be entertained the way they do now. Oh, we went fishing occasionally. I remember we had a fish fry at Silver Springs. (You had to cross Lassiter Creek Bridge in front of [his cousin] R.G.'s house to get there.) The Sunday School at Middle Swamp Baptist Church had a picnic there. We boys drove an old mule named Pete that Papa had raised. Every year Pete's neck would just get eaten up by yellow flies. Papa and Mama went in a buggy. Anyway, the water in the swamp was up and when we went over that swamp, the water was so deep; it came up in the back of the cart. I was scared to death! What times we had back then!"

Daddy (far right) with his brother Gladstone and sister Edith

That's most of what Daddy ever told me about his childhood. I have read and reread this, trying to imagine the Daddy I knew as a child riding in a mule-drawn cart in eastern North Carolina. The picture above shows Daddy as a child of about three (on the right) with his brother Gladstone and little sister Edith probably in the yard of the house where he was born. It seems like his childhood is a million miles away from where I sit now typing his story on a computer. But though Daddy and all the people he told me about are gone, they live again in the stories he told me. As long as we tell their stories, our loved ones live on.

CHRISTMAS CAROLS

s I write this, I am watching online the Sunday morning service at First Baptist Church, Alexandria, VA, the church my daughter and son-in-law and their boys attend. The service is broadcast at a time when Paul and I have returned from our own early church service at Zion Lutheran Church. We love our tiny church but I do so enjoy the large church service at First Baptist. The pastor always presents wonderful sermons. And the music there is beautiful with an orchestra each Sunday and huge choirs of different ages. The beautiful carols that have been sung during the holiday season have reminded me of two times in my history when I have been moved at the playing of carols.

One occurred when I was living on a farm in North Carolina. It was Christmas and I was, as usual, having a hard time making ends meet. I was a stay at home mother at the time and my farm was on the market. It was the very middle of the farm crisis of the early eighties and I had very little money to provide some Christmas gifts for my son Tom. Yet I went to the little town of Suffolk, VA nearby to do some Christmas shopping. It was a bitterly cold day and there, outside the dime store in town, I met a member of the Salvation Army. He was wearing the uniform of the Army and stood beside his red kettle. In his hand was a shiny brass trumpet. I nearly passed him by, my own money woes surpassing all thoughts of charity. But then he put the trumpet to his lips and played the clearest, most beautiful version of "O Little Town of Bethlehem" I have ever heard. I wondered that someone could stand in the icy cold and make such beautiful music. Of course I was moved to donate what little I had to his kettle.

Some years later, I was living in northern Virginia and doing some shopping at Costco just before Christmas. The store was very full, so I decided to get a hot dog before I shopped. I was seated in the middle of the raucous crowd, everyone focused on grabbing a bite to eat before securing a bargain. Suddenly a man of Korean descent stood in the middle of the restaurant area and began playing the same carol, "O Little Town of Bethlehem" on his trumpet. The crowd, whose noise only moments before threatened to drown out all conversation, suddenly became completely silent. The musician played a couple of verses, then took his mouthpiece off the trumpet, quietly put the instrument in its case and walked away. There was utter stillness for a minute. Then suddenly, the gathered crowd stood as one and gave the musician a standing ovation.

The two performances of that old carol happened literally decades ago, yet I have never forgotten them. It took courage on the part of the musicians to proclaim their faith so publicly. It took commitment. I'm grateful for those two men and their talent. And I'm grateful for the tiny Baby who came to earth so many centuries ago to change the world.

CHRISTMAS LIST

'**ve** been spending the day trying to figure out what to get for my grandchildren for Christmas. This year, for the very first time, we've decided to draw names so that each person only has to give to one other person in the family, but of course I am breaking the rules and giving to my grandchildren too because, as Nana, that's how I roll. In the drawing, I got my son in law Ben Bond's name. I'm hoping he'll enjoy the complete box set of "Days of Our Lives" since 1965 that I ordered for him. (Ha!) The grandchildren are still young enough that it's fun and easy to shop for them. And since the coming of Amazon Prime, I don't even have to leave the comfort of my own home, fight the traffic and the lines, to get even these few gifts bought.

But there's something to be said for the old ways of shopping - going downtown (not to a mall) and seeing strings of lights across the street, decorated shop windows in all the department stores, smelling perfume at the cosmetic counters and checking my wallet to see if I have enough. That's how it used to be.

In years past, on the third floor of most big stores near the children's department, an area was transformed overnight into a winter wonderland where Santa himself sat, with one after another little Southern child perched tenuously on his knee. I don't recall ever sitting on Santa's knee as a child. (The minister's family was geared more toward the Nativity story rather than the North Pole story.) But still there was excitement in the air.

In the years I lived on my farm in North Carolina, shopping was a simple task. One year, I bought Rocket Nutcrackers from Rountree & Riddick general store for all my family and handed out bags of pecans picked from the eight pecan trees in our yard. I took Tom to the big town of Ahoskie to look at tricycles in the Western Auto Store window. One year on the farm, I hand quilted pillows for all the women in my family.

But none of these memories surpasses the memory of the year I was fourteen. I lived in Savannah then with my parents and sister Jerry. My older sisters Louise and Martha Jean were already married. I had little babysitting jobs and took handouts from my daddy from time to time. But basically, as Daddy used to say - it was "hard times." So that year, 1962, I decided to save a little bit of money as often as I could for my Christmas gifts. I kept a typed record of my account with the list of gifts I finally bought - proof positive of the nerd I would become in later years.

When I was fourteen, I kept a list of what I spent on Christmas gifts. You would be amazed to see that I was able to purchase two shirts for my daddy for the astounding price of $6.20, kid gloves for my mother for $4.11 and walkie-talkies for my sister Jerry for $2.25 - these came with the added bonus that there were two of them so...one for me, I guess. I was as poor an accountant then as now because the expenditure ($24.36) far exceeded my cash on hand ($15.01) I have no idea how I made up the difference. Nevertheless, it must have been a successful Christmas, because I have the record as proof fifty three years later.

MAMA'S BED

 couple of years ago Paul and I took a trip to Colorado Springs to meet our new grandson Henry Daniel Bond. While there, we stayed in the lovely guest room daughter Caroline and son-in-law Ben have prepared for their visitors. Ben is a Navy Lieutenant who, at the time, was working on an assignment with the Air Force there and Caroline is a stay at home mom. They also have another son Will, a four year old who loves all things cowboy.

Anyway, back to the guestroom. The centerpiece of the room is a mahogany bed which they inherited from Paul and me and which I in turn inherited from my parents. It came to me after the passing of my father and after my mother's stroke, when my sisters and I divided up their things.

I have many memories of this bed. I recall as a child of the 50s, snuggling down under the covers, when I stayed home from school sick with a cold. Mama brought me comic books to read and took my temperature with the thermometer she kept in the drawer of the bedside table. I remember sitting on the bed late one night as a young teen and listening to my father, a minister, as he counseled by phone a man who was an alcoholic and was in distress.

My mother slept in this bed at my home after the stroke which robbed her of her mobility and speech. Most of the time she stayed at Jerry's home, but my other sisters and I tried to give her a bit of change by bringing her to our homes. I remember with sadness watching my then-husband lifting her tenderly into the bed for her night's rest.

But the memory that warms my heart most is the one I can't really recall. I just know it happened from a picture you've seen in this book. In the bed, my mother, a quiet woman of thirty-three, cradles tiny twins, my sister and me in her arms. We'd just been born and had been a surprise to everyone except Mama.

When she came home from the hospital, Mama came to the very bed I slept in at Caroline and Ben's home and cradled Jerry and me as tiny newborns in her arms. Fast forward nearly seventy years and I am now a grandmother of eight sleeping in that very same bed.

Somehow it was a comforting thing to think of all the family history tied up in that bed. I hope Caroline and Ben have as good and happy a life as my parents did. I hope they know how much I enjoyed being with them as they brought little Henry into their home. And I hope in some way that Mama and Daddy were looking down from Heaven to see their family continuing to grow and thrive.

YOGA LADY RETURNS

Today was my day to go to town. Now that I live in the country, I don't often get into the big city of Fairfax, so when I have a hair appointment, I usually make a day of it - the mall, a lunch out, and (maybe) a little something for me. I was well on my way to accomplishing all of those goals today when I met up with an old foe - Yoga Lady.

You may perhaps recall my first meeting with Yoga Lady, clad in skin-tight yoga pants and midriff-baring tee shirt, in Costco, when I may or may not have slipped a giant bag of M&Ms into the cart she had filled with juices and fresh vegetables. Then there was the time she was in the drug store ahead of a long line of senior citizens (one of whom was me) waiting to make our Geritol purchases while she regaled the clerk with tales of her latest spinning class.

Today I was in Lord & Taylor feeling really spiffy now that I'd had a couple of blonde streaks put in my hair - Yesirree Bob, I am still one of the Pepsi Generation. All of a sudden, along comes Yoga Lady prancing down the aisle. To put this into perspective, I was wearing a pair of khakis, a white tee shirt and a long sweater (to cover the hips, of course) as well as a comfortable pair of flats. I caught my reflection in one of the mirrors and managed to focus solely on my coiffure.

Then here comes Yoga Lady - Picture this. She's wearing the color maroon (a dark garnet color) from head to toe. On her legs are the skin tight yoga pants I've come to expect from her (in maroon.) Atop the pants is a fashionable sweater, not too tight, not too loose, also in maroon. Her feet, definitely no larger than a size six at best, were encased in 4 inch spike heels in her signature color - maroon. Her hair, a frosted blonde, was pulled back into a tight, high pony tail. Her carriage was upright and there wasn't an extra inch of fat anywhere on her. Even the shopping bag she carried was maroon. I both hated and envied her the minute I saw her.

Here's my question - WHEN DID I GET TO BE SO OLD????

THE SPA AS SANCTUARY

esterday I went for my monthly update at the local Elizabeth Arden Red Door Salon. I've been going to this particular salon for over ten years, seeing the same specialists - Corey for hair color (yes, I do!) Wendy for cut and style and Kelly for brow waxing. For years I have laughed and cried with them, young women of the age of my daughters, listened to their stories about their children, and shared pictures and stories about my dearly loved children and grandchildren. It was a fairly typical relationship for years. "What are you doing for the holidays?" "Want to see the latest pictures of my grandchildren?" Or from the girls, "You'll never guess what my little boy did in school this week!" The stories we shared were funny or sweet. I usually leave each of them with a hug or a handshake along with my tip. The hour or two I spent in the spa each month were more for relaxation and beautification than anything else. But for me, anyway, it all changed after the passing of my grandson Camden.

The girls (for that's how I think of Kelly, Wendy and Corey) have followed the births of each of my grandchildren. They ask about them each month just as I ask about their children. But since Camden's death, something is different. We are looking deeper into each other. That was brought into sharp focus when Wendy appeared at the visitation for Camden at the funeral home. She was just off from a day at work, but said she had to be there for me. Pressing an envelope into my hand, she said, with tears in her eyes, "These are for you and Katherine." They were coupons for a massage for each of us at the salon. "Whenever you're ready," Wendy said. The salon manager Pam had insisted that they wanted to do that for us.

About a month after Camden's passing, I went back for my monthly re-do. After Kelly, a beautiful, quiet, wispy Asian girl, finished my brows, she said, "If you have nothing else to do this afternoon, please let me give you a facial. I want to do something for you." We had not talked so much about Camden's passing, but she knew his story and wanted in her quiet way to help. I agreed and felt more completely relaxed than I had in months, her slim hands massaging away the sadness of the past few weeks, for a little while anyway. Corey, meanwhile, as she was applying my new color, asked me about the family, listened to me as I talked about our loss. That's one of the beautiful things about women - we have such wonderful ways of sharing burdens, uplifting each other, listening to our cries, and laughing and rejoicing at our triumphs. Corey has a way of listening and asking the right questions at the right time that allows me to unburden myself without feeling uncomfortable.

Wendy, who is a cancer survivor, keeps me in stitches each month with tales of her wacky family and listens with delight, it seems, to my stories of my own family. Yesterday, she distracted me with a story about one of her children. It seemed to me that she was asking my opinion (since I'm a former teacher) about an issue, but knowing Wendy as I do, I would say she has it all under control. All the while she is talking, her skilled hands are shaping my limp, thin hair into something better.

When the afternoon at the spa was over, I went to pay my bill, and the young woman behind the counter looked at the computer and said, "This can't be right," and called another young woman to look at the screen. She stepped away for a moment, then returned and said, "The clinicians wanted to provide their services to Mrs. Belvin at no charge today." As you can imagine, tears came to my eyes again as they did so frequently then. I asked if I could speak to the salon manager and Pam came out. I expressed my gratitude and pulled my phone out to show her a picture of Camden. She said, "Oh, I've seen all your photos. [Wendy and I are Facebook friends so she had shared our family's saga with Pam.] I even knew the morning when Camden went into surgery."

I came home thinking about the importance of the salon as a sanctuary, a place where the cares of the everyday are washed away for a bit. Framed in the context of multiple mass shootings which seem to occur weekly in our country, I was struck by the contrast between the compassion of so many who comforted us in those days with the evil that also exists in our land. It occurred to me that all of my friends, my family, my salon friends, my college friends, my church friends, my work friends, my high school friends, my childhood friends - all of you are God's grace gifts to me. In the Bible, the book of John 14:18, we are told:

"I will not leave you comfortless: I will come to you."

God did come to me in the guise of all of these dear friends and family. I will always be grateful for them.

A SAD BIRTHDAY

y birthday in 2015 was the saddest birthday of my life, but it was made a little more bearable by the support and love I received from friends and family. Since the passing of my grandson Camden, I have had a tough time. I am a Christian and publicly profess my love for Jesus as my Savior. But I have a tough time understanding why it was necessary to take little Camden, who never did a thing except express pure joy to us. I have done lots of reading since then, especially in the Bible, and looked particularly at the passage in John 11:1-46 where Jesus raises Lazarus from the dead. Like Mary and Martha, I have questioned why Jesus didn't come to that hospital

room to heal Camden. Why did God allow Camden to die? That is the big question I have pondered. Certainly Jesus knew of Camden's heart defect. Why didn't He heal Camden? It was not because He was unable to heal him. I fully believe that. He was able to heal lepers, give sight to the blind, make the wind and waves obey His voice. Why not heal Camden?

I don't have the answer to that question. I just don't know. But there is a passage in 1 Corinthians 13:12 which says:

"For now we see only a reflection as in a mirror; then we shall see face to face. Now I know in part; then I shall know fully, even as I am fully known."

In other words, all this will be made plain to me when I get to Heaven. That, of course, brings up another question - the question of Heaven. I've never seen it. I only know of its existence by what I have heard and read in the Bible. What am I to make of that? Of course, if I choose not to believe in Heaven and eternal life through Christ, what else is there? So I must believe. And though my heart is broken from saying goodbye to Camden, I must believe I will see him and know him again in Heaven for all eternity.

I am trying to recover from the loss of this precious child, though my grief is as nothing compared to his parents' grief. I have good moments and then moments where my heart sinks to think of this great loss. But I do believe Camden completed a great work for God in his eleven months on earth. He brought love. He reminded us to cherish life and each other. He reminded us of the necessity and power of prayer. He reminded us that we are only promised today so we should cherish every moment and serve God for as long as we have.

In the Gospel of Mark 9: 1-29, we are told of Jesus' healing of a boy afflicted with epilepsy. The boy's father begs Jesus to heal his son, yet though he wants it desperately, the father still has some doubt. After all, the boy has been ill for so long. The father tells Jesus, "I do believe; help thou my unbelief." I am praying for my belief to be strengthened in the midst of my grief. There is just no other way.

Camden

NANA'S EULOGY FOR CAMDEN

I was blessed to love this sweet baby boy, my grandson Camden, for every one of his 338 days here on earth. Katherine and Shon were such loving parents, and such loving children to me. It was an honor to eulogize Camden at his funeral. I wrote this eulogy to be read by one of the pastors.

CAMDEN ANDREW KLEGIN

September 9, 2014 – August 12, 2015

Written by his grandmother Janet Morris Belvin

I first learned of my grandson Camden's existence when Katherine told me that she and Shon were expecting twins. This was truly a double blessing, as Katherine had experienced an ectopic pregnancy months before and lost her baby. Because of that miscarriage, Katherine received more than the usual amount of monitoring and ultrasounds to make sure all was well. On one of those visits, Katherine and Shon learned that the doctors could not see a significant part of Baby B's heart (as he was then known.) So, many more trips for ultrasounds were made, and on one of these we learned that Baby B, by then named Camden Andrew Klegin, would be born with a very serious combination of heart defects known as Tetralogy of Fallot.

Tetralogy of Fallot affects the structure of the heart, causing oxygen-poor blood to flow out of the heart and into the rest of the body. Katherine and Shon learned after he was born that Camden also had a condition known as Alagille Syndrome, a condition which affects organs such as the liver. Luckily, Camden's place on the spectrum was low enough that medication would normalize his bile count rather than having the necessity of an organ transplant.

Nevertheless, Katherine carried the babies successfully and when they were born, we were hopeful. After the birth of Camden and his twin brother Hudson James, an ultrasound revealed a blockage in Camden's bowels so he underwent surgery to remove the dead portion of his bowels and reconnect where the blockage had been. The surgery so soon after birth caused his tiny body to swell. He required a level of care that the NICU was not comfortable with, so he was transferred to the PICU (which includes a cardiac wing.) After his transfer there, Katherine and Shon went through many ups and downs and Camden remained hospitalized for the first two months of his life.

But it was a joyous day in our family when Camden finally came home to join his big brother Nolan Thomas, his twin Hudson and his mom and dad. Over the next nine months of his brief eleven month life, all of us who came to know him fell under the spell of his enchanting smile and sunny personality. It seemed that no matter who came to see him, Camden always greeted his visitor with the brightest of smiles. Katherine and Shon shared him generously with all their friends and family through their frequent posts of photos and videos on Facebook. Hundreds of people have told me and others that, though they never met Camden, they came to love him and grieved at the news of his passing as though he were a member of their family. Paul and I cherished the once or twice weekly visits we had with him and his brothers, one of the joys of our being retired.

Soon Camden began delighting us with his babbling, attempting to talk quite a bit sooner than Hudson, who was more the strong, silent type. With his tiny hands he high-fived his mother and learned to toss a ball to his dad and big brother. He had begun to crawl a bit too, although, as many babies do, he started out going backward. He had even begun baby signing which delighted his parents.

Always in the back of our minds, though, we knew there would be a day for open heart surgery, a date which was set and reset because of illness or other factors. The day finally came on August 12 and I was called upon to keep Nolan and Hudson that day. I watched as Shon and Katherine gathered their things to take Camden to the hospital. His smile and active little limbs were in motion as he said goodbye. Little did we know then that the day which had begun with such bright promise for a complete healing for Camden was to end in a different kind of healing.

As our hearts broke to learn the news of Camden's passing, we mourned and cried over the thought of never holding his tiny body in our arms again. We looked at twin strollers and cribs, one of which would now remain empty. We thought of the empty high chair at the table. Eventually, after the fierce pain from the loss of our little Camden subsided, we realized that he received the healing after all – just in Heaven, not on earth. We rejoice to think that Camden will be a boy in Heaven for all eternity, never having to suffer the heartaches and pain that life on earth can bring. We will remember his thousand watt smile, his brave heroics as he went through one procedure or surgery after another with patience and good humor.

 In the few months that God lent Camden to Katherine and Shon, they provided for him a lifetime's worth of activities and love. Whenever he was not quarantined for health reasons, he went to a Major League baseball game, or he visited with family and friends, he shopped with his mom and dad and most importantly, he went to church with his family. The faith that his parents shared with their children is the faith that sustained them as they got used to life without their precious Camden.

I have come to believe that in his brief stay on this earth, Camden had more influence and touched more hearts than I have in my nearly 70 years of life. Our hearts have been broken by his passing. I would have given him my heart if I could. He already owned it anyway.

THANATOPSIS

hen I was a high school student laboring under my beloved English teacher the late, great Beulah Harper, I was assigned the task of analyzing the poem "Thanatopsis" by William Cullen Bryant. To my fifteen year old self, never having lost a loved one, the poem was a complete enigma. I remember stomping down to the breakfast table where Daddy and Mama sat waiting for their daughters to join them. Daddy tried in his usual jovial way to tease out of me what was my latest teenage woe.

"I have to learn this stupid poem, and I have no idea what it means," I pouted.

"What's the poem?" Daddy asked me gently.

Knowing full well he could never help me, I told him it's something called 'Thanatopsis" or something like that. What could he possibly know, I thought. Imagine my surprise when there, over his bacon and eggs, Daddy began quoting from memory the poem itself. My jaw dropped and my eyes bugged.

"Yes," I told him. "That's the one. I have no idea what it means."

So Daddy sent me for my literature book and began to explain to me the deeper context of a poem about the universality and mystery of death. But in explaining it to me, he focused on the last few lines, lines he quoted frequently in the funeral services he conducted for his parishioners. To say I was astonished at the breadth of my father's knowledge is an understatement. But I know that my Heavenly Father knows even more and the day we laid Camden to rest was a part of God's plan, a plan which I will not understand until I join Him and all my loved ones in Heaven. These are the last lines of the poem -

> "... *So live, that when thy summons comes to join*
>
> *The innumerable caravan, which moves*
>
> *To that mysterious realm, where each shall take*
>
> *His chamber in the silent halls of death,*
>
> *Thou go not, like the quarry-slave at night,*
>
> *Scourged to his dungeon, but, sustained and soothed*
>
> *By an unfaltering trust, approach thy grave,*
>
> *Like one who wraps the drapery of his couch*
>
> *About him, and lies down to pleasant dreams."*

LETTERS FROM MAMA AND DADDY

Yesterday, I went out to the barn to see if I could find something to do. I had found the key to the heavy metal trunk I had taken with me to college, so I decided to explore that. Imagine my surprise when I found a box of letters from my Mama and Daddy, all sent to me while I was a college student.

I don't think I had seen or read those letters since receiving them nearly fifty years ago. About half were from my daddy, written on the letterhead of the church he served. His distinctive slanted handwriting, scrawled in the Shaeffer's fountain pen he used back then, was very different from the delicate penmanship of my mother who wrote, more often than not on pink stationery with a plastic Bic pen. There were also more than a few postcards from places like Houston, New Orleans, Louisville, and various small motels in Southern towns where Daddy held revivals.

The letters invariably mention how much Mama and Daddy missed me and how quiet and clean the house was without Jerry and me. They always included a small amount of money - $2.00, $5.00, never more than $10.00, with instructions to make it last until they could afford to send more. Mama's letters often mentioned a dress or jumper she was sewing for me, saying that she would have it in the mail soon. In one she writes delightedly of the new General Electric hair dryer she just got with her S&H Green Stamps, and says Jerry and I will probably take it back to school with us.

They remind me to study hard and not stay out too late on dates. Mama reminds me not to go out alone on a blind date but to go with Cindy or June. She asks in another letter how my weekend was at Wake Forest when I went to a football game with Paul. She frequently mentions how glad she was to have Anne or Cindy or June (my roommates and suitemate) come home for the weekend with me.

Daddy writes about how lonely he is with Mama gone to help my sisters Martha Jean or Louise when they had new babies. He tells me that to kill time, he goes to his farm in Gates County, NC to do some plowing, but has to get back for preaching on Sunday. They write once of coming to Raleigh to take me to the NC State Fair and later, of how much they enjoyed seeing me.

I must have told Mama about all my dates because she comments on how much she enjoyed meeting them or how nice they sound. But there is always the reminder to be a good girl and stay out of trouble.

My heart breaks to think of how quickly I read these and tossed them aside after extracting the dollars inside. I didn't know then how quickly life passes and how soon my parents would be gone. Still, I'm comforted by the fact that Mama and Daddy mention in almost all their letters how much they appreciated the letters I wrote them. I hope I was a good daughter.

Now I am a grandmother myself and I am the one helping my own children with their children. My house is now the quiet and clean one. But just for an hour or so today, I was a college girl again and Mama and Daddy were still alive, still sending me all the news of the family, still looking after me. I feel like I just discovered buried treasure.

DESTINATION SAVANNAH

If you travel 626 miles from my home outside Lovettsville, Virginia, through the rolling pastures full of grazing horses and the cityscapes of northern Virginia, through the corn and tobacco fields of North Carolina and the dense forests of South Carolina that run alongside I-95, you will eventually arrive in Savannah, Georgia, a place of such great natural beauty that you will think you have time travelled to the past. In a way, that is exactly what I did this weekend when I drove alone to Savannah for my (gulp) 49th high school reunion.

If you have never been to Savannah, I highly recommend that you put it on your To Do list. The architecture of the homes and buildings there is incredibly diverse. You can find everything from tiny board and batten cottages and Victorian houses in bright colors to grand mansions which might well have been Tara. The streets of Savannah are paved in the same concrete that perhaps my Daddy and Mama drove on in the fifties, very different from the asphalt I see here at home. The city streets still bear the same orange oval bus stop signs. I caught the bus at those signs when, with my sister Jerry and friend Terri, we went downtown unaccompanied at age 10 or so to see a movie at the Lucas theater.

Jerry, her husband Larry (who also came to Savannah for the reunion) and I met with Terri and her husband Marion and our other old friends Beth Everette and Derry Stockbridge for breakfast and lunch on two days. During both meals we laughed and told old stories and memories nonstop, amazing because we have spent so many years apart. Old friends are truly some of the best of the many rewards that old age brings.

We also visited with our sister Louise and had a lovely lunch at the Crystal Beer Parlor with a shopping trip afterwards to a fabulous shop called One Fish, Two Fish. I loved that the shop clerk was so friendly, something that I noted wherever we went in Savannah.

At the main event of the weekend, the reunion Saturday night gathered 80 members and guests of the over 600 members of our class of 1966. I loved seeing so many dear faces from the past. We were older, some of us gray, some not (thank you to my hair salon). Some of us had had difficult lives; some of us seemed to have had it easy peasy. But we hugged. We laughed, and we talked nonstop about old memories. We learned of the passing of old friends, we shared grandchildren's photos and news of upcoming retirement and hopeful news of medical advances. The night was over all too soon, but not before a few stalwart souls gathered on the deck of Tubby's Tank House, the reunion locale, for a cigar (banded with the Class of '66 logo!) Afterwards, Jerry, Larry and I stopped by the Krystal for old times' sake and got a few of their tiny hamburgers for the road. What delicious memories they evoked!

The next day we went to Bull Street Baptist Church, the grand church my father pastored in the fifties and sixties. We even saw a couple of old friends, Gloria Harrison Tootle and Linda Carmichael Howard, from the good old days. Lunch at Carey Hilliard's afterwards brought more delicious memories with friends and family. After lunch, Jerry and I went for a walk down River Street, the cobblestoned boulevard beside the Savannah

River to get a box of pralines from River Street Sweets. I also bought a few bags of Byrd's Scotch Oatmeal cookies as a reminder of the days back in Charles Ellis Elementary School. We could buy them for a treat then for just a few cents.

Leaving the city yesterday morning, I marveled once again at the huge live oaks lining the streets, their massive arms dripping with grey Spanish moss. Practically any house so adorned with these beauties could be the setting for a Gothic novel or movie. No wonder Savannah is such a big travel destination. But more than its beauty, I love the people I knew there, the people I know there now and the people I met there. All of them are full of that great storied Southern hospitality. Everyone speaks to you. Everyone smiles. The men at the reunion call the women "darlin." The women at the reunion shared stories that were fascinating in their detail. Southerners are great storytellers!

On the way out of the city yesterday morning, I turned on my car radio and found, incredibly, the Big Ape - WAPE in Jacksonville, Florida, the radio station we listened to as we tanned our bodies on long towels on the sands of Savannah Beach (now known as Tybee) so many years ago. The music was not the same, of course, and I am many years away from those happy years. My life has ebbed and flowed like the waters of the marshes surrounding the city, but in one brief weekend, the memories all came rushing back to me.

PARKER'S BARBECUE

ast Monday I drove back home from Savannah all in one day. It was a long drive but I broke it up by stopping for lunch at Parker's Barbecue in Wilson, NC. I have eaten barbecue in Virginia, Georgia, Kansas City, KS, and probably a few other states and, in my opinion, it is hard to find a plate of barbecue that isn't delicious. But if I had to choose, my very favorite would be the barbecue I got right there at Parker's, eastern North Carolina-style with that wonderful vinegar-based sauce.

Parker's opened in the 1940s but I didn't discover it until the late 1960s when I went there on a date. Inside the restaurant, a white frame, flat-roofed building, customers sit at Formica-topped wooden tables in sturdy wooden chairs that look like they came out of a school from the early twentieth century. The servers are clean-cut young men in khaki pants and short-sleeved white button down shirts. They wear paper caps that resemble the hats of soda jerks from the fifties and they are just as friendly and polite as you would expect. The whole experience of dining there is like a trip to the past with your Mama and Daddy. But the best part of the whole experience is the food itself.

For $6.06 + tax, I got the most amazing barbecue dinner in the history of barbecue. The hallmark of a dinner there is the finely chopped pork covered in the thin watery, vinegar sauce that is the calling card of Eastern North Carolina barbecue. Beside the barbecue, there are boiled potatoes, hush puppies, and the most delicious finely chopped coleslaw you've ever tasted. And the tea is so sweet it sets your teeth on edge, with the tiniest of ice cubes to keep it cold.

Businesses come and go. There are few places that stay the same through decades. But Parker's is one of those unique places that haven't changed, because it doesn't need to change. You should put this restaurant on your bucket list. It's that good.

FIFTY YEARS

hen you reach my age, you have a lot of anniversaries. Already this year, I've gone to two college reunions and a get together with old friends from the past. It won't be long before I will attend another reunion. But I will probably never have the luxury of having a fiftieth wedding anniversary with Paul. We have been married for twenty-four years, but unless medical science makes some real advances in the next few years, I doubt that we'll see our golden anniversary. But today I am celebrating our fiftieth anniversary. Here's how:

Fifty years ago, my parents moved my sister and me to Hampton, VA during the summer before my senior year in high school. My father had accepted the pastorate of a church there and so, of course, we moved. To say I was distraught is a huge understatement. One's senior year in high school is supposed to be the year when you're at the top of the heap. Yet here I was in a strange place, knowing no one.

To the rescue came Paul, like a knight on a white horse. Of course, he likes to say that he and Dean Majette, his buddy from high school and church, were "scoping out the new talent." On the first Saturday that my family moved in, Paul, Dean, and two other girls from church, came over to meet us. They introduced themselves awkwardly, then drove us to

Shoney's, all six of us crammed into Paul's white Ford Falcon. After stuffing ourselves with strawberry pie, we came back to our home and looked at my high school annual (nowadays they call them yearbooks) from Savannah High School. Mama served us Co-colas and cookies.

Paul and me in high school

And that's how I met Paul so many years ago on June 5, 1965. We were instantly intrigued with each other and dated off and on through the next few years. I always found him the most interesting man I ever knew. But after college, we went our separate ways and married others. When those marriages failed, I was in the midst of other personal tragedies - my mother's devastating stroke, and my father's death in a car wreck while on his way to the rehab center to see Mama. Paul, who had become an attorney, came back into my life offering to help with the legal matters that erupted as my sisters and I struggled to care for our invalid mother.

And then, we realized that we were in love, and probably should have been together from the start. We married in 1994 (in a wedding officiated by Dean who became our minister) and Paul took on the task of helping to raise my three children, whom he came to love as his own. Now they have given us eight wonderful grandchildren. So it's true that Paul and I may never celebrate our fiftieth wedding anniversary. And it's true that Paul was not my first love. But he will be my last. Happy 50th anniversary, Paul.

THE CLASS OF 1970 – FOREVER STRONG

hen I left Meredith College in 1970 as a brand new college graduate, I was 21 with a teaching job already lined up. I weighed 125 pounds and didn't have a wrinkle on my face, an extra pound on my torso, or a serious thought in my head. All I knew was that I was now free to be a grown-up.

Fast forward 45 years and things are slightly different. I'm now retired from a teaching job that put between two and three thousand middle and high school students in my classrooms over the years. I like to think I made a difference in their lives, but truthfully, I know there were some I couldn't reach, some I could never help. My weight is...well, let's just say it's more than 125 pounds and I have quite a few wrinkles and grey hair (if I don't make my every four week appointment at the salon.) Those are all pretty negative things but the silver lining is that none of that mattered on the weekend I met with several dozen of my former classmates from the Class of 1970 for our 45th reunion.

This was one of many times I have gathered with the Meredith girls (Meredith is a women's college) but for the first time, it felt different. There was a spirit of joyfulness among all of us, a real feeling of gratitude that we had survived so much and were together again on that beautiful campus. I would venture to say that at some point during the weekend, every one of us had a fleeting moment of desire to go back in time to when we were college girls again. Of course, that time is lost ("temps perdu" as Marcel Proust called it in Remembrance of Things Past.) But the memories of those heady days in the late sixties were all around us this weekend. We might have wrinkles and grey hair, we might be battling cancer or Parkinson's disease, and we might be dealing with aging parents or grieving lost loved ones, but for two precious days, we regained all those lost hours.

We were living again with suitemates and roommates in Vann or Stringfield or Faircloth or Heilman dorms. We wore Pappagallo shoes and Villager sweaters over our McMullen blouses. We listened to the Temptations and read *To Kill a Mockingbird*. We worked in the chemistry lab or solved math problems for our professors. We went to fraternity parties at NC State or drove to Chapel Hill for our dates at UNC. Frantically, we typed our term papers on portable Royal typewriters provided by our parents who were still living and paying all our bills. We called out "Man on the hall!" when our daddies lugged trunks up to our dorm rooms and sat by the only phone on the hall, a pay phone, to wait for our dates to call.

On campus, we sunned on the roof of the breezeway (Skin cancer? Not us!) We attended our early morning classes in pajamas underneath our London Fog raincoats. No need to worry - there were no men in our classes. And in our sophomore year, a new tradition was born out of our rebellious and crazy natures - an original singing group called "The Bathtub Ring." Forty-five years later, there is still a Bathtub Ring on campus, but now you have to audition for it. The members of the original Bathtub Ring were on campus on this particular weekend and serenaded all of the classes with their signature song, "Cigareets and Whiskey and Wild, Wild Women (They'll drive you crazy, they'll drive you insane!)" It was quite scandalous for a Baptist college in 1967. Needless to say the crowd went wild. Sadly it was to be the last performance of the original three as one of them, Betty Johnson, lost her battle with cancer soon thereafter.

The last precious hours of our reunion were spent in hugging and laughing, taking photos and promising to get together for our fifti-eth, though I'd be willing to bet we won't wait that long. Life has given us many lessons in the forty-five years since our graduation. We've mar-ried, divorced, given birth, and buried parents and children, had careers, made homes, had spectacular successes and spectacular failures. But for the few hours when the Class of 1970 was together again on that magnifi-cent Raleigh campus, none of that mattered. We were ageless and time no longer mattered. All we knew for that wonderful weekend was that we were together and we had friends for life. As the motto for our wonderful Alma Mater states, we are "Forever Strong."

THE SOUND OF MUSIC...AGAIN

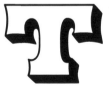 he year 2015 marked the fiftieth anniversary of the musical "The Sound of Music," a movie which has been for one reason or another important in my life through the years. It was being shown on the big screen of one of our local movie theaters so I told Paul I had to see it again. When I did, we were as delighted by it as the first time we saw it. The movie was a little late starting because of some technical difficulties, but the audience was in a good mood. Someone began singing "Do-Re-Mi" and everyone laughed and joined in. A couple of people in the audience came dressed in the alpine costumes of the movie, though I didn't see a single nun. I

especially loved the marionette scene - I've always been a sucker for marionettes and Bill and Cora Baird, famous puppeteers, were behind the magic
in the Lonely Goatherd scene. I was charmed by Maria and the Captain
dancing the Laendler, an Austrian folk dance. (Check out the actual dance
from the movie on You Tube if you've never seen it.

At the end of the movie, as the Von Trapps crossed the grand sweep
of the Austrian Alps, the audience erupted in applause. It was a great
moment. The audience knew every line of dialogue but we all loved it.
There is just something about seeing a big film like this on the big screen
rather than on one's television.

I first saw the movie when it came out in 1965. I went, as my high
school diary reports, with Paul on Saturday, May 14, 1965. We were seniors
in high school, a couple of weeks away from graduation. He had asked me
out on Wednesday, May 11 and I was very excited to go as it was the hot
ticket in town. We saw it in the brand new Newmarket Theater in Hampton,
VA. Paul even bought me a souvenir book afterwards, which, you will not
be surprised to hear, I still have. A few weeks later, I was wearing Paul's
high school ring with melted wax to make it fit.

Some years later, I was married (not to Paul) and bought the videocassette of the movie. In time, my marriage failed and I was, for a time,
a single mother with three children. Caroline, my youngest, was a pre-
schooler at the time and absolutely fell in love with the movie, especially
Maria's wedding scene. I can't count how many times she and I watched
that scene together while her siblings were in school. Each time, she put
a blue tutu on her head, grabbed a fake bouquet and walked down the
middle of our den to the music of that grand pipe organ, as though she
had become Maria on her wedding day. I admit that tears came to my eyes
today as I watched Maria walk down that aisle on the movie screen. So
many years had gone by.

Through the years, I bought the LP soundtrack, then the CD
soundtrack when the LP became too scratched. It seemed I couldn't get

enough of the story and music. Fast forward to 2006. The videocassette of "The Sound of Music" finally wore out when I brought it out again for the movie's 40th anniversary - the tape just snapped. So the next Christmas, in a replay of that high school date so many years before, Paul bought me The 40th Anniversary edition of the DVD including OVER 6 HOURS OF EXTRAS and a companion 184 page book. You can well imagine that I have enjoyed that.

Many things have changed in my life. I am now, not a 17 year old high school senior but a grandmother of eight. Paul and I have been married for 24 years. Caroline is now married (as are her brother and sister) and the mother of her own little boys, my grandsons Will and Henry. My life today is very different from when I first became enchanted with this story. Yet almost fifty years to the day when I first saw it, this nearly three hour movie wove its magic again and the hills (of Loudoun County, VA) were alive with the sound of music one more time.

SAVANNAH SAFARI

very so often I enjoy going back in time, either through looking at old photos, reconnecting with old friends or seeing places where I used to live. Lots of people don't enjoy looking back, but for some reason, I do. This weekend, I went back to Savannah, my home from 1955-1965 when I was age 7-16. I had come to help my sister move into a new apartment and after the work was done, I took my camera out and went on safari.

My first stop was Bull Street Baptist Church. I was a preacher's kid, so BSBC was practically my second home. Sunday School, Morning worship, Training Union, Evening Worship, Youth Fellowships after Sunday evening church service, Family night supper on Wednesday followed by GA's (Girls' Auxiliary, now known as Girls in Action) then Prayer Meeting. Add to that choir practice for whatever choir I was in and Vacation Bible School in the summer - there was absolutely no time left for me to get into trouble. I think that was part of the plan.

The church building was sparkling, most of its interiors having been refurbished to bring it up to date. Granite counters and polished fixtures in the bathrooms; slogans painted on the wall in the youth area; clean and freshened nursery rooms - all to make the church ready for the twenty-first century. The church itself is a magnificent stone structure with huge columns on the front porch atop impossibly tall steps. The service was quite different from what I remembered when my father was the pastor so many years before - it included drums, cymbals, guitars, and hymn lyrics projected onto a screen coming down from the ceiling. Yet the heart of the church, the warmth, was still there. Though I had not attended a service there in decades, quite a number of people came up to me, gave me a hug and introduced themselves to me. At the end of the service, I found myself in tears for the memories of all those days gone by.

I drove past the old Lane's Drug Store where my friends and I went between Sunday School and Church for a quick cherry Coke. Frequently we had to sneak into church onto the back row, praying that Daddy didn't see us coming in late. He did one time, though, that I will never forget. The teenagers I hung out with were sitting one Sunday night on the back pew chattering away while Daddy preached from the pulpit. Suddenly we noticed that he had stopped his sermon and directed his attention to us. "Will all the young people on the back row meet me in the church parlor after the service?' he intoned in the voice of God Almighty. We knew we were in for it. I have blocked from my memory most of what he said, but I remember I was praying to be swallowed up by the carpet.

I saw the old Telfair Hospital where Daddy used to take me for his pastoral visits. I passed by Forsyth Park where I used to go for my gym class as a student at Richard Arnold Junior High School. Back then it was just a long hike from the school, but now I see what a place of great beauty it is.

Hundreds of people were in the park - on blankets sunbathing or picnicking. Oddly, some twenty or thirty people were bouncing into each other from inside huge clear plastic balls - it looked like fun.

Next I had breakfast and supper with old high school friends from Savannah High School. Forty-nine years before we had been teenagers and in the years since, we'd all had different experiences, led different lives. Now here we were still laughing over the same things, still interested in each other's lives. It touched my heart that these high school friends made time to see me for meals while I was there. Southern childhood friends are for keeps, I think.

I passed the Pirate's House, my favorite childhood restaurant, the old Annette's Dairy, whose horse-drawn wagons clip-clopped onto our cement streets to deliver milk in clinking glass bottles to our door. And finally, I drove down my old street, the streetcar rails in the middle where I fell one day, long since cemented over. And there it was at last - my old house where I lived for ten years, perhaps the most formative years of my life. The brick exterior has been painted now, a lovely cream color. The grapevine which sheltered the graves of so many of my goldfish is long gone. In the place of the swing set where I imagined a circus career as a trapeze artist, a lovely pool welcomes swimmers and sunbathers. The playhouse that housed my dolls and toy stove has been made over into a beautiful pool house. The current owner of the house was gracious to show me all these things - her Southern gentility and hospitality making me feel right at home, though I had not walked on those floors for fifty years.

I drove past Charles Ellis School, Richard Arnold School and Savannah High School - where so many of my Savannah memories took root and so many friendships were formed. I passed the old Central Pharmacy and Cheatham's Grocery where Daddy and Mama took their business. Now the building holds a barber shop and another business I couldn't figure out.

I drove down to the historic city center where so many squares confound the unaccustomed driver but whose moss-laden trees shelter lovers and dreamers, tourists and the homeless. And wherever I went, I was greeted with the slow flattened cadence of Southern tongues from smiling faces. Everyone was so incredibly friendly and polite.

Finally it was time to come home to Virginia. I did so with a mixture of sadness and longing. I love being a Virginian and living with Paul. But a part of my heart will always remain in the Deep South where I grew up - the beautiful "city by the sea," as our high school annual dubbed it. I'll be back, Savannah.

HORSEBACK RIDING
WITH DADDY

 fter feeding some carrots yesterday to the horses that live in the pasture next to our house, I remembered an adventure I had with my father over forty years ago. Daddy was 60 at the time, ten years younger than I am now, but I thought he was ancient. He and Mama had just moved back to Gaffney, SC, his favorite place in the entire world. He was taking up the pastorate of West End Baptist Church, his last full time assignment before retirement. I was devastated as it was the first time I had lived in a different city from my parents other than the semesters I spent in college. I was still a newlywed, teaching at a junior high school and was not ready to have my parents live so far away.

So when spring break came around, I took the bus by myself to Gaffney and settled in comfortably into Mama and Daddy's guest room, surrounded by the furniture and things I remembered and loved. For a week, I shopped at mill outlet stores with Mama, ate her delicious home cooked meals and visited in the town where I was born. On Thursday,

Daddy woke me up early and said, "Get into your jeans. We're going to see somebody."

While Mama stayed home, Daddy and I went to see one of his church members, a Mr. Webb who owned a farm on the outskirts of town. Mr. Webb had been after Daddy to ride his horses ever since they'd moved to town. So when he suggested we do that, I jumped at the chance for some alone time with Daddy. When we drove into the barnyard, Mr. Webb came out to meet us, a short man of about 65 or so wearing overalls and a gimmee cap. He led us to the stable and saddled horses for all three of us. I was a little in awe of the fact that my daddy was riding. A big man who stood 6'2" and weighed right around 200 pounds, Daddy climbed easily into the saddle of a sturdy plug that looked like he knew how to pull a plow. It occurred to me then that Daddy must have ridden horses and mules quite a bit from field to barn, growing up on a farm as he did. Mr. Webb settled me on a mare that showed a little more white in her eyes than I was comfortable with. She was dancing around in the barn lot, the metal rings on her bridle jingling as she tossed her head back and forth. It occurred to me that I might have oversold my riding ability to my companions, but it was too late to admit it. Mr. Webb tightened the girth on my horse, swung up nimbly onto his own and clucked loudly.

Our horses followed, one after the other, behind Mr. Webb's horse, on dirt paths around his pastures and through woods, on the red dirt rutted trails through corn fields and grassy passages near the highway. Daddy spotted a snake once, but fortunately our horses did not. My horse was already looking for spooks and found one, an intimidating piece of paper that flew up in front of her. My heart leaped into my throat as the mare attempted to rear. Luckily Daddy was riding just beside me and reached out, grabbing my horse's bridle, settling her and me.

The rest of the ride was uneventful, a peaceful and beautiful April afternoon that gave me a sweet memory all these years later. I like to remember that as long as he lived, Daddy was always there, giving me adventures and protecting me from harm. We rode together a few more times in the years Mama and Daddy lived in Gaffney, but this was the first time, and I have never forgotten it.

BARN LOVE

ome of the happiest moments of my life have been connected to barns. Whenever I travel in a rural area, I always photograph any barns I see. I do this because I know they are a dying breed. A barn on a farm was built as a workplace, a place to house farm animals and equipment, and ultimately a play place for farm children. Yet, when agricultural techniques changed, the barn lost its identity. Draft horses lost out to high powered tractors and combines. Farming practices changed, prohibitive costs made dairy cattle impractical, and tobacco growing developed a stigma, so the barns lost their purpose. Yet farmers either couldn't afford to or couldn't bring themselves to tear down the old barns. So, in many cases, they stand - silent reminders of days gone by.

Lately, there has been a new appreciation for old barns. There is even a program called Barn Again! created by the U.S. National Trust for Historic Preservation and Successful Farming magazine to promote restoration or adaptive reuse of old barns. This is heartening to me as I have always loved barns

One of the first barns I recall was the giant wooden barn on my granddaddy Dever's farm near Gravel Switch, KY. I visited there once each year, usually in August. My granddaddy raised a herd of Black Angus cattle and a few dairy cows as well as tobacco and other crops. My grandmother often shooed Jerry and me out the door and told us to get out the Parcheesi board or go play in the barn. The barn, dark and cool in the hot days of August, held many charms. There was the corn sheller, a magical contraption that, by turning a crank, would change ears of corn into buckets of kernels. There was nothing so interesting in our city home in Savannah. There were numbers of stalls, filled with hay and tools. Chains hung from rusty nails in the timbers. These chains became shackles of captivity in the pirate ships of our vivid imaginations. The first stall, the one nearest the wide door, was our special playroom. It contained old furniture, feed bags for tablecloths and, most wondrous of all, an old wall-hung telephone, the kind you have to crank to use. Our imaginations took flight and we were no longer 8-year-old city girls, but pioneer women or Roy Rogers getting corn for Trigger. Though my grandparents' house is long gone, the barn still stands, a looming reminder of happy days of my childhood.

Granddaddy's barn

My other grandparents, who lived on a farm near Gates, NC, grew tobacco and peanuts as well as corn. The barns on their farm were smaller than the Kentucky barns, but no less fun. In the early days of my visits there,

Granddaddy kept horses and mules, one white and the rest brown, in one of the barns. They were used for plowing until a tractor took their place. Uncle Thurman would give Jerry and me rides on the white horse which was the only gentle one of the bunch. I remember having great peanut wars in the barn with Jerry and my cousins J.C. and Walter. We'd take sides, and then position ourselves behind peanut hay bales. Plucking peanuts off the vines or from the sandy floor of the barn, we'd fire them at each other, yelling "Bombs away over Tokyo." Growing up only ten or fifteen years after the end of World War II, we played soldier endlessly. Poor Walter always had to be the Nazis or the Japanese as he was the youngest in our group. When we tired of war, we could always pedal the grinding wheel, which was set up like a bicycle. How many hoe blades or knives did my grandfather sharpen there?

One of the barns at my grandparents' farm in NC

The smells of the barns were comforting - the odors of hay and straw, leather harnesses and saddles, and the sweat of horses and mules and cattle, most long gone. Dried cow patties littered the floor, to be picked up and used as ammunition against the dirty Nazis or the pirates or whoever Roy Rogers was fighting that day.

When I owned a farm in North Carolina, my daddy built a small barn for me. It was sheathed in tin, which we painted red. The doors were framed in wood painted white. Inside, Daddy constructed a rough wooden workbench where one day, I used a hammer to repair something, causing a swarm of yellow jackets to emerge and land on my knee. I spent days afterward resisting the urge to scratch the terrible itch that ensued. Daddy got rid of the yellow jackets, taking care of me as he always did.

Finally another barn became important to me but for a very different reason - When our son Tom was married, we held his rehearsal dinner in a barn at a reception facility called Great Country Farm. We had catered barbecue and fixings brought in and hired a square dance caller to teach us how to dosey do. It was a happy night when all my family was gathered around me.

Barns will always be a happy sight to me though they may no longer serve their original purpose. Now, more often than not, when a barn is allowed to stand empty and rot, a farmer will let it fall down, thankful to be able to make a better use of the land. Any buildings they replace them with will be squatty, featureless buildings with no character. In another twenty-five years or so, my grandchildren may never see the great wooden buildings I came to love, except in photos. The end of that era will be a sad reminder that the days of the small farmer are over, replaced by colorless, soulless agribusiness. Till then, I'll keep taking pictures of barns.

HOME

'**ve** lived in lots of places in my lifetime but I remember specifically the homes of my parents where I was raised and where I came home to as a young adult. I remember in particular, going home to spend time with Mama and Daddy when they were living on their farm in Gates County, NC.

They were getting older (in their 70s – not much older than I am now!) and I was coming to the realization that I would not have them forever. Most of the family would gather in that old house where generations of Morris's had lived and loved and gathered since before the War Between the States. Mama would cook platters of country ham and turkey which Daddy would slice with an old butcher knife he'd sharpened on a whetstone. The knife's handle was held together with electrical tape but the blade was sharp enough for surgery. There'd be deep bowls of corn, butter beans, applesauce, and tomatoes, all canned or frozen by Mama from Daddy's huge garden. I was naïve enough at the time to believe that all this appeared as if by magic, never really taking into consideration the hours of labor and love involved in the bounty on their table.

I remember in particular one time when my sister Martha Jean and her husband Hines came home from a foreign country just in time for Christmas. I was a young mother with two children and most of our family had gathered at Mama and Daddy's house for the holiday. Mama had put up her Christmas tree in the living room and set a beautiful table. She served her dinner and Daddy beamed the whole time – surveying his treasure – his children and grandchildren, because he surely never had much in the way of material wealth. The love around the table was so strong it was almost palpable. After dinner we gathered around the tree where my son Tom, a lad of around four at the time, and his cousin Ellen who was five, distributed the presents to everyone. Then such chaotic tearing of wrapping and ribbons flying you have never seen. Children were shrieking and oohs and ahhs escaped our mouths as gifts were admired. After the deluge of gifts, Mama began cleaning up the wrapping paper and Daddy took it out to the oil barrel out back to burn. Some of us (not me, usually) went to the kitchen to do the dishes and others went outside to stand around the barrel and watch the sparks fly up to the sky. The stars on that particular night were brighter than usual and before daylight, there would be a thin coat of snow on the ground. I remember wanting the night never to end.

Though I lived just five or so miles away, I remember spending the night on my Mama's couch because I didn't want to leave. I just wanted to have everyone around me for a while longer. I still remember my mother tucking a sheet and blanket around me and placing a pillow under my head on the couch. The pillowcase had been hung on the line and ironed smooth by my mother so that it had a smell of sunshine and fresh laundry detergent. Outside the moon and stars winked at me through the window. The house settled and my eyes closed. For one night, I was Mama and Daddy's little girl again, safe under their roof. Though they are gone and I can no longer go home again, I carry that memory in my heart.

MY BABY LOVES THE WESTERN MOVIES

 hen I was 10 years old in 1958, rock and roll radio stations played a song called "My Baby Loves the Western Movies." It was recorded by a doo-wop group called the Olympics. The song was the lament of a

young man who couldn't get any attention from his girl because she was so caught up in Westerns. I heard this song this morning and it reminded me of the cowboy phase I went through back in my childhood. It's now over sixty years later (I know...I can't believe it either!) and I'm still hung up on Westerns.

It's Saturday morning and I'm reading the *Washington Post*. Page after page is filled with death and destruction, wars and rumors of wars. Yet on TV (the COZI channel here in the Washington, DC area) it's the 1800s again and the landscape is decidedly desert-like. Every Saturday morning you can see Hopalong Cassidy, The Rifleman (Lucas McCain who thought it was completely normal to carry his rifle when he went into town to get feed for his cattle or food for his son Mark - played by Johnny Crawford, an early boyfriend of mine though he didn't know it,) Daniel Boone, Matt Dillon (one of my favorites who, along with his sidekicks, Festus Hagin, Kitty and Doc, brought law and order to Dodge City,) Wanted Dead or Alive, or Rawhide. Ahh, Rawhide with the young Clint Eastwood as Rowdy Yates. His chiseled face made it into many of my elementary school dreams back then. Me and Rowdy cooking our supper over an open fire. Rowdy saving me from marauding Indians, Me and Rowdy wrapped in a blanket... oh wait ...that came much later.

Our family loved Bonanza. It was the first TV show I ever saw in color on our brand new color TV set. To see the three Cartwright boys and their father Ben come riding across the Ponderosa "in living color" was thrilling beyond words. Those who are young enough to have only known color TV will never understand how amazing the first color TV programs were after years of black and white. My favorite Cartwright, of course, was Hoss, a big, goofy guy who was gentle and kind. Woe to any females who fell in love with any of the Cartwrights, though - they were destined to die of a disease or to be found out as villainesses.

Daddy always liked Have Gun, Will Travel so we watched it every Saturday night, presumably after he had prepared his Sunday morning sermon! I always thought it was cool that he had a calling card with a knight chess piece emblazoned on the card. But for many years I thought his first name was "Wire" as the card instructed potential clients to "Wire Paladin" for help in ridding themselves of bad guys. Daddy also liked the rotating shows of Bronco (Daddy later named one of his ponies Bronco!) Cheyenne (How big were Clint Walker's muscles, anyway?) and Sugarfoot (the story of a tenderfoot who went west to become a lawyer.)

But probably my all-time favorite was my earliest Western hero - the king of the cowboys - Roy Rogers. I played for hours in my daddy's back-yard garden with my Roy Rogers Double R Bar Ranch play set and named my bicycle Trigger, stabling him each night in our garage-cum-stable. I wanted more than anything to have a fringed shirt like Roy's and to ride off into the sunset with Roy. Dale didn't even make it into my daydreams.

The years since those halcyon days have been more than a little rocky. There have been deaths, divorce, financial problems, as well as sweet days with three children and now eight grandchildren. And there was the sweet rekindling of love in my heart with my marriage to Paul. But through all those things, through good and bad, the Westerns have always been there, cleaning up the West, making it safe for good folks everywhere to drink sarsaparilla, pick up some supplies at the general store, and wear the same clothing week after week. (Adam Cartwright's all black attire, Hoss's brown suede vest, Matt Dillon's faded pink shirt and brown vest!)

It may be 2018, but in my heart of hearts, every Saturday morning, it's the 1870s, and I'm living in the old West. Yee haw! Rolling rolling rolling, keep them doggies rolling!

THE HOME SHOW

t's pretty clear Paul and I have officially become curmudgeons. We woke up this morning and decided to go to the annual Washington Home + Remodeling Show, not because we are planning any remodeling, but because we are retired and are constantly looking for amusements. It is being held at the Dulles Expo Center in Chantilly and we thought that, by going EARLY on a Friday morning we'd miss the crowds. BIG MISTAKE!

Because there were so few people there, EVERY single exhibitor from Thompson Creek Windows to Little Giant Ladders practically attacked us with their sales pitch as soon as we came in the area of the aisle in front of their booth. As soon as we had rounded the first corner, Paul was already turning to me saying, "I think we've made a mistake." By the end of the next aisle, it was "Don't make eye contact, Janet!" Yet without fail, each exhibitor practically reached out and grabbed us to look at their product or take a brochure.

"What home improvement plans do you have?" they all said, as though they were reading from a prepared script. One of them, whose product was some kind of massage item, yelled out at me as I passed, "What size shoe do you wear, ma'am?" I mean, really, what possible reason did she have for needing to know that for a massage product?

We finally did stop to listen to the sales pitch for a steam cleaner. It sounded pretty good to me and I was thinking maybe we'd think about getting one. So Paul did what Paul always does - he walked me around the corner and looked up a review of the product online - nope, not happening.

It was cheaper online and the reviews weren't that great. If the "special show price" wasn't really so special, I was beginning to wonder why we'd bothered to come out. Though I know these sales people have got to make a living, hard sales like that just don't work on me. So the morning was a complete bust.

But wait, not a complete bust. Our daughter Katherine texted us to meet her and the boys for a hot dog lunch at Costco. What fun! On second thought, I'll suffer through a barrage of in-your-face sales pitches like that for a chance to see my grandchildren any day of the week. Maybe I'm not such a curmudgeon after all.

A MEMORIAL TO THEODOSIA ELLEN DEVER MORRIS

January 21, 1915 - January 10, 2000

I wrote the following eulogy for my mother's funeral. Because of my emotion, I was unable to read it, so my niece Suzanne Purdy filled in beautifully for me. I hope you can hear me reading it today, Mama. I still miss you so many years later. We were lucky to be your children.

How did you know the woman you are here to remember today? For many of you, she was Mrs. Morris, the quiet, dignified minister's wife who followed her husband Frank Elliott Morris to serve churches in states all across the Southeast. Others, a few, called her Doty. For you, she was a friend, constant and true but always reserved. For five tall, beautiful Kentucky girls, Doty was the sister who was next to the youngest in age, the only one to live outside of Kentucky.

My mother

For ten grandchildren and six great grandchildren, she was Nana. And for four of us, she was our mother. Two of us called her Mother and two of us called her Mama, but to all she was a stable source of strength, a banked fire to serve as counterpoint to our father's cheery flame.

For the last nine years of our mother's nearly eighty-five years of life, she was confined to a wheelchair, crippled by a disabling stroke which stilled her voice and immobilized her right side. It was a disability she bore with as much patience and dignity as possible, enabled by the tender loving care of Jerry Ann, the daughter who was her caregiver for most of those years.

But even the stroke years were unorthodox, for Mama was a woman who expected certain things out of life and generally got them.

When doctors told her, for example, that she was no longer able to swallow and could not take food by mouth, Mama reacted by first removing the feeding tube they'd inserted and later, accompanying Jerry to the Trellis Restaurant in Williamsburg to eat an entire plate of filet mignon and scallops!

Often the rest of the family would call or drop by to check on Mama only to find that she and Jerry had set off on another adventure. She accompanied Jerry all over several states as Jerry worked at her job. Mama would sit patiently in the car while Jerry visited her places of business. Then she and Jerry would set off on another trail, sometimes to visit Louise in Savannah, or Martha Jean at her home. Once she even flew with Janet to Kentucky to visit her sisters. Just as you'd expect, the airline bumped Mama up to first class!

Sometimes the adventures were less than dignified, how-ever. When Paul and I moved with our children to northern Virginia, we left behind a trailer load of belongings which Jerry and Mama volunteered to bring up later. The sight of Jerry and our mother as they turned into our quiet neighborhood in a car pulling a trailer loaded with boxes, clothes, a dog box, a mutt named Reckless straining at her chain and baying at passing cars, and Mama's wheelchair hanging off the side was one never to be forgotten. More typical, however, were quiet mornings when Jerry would bring coffee in china cups and saucers to our mother and her roommate in the nursing home.

But even the last few months spent in the nursing home were out of the ordinary for our mother. She would accept no less each day than to be completely dressed right down to the proper foundation garments. And don't think you could get by without a full make-up session daily and hair appointments every week. But for those of us who took care of her, it was a labor of love, a small down payment on the monumental debt we owed her for raising us. And here we want to pay tribute to Jerry Ann for the years of selfless service to our mother. Jerry gave her a life that was relatively pain-free, active, adventurous, and comfortable. Thank you, Jerry.

But we have other memories, too, of other long ago times. We remember our mother as the best of Southern cooks. We remember always coming home from school to find cookies and milk or, on days when we deserved a special reward, her fried apple pies. I'm half embarrassed today when I set a bowl of Cheerios in front of my children as I recall the daily offerings of my mother at our breakfasts - fresh ground sausage patties or bacon with scrambled eggs and homemade biscuits and molasses. And for dinners and suppers, there were platters of fried chicken, steaming mounds of real mashed potatoes, turnip greens, corn, butter beans, tomato pudding, all canned or frozen by her and finally peach cobbler or apple crumb pies or banana pudding. On most days, life was good and we'd even be likely to come to the kitchen to find Mama in her dress, cooking up a storm and dancing the Charleston in front of the stove.

Our mother was also an accomplished seamstress, sewing clothes for all four of us girls and also for her grandchildren. Many nights she stayed up long past midnight to finish a hem or sew on buttons to make sure we all had new dresses for church. She also made curtains for our newlywed apartments, crocheted receiving blankets for her grandchildren, and mended our clothes when we were too busy as young adults or too lazy to do it ourselves.

She came to our homes for a week or two after the birth of each grandchild to show us how to bathe our newborns, to cook and clean for our families, and to diaper the babies when we were too sick or too tired to do it ourselves.

We remember the pots of homemade soup she brought over on nights when our own days at the office were too long. We remember standing at the sink by her side drying dishes and spilling out our teenage angst to her listening ears. We remember her stately presence at each of our weddings and the fun she had when new sons-in-law joined the family. At long last, after four girls, she had sons who called her Mom and teased and flattered her. Our mother could deny them nothing and filled their stomachs with fried apple pies.

We remember the funny stories she told us of growing up without a mother in Kentucky in the early days of this century - of driving a Model "A" Ford to school at age 14! And of getting into mischief with her five sisters. Her mother passed away when Mama was just four. So the six young girls were often left alone while their father was out farming. Mama often regaled us with the tale of the day the sisters made biscuit dough, and then threw the dough in great gobs onto the kitchen ceiling just to watch it fall. We remember our mother's laugh as she told the story.

We remember, finally, our mother's hands. Always small and soft, they were constantly busy. For us, they cleaned and cooked, they applauded and corrected. But they always caressed us with the love that was her main ingredient.

And as today as we give our mother back to God, we thank Him for His mercy in lending her to us for so long. We will never forget you, Mother, or your words to us. We'll remember, Mama, to stand up straight, to be kind to others, to say our prayers, to hold in our stomachs, and remember who we are. We'll remember, Mama.

THAT TERRIBLE DAY IN 1963

 n a perfectly normal day in November, 1963, like many of my Savannah, Georgia friends, I was a Savannah High School sophomore. I lived in a bubble of safety, unaware that the world was about to change around me. I went to school as usual on that day and had just about completed my World History class with Mrs. Madeline Boney when all of a sudden, my classmates and I heard the crackle of the intercom interrupt our lesson. Oddly, it was not Dr. Moseley, our principal, who came on the intercom, but the garbled sounds of a radio. Haha, I thought. Some goofball in the office has turned on the intercom by accident and had the radio playing. It soon became evident, though, that something very different and infinitely more awful was playing out.

We heard the doleful voice of a reporter saying the awful news that President Kennedy had been shot. Where there had been laughter and talking in the classroom, there was suddenly stunned silence. People whispered, "Is this real?" Mrs. Boney looked shocked, as though she had been punched in the gut. Soon Dr. Moseley came on the intercom, interrupting to tell us to move to our next class. I went directly to Mrs. Beulah Harper's English class, the room where I felt most at home in the school, only to find Mrs. Harper distraught. There was obviously no English lesson that day.

We listened to more news from the intercom and were soon let out to go home. There at home, we glued ourselves to the television, the horror story unfolding in black and white before us. We stayed there for days watching as the nation prepared to bury its President, our hearts saddened for the beautiful widow and her little children. We were fearful for the implications for our nation. Was it a conspiracy? Was there more to come?

Sadly, there was more. My family was coming home from church on Sunday and heard the news of Jack Ruby's murder of the suspected assassin Lee Harvey Oswald. It seemed as though it would never end. It did end, though and the nation returned to normal. We would be assaulted time and again through the years with more tragedies – the Vietnam War, the Challenger disaster, the 9-11 attacks on America, just to name a few – but the nation still stood strong.

On an anniversary like November 22nd, I have to look a little harder to find something to be thankful for, but I do find it – I am thankful today for my country, for its heroes, for those who give their lives in its service, for the citizens who live by the rules, for those who protect us from wrongdoers. On each anniversary of this terrible tragedy, I am thankful for my country.

JERRY AND LARRY

y twin sister Jerry has been at my side longer than anyone else on earth. She is younger than me by five minutes, a fact she has trumpeted for years. I complain about the fact that she has always been the cosseted baby of the family, yet in reality, nothing could be further from the truth.

Jerry is maybe the most unselfish person I have ever met. She has spent her life caring for others. For about ten years, Jerry was the primary caregiver for our mother who had suffered a devastating stroke. She and her husband Larry moved Mama into their home and became physical therapists, heavy lifters, counselors, and maids for the woman who had been the same for us for so many years. Before that, though, Jerry had helped Larry care for his mom who had early stage dementia before her passing. They also frequently welcome into their home Larry's older brother Steve, a developmentally disabled man who is becoming more and more physically disabled. As a final challenge, Jerry has become the eyes for her husband Larry who lost his vision in his thirties as a result of a terrible disease called Retinitis Pigmentosa. An important fact about Larry is that in ALL the years since he lost his vision, I have NEVER heard him complain.

In Larry, Jerry married perhaps the only other person on the planet who is as humble and genuinely good as she is. Together they make a perfect team. Walking beside them, you can hear Jerry quietly telling Larry when to step up or down. You can hear Larry repeating something he has heard to Jerry (whose hearing in one ear has deteriorated.)

Such difficulties as Jerry and Larry have faced would have defeated and angered me years ago. I would have shaken my fist at the universe and retreated into a black void. But that is not the path Jerry and Larry have taken. At any given time you will find them in their church's kitchen preparing a meal for 200 people, hosting their church prayer group in their home or keeping the nursery. Jerry teaches a weekly art class and runs a children's art camp in the summer. Until recently, Larry ran a successful tire business in Raleigh. Many people who met him never realized he had RP.

Playing the hand they were dealt is just a way of life for Jerry and Larry. They are surrounded by friends and family who love and admire them. Their son and daughter, their spouses and four granddaughters love them and realize just how special they are.

When we were younger, Jerry and I always had our pictures taken and Jerry always put her hand on my shoulder. I always complained. When we slept in the same bed, I drew an imaginary line down the center of the bed and dared her to cross it. I was then and always will be, in truth, the evil twin. It's hard for me to be as physically demonstrative as Jerry to those I love but I CAN write how I feel. This is me, putting my hand on your shoulder, Jerry. I love you and Larry.

MAMA - THE GOOD SPORT

I have found it much easier to write about my father than about my mother. Like me, he was an open book. We were kindred spirits, loving to talk and meet people, telling stories and Southern to the core.

Mama was always more of an enigma. She was quiet and a little shy, preferring to stand in Daddy's shadow but always available in case he, or any of us girls, needed anything. Her rules were a little stricter than Daddy's; her voice could be a little sharper. But if I ever had a problem with boys, or homework, or life, she's who I went to first. I've often said that I loved the days when our dishwasher was broken or full, because then I got to dry dishes beside my mama. She would wash the pots and pans quietly while I unburdened my soul to her. This quality of hers, living in the background, led us often to overlook her.

So I never really appreciated the core of strength within her until she had her stroke. I marveled at her ability to smile in spite of her limitations. She no longer had a home of her own, her husband had passed away and she was imprisoned by her body which no longer worked on one side. Yet after the initial hard few months while all of us came to the realization of the way it was going to be, Mama adjusted beautifully. She was, in fact, what we realized she had been all along - a good sport.

Through the years, Daddy had decided where they'd live, where they'd shop and where they'd vacation, among other things. And time after time, in the way of women of that time, Mama would acquiesce. Summers would find her cooking amazing meals in tiny rented cabins on the Outer Banks. She would adjust to a new town only to find a few years down the road that Daddy felt a pull from God to go to another place. So she'd have to adjust all over again.

After her stroke, I thought she'd never smile again. I thought I'd never smile again. But we all made the adjustment - we learned that we had to in order to survive. So today, I praise Mama for her ability to adjust no matter where she was in life. She was truly a good sport.

MAMA AND HER GRANDCHILDREN

ama had four daughters and ten grandchildren. After the birth of each one of her grandchildren, she came to her daughters' homes for several days to help out around the house, usually giving the babies their first baths, washing mountains of diapers (no Pampers back then!) cooking delectable meals for her sons-in-law, taking care of the new baby's siblings and getting some up close and personal time with her new grandchild. She kept this up for twenty-three years starting with the birth of her first grandchild in 1963 until the birth of her last in 1986.

She never once complained, although Daddy whined a bit about losing his girl for a few days. He was never much good without her. But she delighted in her grandchildren, crocheting crib blankets for each one. She taught their mothers how to diaper a baby without sticking them with diaper pins. She stocked our freezers with homemade vegetable soup and her famous spaghetti sauce to eat after she had gone back to Daddy. She cleaned our homes and washed our dishes and laundry. She gave us rest.

Finally in 2000, after a massive stroke, her body gave out and we laid her to rest beside Daddy in the little family cemetery in the country. We had her funeral in Middle Swamp Baptist Church, the tiny building where so many of my ancestors had worshipped, been baptized and finally had been given back to God. On that solemn day, all ten of her grandchildren were Mama's pallbearers. The six boys, Johnny, Skip, Frank, Mickey, Chip, and Tom, carried her coffin. They were all so tall and handsome, dressed in black suits and wearing somber expressions. The four girls, Jean, Ellen, Katherine and Caroline followed behind the coffin, each carrying a long-stemmed white rose. All four girls were so tall and slim and pretty, wearing slender column dresses. They looked impossibly beautiful in their grief. It was heart-rending, really, to see them carrying the one who had carried them all at their birth.

With the loss of Mama, I felt for a time like an orphan, which I guess I am still. It was dreadful to lose her quiet presence in my life and I still think I want to call her every weekend the way I used to. Many people are sure that their mothers were wonderful. But for the nearly 85 years that I had her, I know I had the best mother of all.

MAMA LEAVES HOME

In spite of losing her mother at such an early age, my mother did have a happy childhood. She told me often of the pleasures of lambing time in the spring on the farm. For a time, she was sent to live occasionally with her Aunt Arie and Uncle Dave, a childless couple who lived nearby. I'm sure it was to relieve my grandfather of the burden of so many girls, but I imagine Mama was lonely for her sisters and father. Mama was probably the quietest of the girls so I'm sure they selected her for that reason. Mama remembered being given fabric at

Aunt Arie's and taught to make a quilt, which I still have. She told me that Aunt Arie was notoriously thrifty, passing the butter dish around the table so quickly that no one had time to take any of it. Upon Aunt Arie's death in 1965 at age 97, Mama received a set of her hobnail glasses (which my sister Louise now has,) beautiful cranberry glassware and candy dishes, and, most magnificent of all, a Lone Star quilt. Mama told us the quilt had been hidden in the corn crib during the War Between the States to keep it from the Yankees. (I found that intriguing since Mama's grandfather Phillip Dever had been a Yankee soldier during the war. Perhaps a little revisionist history by Mama since she lived the rest of her life in the Deep South?)

Finally though, Mama came back home with her sisters and father. She used to tell hilarious stories of how her cousin Eulalia came to visit while my grandfather was at work on the farm. In a story I have previously mentioned, the girls and their cousin would make batches of biscuit dough, and then throw the dough in great gobs onto the ceiling to watch it fall in stringy, slow messes. I can imagine the girls' laughing with glee as my mother did when she told us this story. But I wouldn't like to clean it up.

Mama (far right) with her sisters Helen and Kelly Mae

I talked once to one of my mother's school friends, Tincy Penn, who owned Penn's Store in Gravel Switch (the oldest country store in America being continuously run by the same family. Check out their website http:// www.pennsstore.com/index.html) She remembered when she, Mama and another teen-aged girl sneaked into the Maccabees' meeting room late one night. (The Maccabees were a highly secretive organization kind of like the Masons.) Tincy remembered that they were disappointed because all they saw was a large chair in the middle of the room. I found this fascinating to think of my mother going on an adventure like this - she was not the daring type as an adult.

Soon though, her Kentucky adventures were over as she married my Daddy in 1936 in the parlor of a minister's home. She often remembered with a sigh her wedding suit which had mink tails on the collar - she was a fashionista all her life. After a year or two in the seminary, Mama moved with Daddy to North Carolina to the first of many pastorates in states across the Southeast - Virginia, North Carolina, South Carolina, and Georgia. She lived with Daddy outside of Kentucky for the rest of her life. Each year on Derby Day, I watched as she battled a lump in her throat when "My Old Kentucky Home" was played at Churchill Downs. No matter where she lived, she was always a Kentucky girl.

I INTERVIEW MY MOTHER

I have always gathered information about my family, so years ago I sat my mother down and asked her a number of questions about our family history. These are the things she told me.

 y mother was born at home, the sixth of seven girls, one of whom died in infancy. Her birth was supervised by Dr. Thomas A. Campbell. She was named after her Uncle Theodore and Uncle Dave Penn's

mother Ellen. She never really liked her name "Theodosia Ellen" and often went by "Doty." She remembered her older sister Helen was called "Cutie" and her younger sister Kelly Mae, the baby of the family, was held a lot. I thought that was a very telling memory from someone whom we in the South call a "knee baby."

She had only one remembrance of her mother who died when Mama was just four. She remembered playing on a double swing in the yard. She had taken the floor of the swing out, leaned it against a tree and was playing with it when she scraped her finger between the swing floor and the tree. She ran to her mother who was churning butter on the back porch. She remembered her mother wrapping her finger. The only other memory she had of her mother was when, at age four, she came down the stairs of their house in Lebanon and saw her mother lying in a casket. Her mother had died on her wedding anniversary of diabetes-related causes. What a sad way for my mother to start life!

Nevertheless, Mama's father was a doting father who made sure that her world was secure. She said she had no worries as a child. Her father didn't have to fight in World War I as he was a widower and a farmer. Mama liked cutting paper dolls out of the Sears, Roebuck catalog. For Christmas, she remembered getting big china dolls and tea sets, raisins and nuts for Christmas.

Mama went to a one-roomed schoolhouse, Caney Creek School, near her home in Gravel Switch, KY from 2nd to 8th grade. Being a teacher, I asked how so many grades in one room were able to function easily. She told me that each of the grades went up by turns to the front of the school to recite. The teachers she remembered were Edna Lankford, Mrs. Boswell, and Ben Wilson. Mama said that during the Depression, they always had plenty of food and she learned to sew. She had a charge account at Lerman's Department Store and wore the same clothes to school all week. She took off her good clothes when she came home each day. She remembered bringing her lunch to school, but sometimes had nothing to eat all day because she had no mother to fix it.

She said she went to school in the town of Lebanon for first grade and high school. Her family made this move because of the death of her mother. (It was thought to be easier to educate the six girls in town, but later they moved back to the farm so her father could get help for the children from a childless couple - Reena and Merrit Cooley and another woman who came in to do washing.)

She remembered being punished only once as a child. Her father cut a switch from a bush in the backyard. Interestingly, Mama couldn't remember what she had done! But she said her father was a good father, very strict and not openly affectionate. But she said he used to take all six girls shopping at The Hub, a store in Danville. He'd sit and watch as the girls tried on new clothes. Mama's sisters often remarked to me that Mama in particular, of all the girls, liked nice clothes. They all remembered a baby blue coat with fur trim that she had.

Each of the six girls had specific chores to do at home. Mama's was to draw water from the well and to bring in firewood and kindling. She also had to wash dishes at night and push the lawn mower. Her sister Helen, a tomboy, gathered eggs, brought the cows in, and milked. Mama remembered that Helen could crawl all over the barn. Cassie acted as a surrogate mother and was very strict with her sisters. She'd clean the house, and then lock the door so the little ones couldn't mess up the house. (They were usually out skating or playing in the creek.) After supper the three little ones, Helen, Mama and Kelly Mae would sing in the kitchen and throw dishrags at each other while their father sat by the fire reading. They used to have a player piano too.

Mama said she began dating at age 15, dating with other couples. When I asked what dates were like, she told me that they went to movies on Sunday night, or to Humpkey's in Lebanon where they had Cokes. (She was careful to let me know this as Humpkey's also sold beer!) Her first date was to a Methodist camp meeting, a kind of revival service.

As a child, she read a lot. She told me she read Jane Eyre and Silas Marner several times. She didn't have access to many books at home, but they did have paperback books. All of her parents and grandparents could read and write, so the children were encouraged to learn.

Mama remembered her paternal grandmother Celia, whom she called Grandmaw, wearing her white hair in a neat bun. Her paternal grandfather, whom she called Grandpaw, was a Civil War veteran, a registered Republican, with a long white beard. Mama remembered visiting them after church on Sundays when all her cousins were there. She remembered that they would go to bed before dark. Mama never knew her maternal grandparents as they had passed away before their daughter married.

Phillip and Celia Dever, Mama's grandparents

Mama took her first and only paying job after graduation from high school around age 19. She was a substitute clerk-typist in the county agent's office.

She made $15.00 a week and, according to her, she was scared to death. She only took one letter of dictation from her boss Mr. G.H. Karnes.

Mama met Daddy at church, at a BYPU party (Baptist Young People's Union.) Daddy's brother Desmond was pastor of Mama's church and he had talked about bringing Daddy to meet her and her sisters. Daddy was a handsome young seminary student in Louisville at the time. It was love at first sight for both Mama and Daddy.

SOUTHERN STORYTELLERS

 y sister Jerry and her husband Larry spent the weekend with Paul and me for what was a quiet, enjoyable, restful weekend, quite different from the usual. I made a pot roast for dinner Friday night (along with chocolate chess pie and a cream cheese pound cake) and cooked eggs and bacon for breakfast on Saturday. After both of the meals, we sat around the table sipping our coffee and talking…just talking. My brother in law Larry is a great story teller. He lost his vision years ago because of Retinitis Pigmentosa and so he picks up on small details to make up for the lack of sight. These details color his stories which are often hilarious and never mean spirited. Jerry and I told stories too, usually about our childhood or family legends. Paul mostly sits back and enjoys the fun, inserting an appropriate remark here and there.

My family, like most Southern families, has always included storytellers, tale spinners of the highest order who could weave marvelous tales of the past, some humorous, some tragic. The stories were told on Grandmama's front porch in North Carolina, on Grandaddy's front yard in Kentucky, or around the kitchen table. Uncle Tommy told car stories; Uncle L.D. told slightly off-color stories; Cousin Blannie remembered stories from our shared family past. Daddy told funny stories.

We've told and retold all of the stories so that they are now bigger than ever. Daddy told us once what he said was a true story of an old fellow who had just gotten an automobile, when autos were brand new. He was scared to death to drive it after having driven horses and mules all his life. He took his daughter Martha with him on the first ride and when he got to a certain hill at the edge of Gates County, felt he was going so fast he couldn't take his eyes off the road to look at the speedometer. So he asked his daughter, "How fast am I doing, Marthy?" [Here Daddy took on the voice of the old fellow, then immediately switched to the prideful voice of his daughter Martha.] "You're setting on twenty, Daddy!" as though he were flying at lightning speed. Daddy told me this tale once as we drove over that exact hill in Gates County. Ever after, I have told the same story every time I have driven over that same hill, to the groans and rolled eyes of my own family. Every time I tell the story, my daddy lives again in my memory. The stories of that weekend were silly and funny and sometimes meaningless, but oh, how they added to the joy of life.

FAKEBOOKING

verybody I know knows I enjoy Facebook. I like sharing pictures and stories about my family and my life and reading and seeing the same about yours. But an article I read in an issue of Health magazine got me thinking. Am I guilty of what they called "Fakebooking?" That's a term to describe editing your pictures and life events so that your life looks better than it actually is.

Of course, everybody wants to be perceived by the rest of the world as smart, interesting, and pretty or handsome. But I like being completely honest so let me just say that most of the pictures of myself which I post were taken years ago before I put on my cushion of insulation against the cold weather. My hair back then was much thicker, my skin was less wrinkled, my eyes were brighter and I was probably much more interesting.

Nowadays Paul and I live a quiet life. Our main sources of entertainment are the TV and the grandchildren. As a Southern girl (and I use the term "girl" very loosely) I do put on make-up and style my hair (what's left of it) every day. But my clothes often feature an elastic waist and more often than not, I wear bedroom slippers as I pad around the house. My cooking most often consists of heating up Lean Cuisines for Paul as he prefers those to the home-cooked meals I tried on him early in our marriage.

We have taken a couple of nice trips but most of the time, our big adventures involve going to Harris Teeter or Senior Day at the movies. And yes, I have fully embraced senior discounts wherever I can find them.

I'll probably still feel insecure when I see all the fabulous places you've been or how you've managed to maintain that slim figure all these years. But I'll just realize that at least some of you are Fakebooking it like I am. And by the way, I'll still probably post only the photos where I look ten years younger.

THE SHEPHERD BOY'S CHRISTMAS

Well, here it is - Christmas again. I had it all planned. It was going to be so glorious to have our three children and their families home for Christmas. But some of the grandchildren are sick and I even woke up this morning with the beginnings of a cold, so of course, the dinner was canceled. So I'll dismantle the table, and save the presents for another day. Paul and I exchanged gifts this morning and they were lovely. But there is one gift we received which is beyond price and it was given over 2000 years ago. A couple of years ago, I wrote this story of The Shepherd Boy's Christmas. In the midst of disappointment that our celebration didn't pan out, I can rejoice in the immeasurable gift of the Messiah to our world.

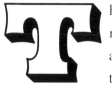he night air was cool and Josiah pulled his thin, ragged robe tighter around his long legs. At 13, he was already as tall as his father Hosea and would probably overtake him in height in another year or two. He kicked at a rock on the hillside and looked to make sure that it hadn't startled the sheep. His father would be angry if it had. Josiah and his father were shepherds and tended a small flock of sheep on the hillside outside of the little town of Bethlehem.

On this particular night, Josiah was nursing a grudge. He hadn't wanted to be outside with his father looking after sheep, not with all the excitement in town. The great Roman Emperor Caesar Augustus had decreed that everyone in the entire Roman world had to be counted, so Bethlehem, known as the City of David for its relation to the great king, was filling up with people who claimed it as their hometown. So many strangers, he thought. Why can't I be there to see them all – the pretty girls, the beggars, the hucksters – they all brought new excitement to the sleepy little village. And here he was on the side of a hill with a bunch of sheep.

He sat down against a large rock and pulled his little dog next to him for warmth. Asa the dog put his head on Josiah's leg and closed his eyes. Josiah looked out at the sheep – all thirty of the animals huddled together near the lead ewe grazing at what was left of the grass. Soon it would be time to bring the animals into shelter for the winter. But Hosea had told Josiah that there would be enough forage for another night or two. So he was stuck on a hillside in the middle of the night with his father, his uncle and two older brothers watching a bunch of sheep. It was an important task, he knew, protecting the sheep against danger. But still he longed for the adventure of the town.

Josiah had been watching the sky for the last few nights. In the upper elevation where Hosea liked to keep his sheep, the sky took on an unusual brilliance and the stars looked so close that you could almost touch them. He'd noticed one particularly large star that had kept the same place in the sky for several days now. It seemed to shine more than the other stars and stood right over the village of Bethlehem, as though it were lighting the way for all those travelers. His father had told Josiah that the star was a comet and Josiah couldn't stop looking at it. The long tail of the star seemed to point the way to Bethlehem, almost as if it were a signpost for all the weary travelers headed that way. Josiah wished that he were one of them.

He sighed, closed his eyes for just a moment and leaned his head back against the rock. Suddenly, he felt Asa lift his head from his lap. Josiah opened his eyes and saw Asa sniffing the air. Asa began barking loudly and, in the sky, the comet seemed to have grown almost incredibly bright, so bright that Josiah lifted the back of his hand to shade his eyes. The clouds around the comet grew thicker, and then seemed to part in the middle. He focused his eyes on the light and saw that in the center of the brilliance, high in the sky was…a being. Josiah jumped to his feet and ran back a few steps to be nearer to his father. Hosea and his uncle and brothers were standing as well and staring fearfully at the sky. The figure in the clouds was dressed in a long, flowing gown of the purest white with a golden sash around his chest. Behind his shoulders, white wings were spread wide. His face seemed to be glowing as though from reflected light. Josiah didn't understand what he was seeing and looked to his father for explanation but his father seemed just as fearful.

As the angel, for that is what it appeared to be, drew nearer to them, Josiah, his father and uncle and brothers bowed their heads and kneeled, their hands grasping their shepherds' crooks tightly. Asa stopped barking and lay quietly at Josiah's side. The angel hovered in the sky near the shepherds and looked at their frightened faces with a look of benevolence. He spread his wings wide and spoke to them.

"Do not be afraid for I bring you good news of great joy that will be for all people," he said. "Today in the city of David, a Savior has been born to you; He is Christ the Lord. If you are looking for a sign, this will be it: You will find the Baby wrapped in cloths and lying in a manger."

Hosea looked at his son in great wonderment. What could this mean? And why had this magnificent being appeared to them, lowly shepherds on a lonely hillside outside the little village of Bethlehem? They were nobodies, Hosea thought. If this Savior we've been promised really has arrived, why didn't He come as a warrior to overthrow the tight hand of Rome. Why did He come as a baby? And why was His birth announced first to poor shepherds, instead of in a palace? Suddenly the sky above them began to fill with a great company of angels, all glowing with white brilliance, all praising God and saying, "Glory to God in the Highest, and on earth, peace, good will to men."

Josiah and the rest of the shepherds watched, speechless, as the angels hovered above them. They seemed to spread a blessing on the men below, and then took flight heavenward. When the angels had left them, Josiah and his father, uncle and brothers looked at one another, their faces still glowing with puzzled looks.

"Let's go to Bethlehem, and see this thing that has happened, which the Lord has told us about," Josiah said and the other shepherds agreed.

So they left their sheep grazing on the hillside and hurried off toward the village, following the star overhead. It soon led them to a stable behind a poor house. There they found a man and his wife. They were near a feed trough whose humble origins had been hidden by the softest hay covered by a cloth of pure white. On top of the cloth lay a sleeping baby, obviously newborn. Josiah and the rest of the shepherds knelt around the sleeping baby and looked on Him lovingly. Mary, His mother, smiled beneficently on the poor men looking at her child and Joseph, her husband, stood guard over his little family. An atmosphere of peace and nobility surrounded the three and it rendered the shepherds speechless. They bowed their heads and thanked God in their hearts for the privilege of seeing this new King. After thanking Mary and Joseph for allowing them to see the Child, Hosea pulled himself up by his shepherd's crook and told the other shepherds that they must go.

"I want to stay," Josiah said. "I want to stay with the Baby."

"No, son," Hosea told the boy gently," "We must tell everyone about this Child."

So they hurried off and told everyone they saw about what they had seen and heard. They told of the great comet in the sky, of the angel's message to them, of the heavenly host singing above them and of the tiny Baby born in a stable. And everyone who heard it was amazed at the story. They were amazed at what the poor shepherds had seen. Finally Josiah, his father and brothers and uncle returned to the sheep on the hillside, glorifying and praising God for all the things they had heard and seen. They couldn't stop talking about the Child they had seen. They couldn't forget the miracle they had witnessed.

Josiah and Hosea and the rest of the shepherds lived over two thousand years ago. Those may not have been their real names but the experience was real and we are still talking about that night today. And so on this Christmas morning as we celebrate once again the birthday of the King, like the shepherds of old, I am in awe of the miracle of Christ's birth. Like the shepherds, I am running to tell the Good News of His birth.

"For unto you is born this day in the City of David,
a Savior which is Christ the Lord."

- LUKE 2: 11

MY CHILDHOOD CHRISTMASES

hristmas has always been the most important time of the year for me. As a child, it was, I expect, because of the anticipation of Santa's visit and the magic associated with the toys he brought - Santa's workshop, the elves, the sleigh, Rudolph! Now, of course, it represents the birth of Jesus, and the hope for the world which He represents. Still, I can't help but recall those happy days of my childhood when Christmas came around.

The tree came first, of course. And it was not the fat, tall giant you see now on Christmas tree lots. It was a thin, sparse fir with ample space between the branches for ornaments to dangle freely. Daddy always got it from the Winn-Dixie on Habersham Street and would be astounded to hear the prices I have paid through the years for my own trees. He never got the tree until a week or two before Christmas. If my own tree is not up by the first couple of days of December, I worry that all the good trees will be gone. Mama decorated hers with boxes of Shiny Brite ornaments, proudly stamped with "Made in USA" on them to let the world know we were not using any glass baubles made in Nazi Germany. We usually managed to break at least one each year. There were strands of glass beads and bubble lights shaped like candles which, when heated up, made bubbles in the liquid they contained. The lights on the tree were always multi-colored and giant sized. I still have a string from Mama and Daddy but I never use them. Everyone of a certain age remembers how, when one light on the string blew out, all the rest of the lights went dark.

The ornaments on the tree were not all round; some were pebbled like a golf ball. Others were elongated or had a large indentation on each side. My favorites were the two plastic birds we placed on the tree, one blue and one yellow. Then came the silver tinsel. Mama insisted we put it on the tree one strand at a time, which we did until she left the room. Then it was time to toss handfuls randomly. Finally, came the angel hair, my least favorite part of the decorating. It looked like drifts of snow when placed properly on the branches. Usually Mama took care of placing this on the tree and the mantel, as angel hair could irritate your skin. It was made of spun glass, after all, whatever that was. Atop the tree was a tiny white plastic angel, no bigger than three or four inches. After the tree was decorated, one of my very favorite things to do was lie down under the bottom branches and look up into the tree, marveling at the lights and shiny ornaments bedazzling our otherwise plain living room.

The tree was only the beginning. Each window of our house bore a candelabrum with at least three to five candles sporting blue bulbs. The mantel was decorated with more angel hair on which were placed little wax candles of choir boys, Santas, angels and plastic reindeer.

I don't remember wreaths for the front door, but I do recall that for several years, my mother covered the front door in shiny foil wrapping paper, and then wrapped it with a big bow to resemble a large package. I always wanted a manger scene but only had one of cardboard from the dime store. You punched out the manger, animals and people and arranged them to your heart's desire. It was like playing paper dolls with Baby Jesus.

The stockings we had were hand me downs from our big sisters Louise and Martha Jean who had outgrown Santa. They were brown cotton stockings given to our sisters during World War II and were very large. We always got a tangerine in the toe of the stocking with a few pieces of hard candy, nuts and trinkets from F.W. Woolworth's. I remember one Christmas I got a Magic Slate on which Santa had written his name. During the day, someone erased his name (by lifting the plastic sheet) and I was distraught. I'd never get another piece of proof that Santa existed!

We got hundreds of Christmas cards each year, a number that astounds me today. No one has time to send them, I guess, but they were very big in the fifties - complete with a Christmas seal on the back (a special stamp, the proceeds of which went to stamp out Tuberculosis.)

Stores didn't decorate so much back then, but one of the things I always looked forward to was seeing the windows of the Western Auto store. Normally filled with auto parts and hardware, for a couple of weeks in December, they sported rocking horses on springs, train sets, John Deere toy tractors, doll babies and shiny red Radio Flyer tricycles, sleds and wagons. The grocery stores began to carry a few toys as well. I remember being dazzled by the Saucy Walker dolls and tea sets that appeared on shelves above the Cheerios.

Radio stations and console stereos played Bing Crosby and the Vienna Boys Choir versions of carols occasionally. My daddy's favorite secular carol was "Silver Bells," sung by the great Kate Smith, a songbird few people my children's age remember. I can still hear him singing along with her. And he dearly loved hearing Bing Crosby singing the religious carols. He called him "Der Bingle" for some reason and so, ever after I have thought of him that way.

Our Christmas gifts were not extravagant - I usually got a few clothes and a doll (a Ginny or Revlon doll.) One year, my mother made the most beautiful green evening dress for a doll I had with flame colored hair. Years later, she gave them away when we moved. I have mourned that doll ever since. When I turned five, Jerry and I got red fake suede cowgirl vests and skirts. We also got two wheeled bikes with training wheels. Of course, my favorite non-doll gift was my Roy Rogers Double R Bar Ranch set which I played with in Daddy's garden. One year I got a Campbell's soup cooking set, but it never stirred up any interesting in cooking for me. We got Howdy Doody chairs once and a metal dollhouse another year. Once I got a set of

Block City building blocks which looked like cement blocks, the dream building material of the 1950s, apparently. Following that, we got a set of American Plastic building bricks (kind of a precursor to Legos.) The last toy I got was a Barbie, one of the first Barbies ever produced.

On the Great Day itself, we got up very early and raced down to see the loot. We tore into the packages, barely taking time to squeal our delight before opening the next one. After a hastily downed breakfast, Mama hustled all of us into our new Christmas clothes and she and Daddy took us to church. It was the only time I was allowed to take a toy to church, our salve for leaving all the goodies at home so soon after we'd received them. I remember Daddy calling all the little girls and boys down to the front of the sanctuary to show off our new toys before sending us back to our pews for his Christmas message. Soon though, the service was over and we went home to enjoy a fabulous turkey dinner with all the trimmings. We spent the afternoon napping or playing with our new toys, and sneaking a piece of candy from the big yellow box of Whitman's Sampler that we seemed to have every year. It wasn't long after Christmas that the decorations came down and the house was cleaned from top to bottom. We'd have to wait another 365 days for another glorious Christmas day of pandemonium.

DADDY'S KNIFE

When Mama and Daddy died, my four sisters and I divided their possessions among us, selling or donating the things we couldn't use. We were fair about it, too - no fights about anything. We made up a pretty good system - we all agreed on four items that were of equal or nearly equal value in our eyes and placed them on the table, so to speak. Then we took turns having first pick of the items.

Louise got first pick of the first group. Then for the next four items, Martha Jean got first pick, and so on. If there was anything that one of us had expressed a really strong desire to have, the rest of us allowed that sister to have that item by choosing something else. We started out with the big items, and then worked our way down to the small, meaningless things. I don't recall a single argument over Mama and Daddy's possessions. We were just glad to be together in our grief. Each item we examined brought back memories or stories to tell or laugh about.

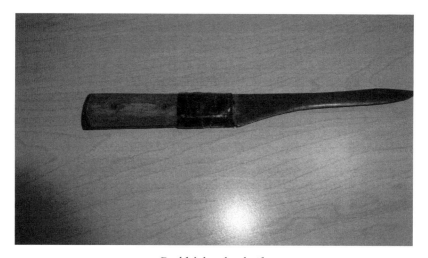

Daddy's butcher knife

One of the meaningless things that I got in the draw was something I wouldn't take anything for - my Daddy's butcher knife. Daddy was a great accumulator of knives. He had a fairly large collection of pocket knives, one for every occasion, so to speak. He had a tiny one he used to pare the fingernails of his little girls. It hurts me to think about this, but in all the "manicures" he gave me, he never drew blood once. He had a larger one he used to slice and peel apples for his little girls or his grandchildren. And he had an even larger one he used to skin the raccoons he loved to hunt or "trim pigs." If you don't know what that means, you didn't grow up in the country. Just ask me about it.

Each of us got at least one representative of his knife collection, but the one I wanted most was his butcher knife. The blade was nearly black from use and sharp enough even now to be dangerous. I can still see him sitting in a chair outside or standing at the kitchen counter drawing the blade back and forth on the carborundum stone he kept in the knife drawer. I remember my grandfather Walter Morris had a grinding wheel in the barn. It fascinated me and I used to sit and pedal the stone like a bicycle wheel. I wondered what it was for. Daddy's handheld stone was the modern day version of that wheel. There was definitely a method to sharpening a blade and he had the knack, for every knife he owned was ground fine. The blade on his butcher knife had been sharpened so often that it was narrowed almost to nothing. Yet it still slices a tomato like nobody's business. You couldn't sharpen a single new knife I own like this now.

Another thing I like about the knife is the handle. Daddy never could abide a knife with a plastic handle - they just didn't feel right in his hand, so if he found a knife that fit, he used it over and over. Daddy's butcher knife lost its rivets years ago, so he did what any child of the Depression would do - he took a roll of electrical tape and repaired it. Good as new.

I expect when I die, this knife will be one of the first things my children pitch in the trash can. But I hope they don't. It's representative of a time when, as the old saying goes, you'd "use it up, wear it out, make it do, or do without." In our throwaway society, it's a good lesson to learn.

LEIGH STREET BAPTIST CHURCH

 esterday for a couple of hours, my father and mother lived again. Paul and I were on our way home from the beach and stopped in Richmond to attend church at Leigh Street Baptist Church, where my father, the late Dr. Frank E. Morris, served as pastor during the turbulent World War II years of 1943-1948, before I was born. I had never been to the church

before except to peek inside one Saturday years ago. But the church has repeatedly invited me to attend their annual Harvest Home Day, a sort of Homecoming and Thanksgiving service. Yesterday was the 93rd Harvest Home Day, so we decided to attend, not knowing what to expect.

The church building itself sits in Richmond's historic Church Hill area, an area of nineteenth century homes near the St. John's Church district. The Church Hill area, whose buildings' period of significance ran from 1812- 1938, is on the National Register of Historic Places. The church itself was listed on individual merit alone in 1972 as the most significant use of the Temple Greek Revival style in the area and was built in 1853 by Philadelphia architect Samuel Sloan. The National Register describes the church as the most remarkable structure with the most extensive use of ironwork in Church Hill. The church's basement was used as a hospital for Confederate troops during the Civil War, perhaps as overflow from the nearby Chimborazo Hospital.

Leigh Street Baptist Church

The church survives today in the same building and neighborhood with a largely older congregation but with a real spirit of servanthood for the area. I was so impressed with the unaltered beauty of the antebellum building and thrilled to the sounds of the massive pipe organ in the sanctuary. Imagine my surprise, though, when an old lady approached me after the service and said, "I heard you say you were Frank and Theodosia Morris's daughter. I remember them so well."

She then proceeded to round up several other old women who remembered my parents, some of whom told me they had pictures of my sisters and me in their own photo albums at home. They remembered my dad as "so dynamic and handsome," and my mother as "shy and beautiful, but a hard worker in the church." One lady told me my daddy had married her and her husband.

It was difficult to leave the church after the luncheon that followed. I kept taking picture after picture. Paul was a good sport and followed along. But I kept seeing my father, a young man of only 30 years of age, preaching in that magnificent structure so many years ago. It makes me smile inside to think that he and my mother left such a mark on that church that they were still remembered some seventy years later. I feel proud to have come from such a heritage.

DEDICATING BABY WILL

 esterday our fifth grandchild, Benjamin William Bond II, was dedicated at Ox Hill Baptist Church, the church where his mother Caroline grew up and where she was baptized. For the first time in quite a while our whole family with the exception of little Camden, who was still hospitalized, were together. You can just imagine how my heart soared to see all those children and grandchildren of mine sitting in the church pews around me.

Baby dedications are done regularly now in Baptist churches, kind of the Baptist version of christenings. They were not done so much when my own children were born but they do have a Biblical basis. In the Old Testament, Hannah presented her son Samuel to be dedicated in the temple and, of course, in the New Testament, Jesus was brought to the temple by his parents Mary and Joseph to be dedicated.

Our Yearwood grandchildren, Leighton, Naomi and Mason attend Zion Lutheran Church with their parents Tom and Julie so they were christened by their pastor. Shon and Katherine Klegin are members of Alexandria's First Baptist Church so when Nolan was born, he was dedicated there. When Camden was well enough, he and his twin brother Hudson were dedicated there as well. Will's parents, Caroline and Ben, were members of a Baptist church in Colorado Springs where Ben was stationed at the time, but since all their family is here, they came back to the church where Paul and I raised the girls (Tom was already in college when we moved here.)

There are baby dedications in many faiths. In the Jewish faith, male infants are circumcised in obedience to Mosaic Law. In Catholic, Lutheran, Episcopal, Methodist and other religions, babies are christened or baptized into the church through sprinkling water on the child's forehead. As Baptists, we do not believe that circumcision is required though many parents choose to do so from a medical perspective. Nor do we believe that infants can be baptized into the kingdom of God, but rather make a conscious decision to join when they are of the age of consent.

For many the practice of dedicating a baby means praying for the child's health and salvation. But I think it is more nearly to the point that, as parents, they are dedicating themselves to God, to the upbringing of their child in a safe and loving home, and helping their child to a relationship with God through a faith in Jesus Christ.

The service for Will yesterday was powerful and meaningful as all his grandparents on both sides, all his aunts and uncles and cousins on both sides (except for Camden and Ben's twin brother Arthur and wife Holly and daughter Annelyse who are stationed in San Diego in the US Navy) were present, surrounding this child with love. We all pledged with Ben and Caroline to commit to providing a loving Christian home for Will, to accept Will as a gift from God and to support his parents in Will's upbringing.

One of the most meaningful moments for me as Will's grandmother, came when the pastor Dr. Dean Majette, who had baptized Caroline years ago, mentioned that it occurred to him that Will's great grandfather, (my own father Dr. Frank E. Morris) was the pastor whose signature was on Dean's license to preach. Daddy had been Dean's pastor when Dean was licensed in the ministry. So he said in a sense it was as though many generations of Will's family were present at this special time.

It was a moment that I will never forget. I am proud of Ben and Caroline and the promise they made to raise Will in their faith. I looked on with love as Dean showed off this precious child to the church congregation. In a time when commitment and ceremony of any kind seem less and less popular, it was a moving time for all of us. I am blessed to be a part of this ever increasing family.

BOOKS OF MY LIFE

In a recent issue of Entertainment Weekly, (one of about a thousand magazines we are now subscribed to as our air miles for one airline are running out,) there was an article titled, "Books of My Life." In which published author Hilary Mandel commented on the following book topics. The idea intrigued me so I decided to do the same thing. Here are the categories and my response to them:

- My favorite childhood book: *Mirrors of Castle Doone,* an obscure mystery which intrigued me with castles, ghosts, and a Scottish locale. The children's librarian at the Savannah Public Library introduced me to it and I was hooked on reading ever since.

- The book I enjoyed most in school: *Jane Eyre,* I was (and still am) a hopeless romantic. The love between Mr. Rochester and Jane set the standard by which all the men in my life were doomed to failure.

- A classic I'm embarrassed to say I've never read: *The Last of the Mohicans.* I don't know why.

- The book that cemented me as a writer: Obviously, *To Kill a Mockingbird* - It embodied everything I ever loved - the South, the Past, a strong father figure, Justice - I wanted to write that book.

- A book I've pretended to have read: *War and Peace.* I "read" it during the late stages of my pregnancy with Tom and during labor. Obviously I didn't give it time.

- The book I read over and over: Other than the *Bible*? (which of course is the rudder for my life) there are several - *To Kill a Mockingbird, Little Big Man, Lonesome Dove, Gone With the Wind, Jane Eyre, A Christmas Carol, Peter Pan, The Reivers, True Grit* and *The Friendly Persuasion*

- The last book that made me laugh - and the last one that made me cry: Same book - *Last Days of Summer* by Steve Kluger, a funny and moving story of a 12 year old Jewish boy who strikes up a friendship with a New York Giants third baseman just as World War II is heating up.

- A book I consider to be grossly overrated: *The Turn of the Screw*

- The books I wish I'd written: *True Grit, To Kill a Mockingbird, Lonesome Dove,* David McCullough's biography *John Adams*

- The book people might be surprised to learn I love: *Band of Brothers*

A VISIT WITH CAMDEN

This little essay was written when Camden was about a month old. Obviously, it is a precious memory to me.

aul and I went to the hospital today and got to spend some time with our new grandsons. And for the first time since they were born four weeks ago, I got to hold Camden. It was a precious moment, made even happier when I got to hold Hudson with him. And once again, I am amazed at the stamina of their parents.

We got to the hospital around 9:30 AM. Shon, of course, was at work. Katherine and Hudson had already dropped off Nolan at his preschool and were waiting for us in Camden's room. Katherine fed Hudson then put him in Paul's arms and turned to her other son. Camden was lying asleep in his crib, attached to a feeding tube going into his nose (called a nasogastric tube or NG tube) as well as to a tube supplying oxygen. He was off oxygen for a while but due to the Tetralogy of Fallot, he is unable to supply quite enough oxygen to his blood. So he gets a little assist and so far he is doing well. They keep a little indicator on his toe to measure his oxygen saturation level. Once this morning, Camden pushed the oxygen tube out of one of his nostrils and he had a moment of desat (low blood oxygen concentration.) Almost immediately, his nurse came into the room, made a tiny adjustment to the tube and his level went up right away. How thankful we are for nurses who are so ready to help when necessary.

As the nurse left the room, I asked rather timidly if I could touch Camden. I had held Hudson several times and I was just so eager to just touch his brother. The nurse said, "Sure. We don't have as many rules as in the PICU. (Camden is in a regular pediatric ward now.) In fact, you can hold him if you want." I looked at Katherine who scooped him up right away and put him in my arms. He's barely as big as a child's football, weighing only about 6 pounds but is so precious. It was a moment I'll never forget.

I asked Katherine what would happen for the rest of the day. She said she wanted to talk to the doctors who were rounding about that time. So Paul and I left to pick up Nolan from school. Katherine soon came home, fed Hudson and changed him. Paul got lunch for us at Chick Fila (the Chicken store, as Nolan calls it) and brought it home. Meanwhile, I did a little laundry for Katherine and played with Nolan. Katherine looked out the window and said, "Look, there's my neighbor cutting my grass. That's embarrassing." (Not at all, I thought. It's another blessing - good neighbors who know the intense burden Katherine and Shon are under and just want to help.) Soon Katherine took Nolan up to his bedroom for a nap and promptly fell asleep along with him. But not for long, as it was soon time for Hudson to be fed.

By that time, Paul and I left for home. But Katherine had supper to prepare, and two boys to take care of. Shon would stop by the hospital on his way home from work to check up on Camden, eat a late supper and help Katherine get Nolan and Hudson to sleep. Tomorrow, it will start all over again. We were expecting Camden to have surgery to implant a shunt in his heart, a temporary fix until he will have the full repair, an open heart surgery, in the days ahead. So many surgeries for such a tiny child who already had one on his second day of life to remove a section of his bowel that was blocked.

Through it all, Katherine and Shon remained steady, upbeat and confident, loving partners in the medical care their son was receiving. Their strong faith as well as the prayer support they have received from friends and families as well as people they have never met undergirded them and prepared them for the marathon they were on. I am in awe of them and grateful beyond words for all who were on "Camden's Team."

WHY I PRAY

I believe in prayer. From the time I was a very little girl, I have prayed on my knees beside my bed every night. I pray other places throughout the day too, but every night at bedside is my ritual. I prayed in thanksgiving to God when my three children were born hale and hearty. When my father died in a tragic car accident, I prayed to God in anger, telling him that I no longer believed in Him. He loved me anyway. I prayed in utter desperation when my first marriage imploded and I was left to raise three children alone. He sent Paul to me. When my mother died after a massive stroke ten years later, I prayed in gratitude to him for relieving her of her imprisonment in her body. When I taught school, I prayed to God each day to put in my way some opportunity to share my faith because I didn't have the courage to seek out people to talk to. He did it with at least one child each year. I remember in particular one girl whose father was in prison. She was failing her classes and came to me after school for help. She told me of her family troubles and asked how I handled disappointments. I was able to share my faith with her. I prayed in loneliness when I moved to my new home a few years ago. I knew no one except my son and daughter in law and grandchildren here.

God sent me Millie, my neighbor, her arms full of preserves and rolls and potato salad. I prayed for two situations in particular - one was my brother in law Larry, who had surgery with the possibility of receiving some sight again after 33 years of blindness. What a miracle that was! And I prayed for Katherine and Shon and Nolan as they faced the birth of their twins, Hudson and Camden. I prayed hard for little Camden who was born with a heart defect requiring open heart surgery immediately, a prospect that hurt me so much I have a hard time even writing the words. I prayed for the nurses and doctors and other technicians who cared for little Camden and I prayed for the strength to be a help to their family. I didn't know what the outcome of all those situations would be. So I simply left it all in God's hands and I kept praying. I believe God likes me to talk with him. And I listen every day for what he has to reveal to me. So I pray.

TV'S GOLDEN ERA

I n an effort to take my mind off other more serious matters of the moment, I have been thinking of old TV shows. We got our first TV in about 1953 but got our first color TV when I was in college. Fair warning: all those born after about 1960 will not get this at all.

- THE HONEYMOONERS – I know it was classic TV but I didn't like the way Ralph yelled at Alice. And I wondered why Norton, the sewer worker had a better looking apartment than Ralph.

- THE HOWDY DOODY SHOW – I loved this show with all my heart. I still love marionettes and have some of my own. I also own DVDs of every episode of Howdy.

- ED SULLIVAN SHOW – Always wanted to see it but as the minister's daughter I had to go to Training Union and church every Sunday night.

- THE LONE RANGER – Never could figure out the mask

- YOU BET YOUR LIFE – Groucho creeped me out.

- THE ROY ROGERS SHOW – I had such a crush on Roy. I loved him and his horse Trigger and had the Double R Bar Playset. I tolerated Dale, Bullet, Pat and Nelly Belle the jeep. I also have the DVDs.

- THE LAWRENCE WELK SHOW – Umm no

- I LOVE LUCY – I loved this show, especially the shows when she lived in Connecticut because I loved the set. (I didn't know until I was an adult that that was the time Lucy and Desi were separating.) I've got all those DVDs too.

- ADVENTURES OF SUPERMAN – Even I wondered how Jimmy Olsen and Lois Lane couldn't see that Clark Kent was Superman.

- THE ADVENTURES OF OZZIE AND HARRIETT – I thought Ozzie and Harriett would have made cool parents. But what was Ozzie's job?

- MY LITTLE MARGIE/OH SUZANNA – Gale Storm's two shows – I saw them only in reruns. It seems like Oh Suzanna was a precursor to The Love Boat

- MAKE ROOM FOR DADDY – I watched this show a lot. But I thought Angela Cartwright was a little too precious even then.

- CHEYENNE – I always thought Clint Walker would flex and tear his shirt.

- WALT DISNEY'S WONDERFUL WORLD OF COLOR – Another loss due to Sunday night church but occasionally I could fake an illness and see it. I loved when the show went to Fantasyland.

- LASSIE – 6:00 pm Sunday – another loss

- FATHER KNOWS BEST – Perhaps my favorite family show. I liked how they interacted.

- THE MICKEY MOUSE CLUB – Wanted to see it but it wasn't shown in Savannah so I only saw it in reruns.

- GUNSMOKE – Watched this with Daddy every Saturday night. I loved Matt and Festus. We also watched Have Gun, Will Travel; Maverick; and Wanted Dead or Alive. Bonanza is a Western that bears special mention. It was in color! It never occurred to me that these "boys" were actually grown men living with their father and never could find a wife – the women always died or were evil.

- THE ANDY GRIFFITH SHOW – perhaps the sweetest show on TV.

- BEN CASEY AND DR. KILDAIRE – I was more of a Kildaire fan. Casey always looked mad.

- DICK VAN DYKE – The show now looks dated in reruns but I thought it was terribly chic back then.

- THE FUGITIVE – Watched this show every week. On the night of the finale, I was a sophomore in college and our dorm mother allowed our dates to stay in our dorm parlor after hours so we could all watch the one-armed man being caught.

- GOMER PYLE: USMC – Never could take him. He was kinda dumb.

- GREEN ACRES – If Mr. Douglas had so much money, why couldn't he have fixed up that house a little better for Lisa?

- THE CAROL BURNETT SHOW – perfect comedy troupe – loved watching them crack each other up.

- STONEY BURKE – Jack Lord as a rodeo rider. He went on to fame and fortune in Hawaii Five-0

- THE MANY LOVES OF DOBIE GILLIS – I thought Dwayne Hickman was cute and his father got mad way too often.

- WAGON TRAIN – Why didn't they ever get to the end of the trail?

- THE REAL MCCOYS – Loved Walter Brennan but why were the two brothers both named Luke?

- RAWHIDE – Sigh ~ Clint Eastwood in his prime!

- JACK BENNY AND GEORGE BURNS AND GRACIE ALLEN – Radio come to life!

There are many good shows today but these early shows were unique!

MY MOTHER

It will soon be Mother's Day and I am thinking today of the wonderful mother I had. My mother, Theodosia Ellen Dever Morris, was born in a rural part of Kentucky and lived for most of her early years on a farm near the tiny town of Gravel Switch. Having lost her own mother to diabetes when she was only four, Mama grew up without a mother to guide her. She and her five sisters, Frances, Daisy, Cassie, Helen, and Kelly May, pretty much raised themselves while their father, my grandfather Mike Dever, pursued farming and worked in a tobacco warehouse.

Legendary in our family lore is the tale of how the six sisters made biscuit dough one morning while their father was at work and threw the biscuit dough, piece by piece, up to the ceiling to watch it fall. I can just hear their squeals as they watched the dough peel slowly from the ceiling and plop to the floor below. Mama graduated from Lebanon High School and went to work for a brief time in the office of the county agent. She told me years later that she hated every minute of her time in the office and never really felt comfortable until she married my father, Frank Elliott Morris, in 1936 and became our mother. Four girls were born to Mama and Daddy - Louise in 1939, Martha Jean in 1940 and Jerry and me in 1948.

I was always amazed at the proficiency, kindness and love with which Mama raised us, having had no role model of her own to follow. She was an outstanding Southern cook, and a wonderful seamstress, making dresses with voluminous skirts for all four of us. She taught us to think for ourselves, to iron, to sew, to cook (some of us less successfully than others) and offered us piano lessons (some of us less successful at it than others!) She accompanied my father, a minister, to pastorates in Kentucky, North Carolina, Virginia, South Carolina and Georgia. A beautiful woman, Mama overcame her natural shyness and taught Sunday School and led women's missionary circles for years. But most important to me, Mama taught us the virtues of Southern womanhood - faith, kindness, intelligence, modesty, charity, and industry. I often cite my father as being an important influence in my life, but if the truth were known, I would not be the woman I am without the guiding hand of my wonderful mother.

WHAT MAMA MISSED

y mother passed away in January, 2000. She lived from her birth in 1915 to see the twenty-first century, but just barely. As the calendar page turned from December 1999 to January 2000, the final massive stroke that would ultimately take her away from us was preparing its devastating blow. And though I had her for nearly fifty-two years, I have often thought of all the milestones in my life that she missed. I even secretly envied the extra time my two older sisters had with her. There were so many wonderful things in my family's life that she missed.

She didn't get to see the births of my eight grandchildren, her great grandchildren. She never got to see the success of my children -Tom who became a mechanical engineer, Katherine who became a marketer and Caroline who became a Navy wife. She never got to meet the three wonderful people my children married - Shon Klegin, our financial wizard who came first, then Julie Keller, our science teacher, then Ben Bond, our Naval officer. So many happy events and wonderful people I never got to introduce to her.

I realized that her own mother, my grandmother, never got to see Mama get married, or meet Daddy, or get to know any of my three sisters or me. My mother was just four when her mother died, so I guess I was really lucky to have had Mama for as long as I did. I remember Mama telling me about her wedding outfit, a burgundy suit with mink tails along the collar. I wonder if she longed to shop for wedding clothes with her mother as my mother did with me. I wonder how she felt on that September day in the parsonage of the pastor in Kentucky who married them. Was she elated, or nervous or wishing her mom was there?

Even though she has been gone now for eighteen years, I still feel her absence every day. I still long to pick up the telephone every Saturday night and hear her voice as I used to do. I long to sit with her and watch another episode of "Days of Our Lives," our guilty pleasure. I long to hear that sweet Southern voice of hers so much that sometimes I replay an old cassette tape I have of her talking to two-year-old Tom.

The good thing in remembering my mother at Mother's Day is that I am reminded over and over how blessed I was to have her. Not everyone has a mother so kind and gentle and caring. I did and she was a grace gift from God to me.

...SO GOD SENT US HENRY

Sometimes it's tough being the youngest (or one of the youngest) grandchildren. The grandparents have seemingly gotten over the newness of being grandparents and, of course, they're getting older. I was one of the youngest grandchildren in both my mother's and my father's sides of the family. To top that, we lived far away from both sets of grandparents, so I didn't have as close a relationship with them as I would have liked. My father was the busy pastor of large churches when I was growing up, so we only had a couple of visits a year with relatives.

Our youngest grandchild, (the youngest of eight!) is Henry Daniel Bond. Henry was born November 5, 2015 and I like to think he was born just when we in the family needed him most. Barely three months before Henry's birth, our grandson Camden Andrew Klegin died tragically after surgery to repair several defects in his heart. Camden was just eleven months old and only weighed 16 pounds. To say that we were devastated is an understatement. Yet God in His mercy knew that we needed joy in our lives again. So He sent us little Henry. Henry lives with his mom and dad and big brother Will in their new home about four hours away from us, so I don't get to be with him as much as I'd like. But this is certainly closer than his previous homes in Colorado where he was born and Rhode Island where he lived for a few months.

You see, Henry is a military kid. (I know they are usually called military brats, but I don't like that term because Henry, like his brother Will, is anything but a brat.) Charming and bright, Henry likes to talk with me on Facetime, that marvelous invention of the smartphone that allows Nanas like me to see and chat with grandchildren who don't live nearby. And though I only see Henry every few months, he smiles and shows off winningly every time we talk.

Henry with his grandfather "Pablo"

Henry's dad Ben is a Navy Lieutenant, currently attached to a destroyer based in Norfolk, VA. And like military families everywhere, Henry, Will and their mom, our daughter Caroline, often go days or weeks communicating with Ben only through Facetime or Skype or whatever method they use.

I never would have predicted that Caroline would have been a Navy wife. But she has not only survived but also thrived, making new friends wherever they live. The boys have adventures with other Navy children and see more of the world than I ever will. I'm thankful for the sacrifice and strength of my Navy kids (all four of them) and proud of them.

And I'm especially thankful for little Henry, the baby who brought joy back into our lives again. Here's to many more adventures with you and your brother, little guy. Nana loves you.

MAMA IN HER CHAIR

Looking at my mother's photo in the picture below, I am struck by several things. First, she is studying her Sunday school lesson. In her lap are a Bible and teacher's manual. Though she was a very quiet, shy person, she always accepted that, as a minister's wife, it was her duty to be a Sunday School teacher. She did it willingly all the days of her life, until she had her stroke.

Second, her clothes were all polyester. She had spent decades ironing dresses, shirts, sheets and pillowcases, and boxers for her husband and four daughters, so when polyester fabric was introduced, she embraced it wholeheartedly.

Third - that hairdo. As long as she lived she had a football helmet for her hair. Every night she slept in a satin night cap and every morning she sprayed the heck out of it with a tall can of Adorn or Miss Breck or Aqua

Net hairspray. Then it was good for the rest of the day. She had it shampooed and set once a week and, in her later years, colored with her color of choice, Roux Fanci-full #41 at either Mrs. Sam Miller's shop in Gaffney or Mrs. Lillian Knight's shop in Savannah or Kelly's beauty shop in Gates.

Mama in her chair

That room - Mama is pictured here in the family room of the old house in Gates County which had been built by my Daddy's grandfather Ephraim Morris maybe 150 years before this photo was taken. Daddy and Mama rehabbed the place to make it their retirement home, covering the walls with plywood paneling which was the fashion of the day (and also affordable to a retired minister and his wife.) Mama decorated the house with such adornments as she could find. In the window, there is an old Avon bottle which, when she had used its contents, she cleaned and filled with colored water. It sat in the southern window of that room to catch the sun.

My Mother never had great wealth or abilities in life. She was not a great public speaker as my Daddy was. Her preferred spot was in the background, supporting Daddy and us four girls. She lived far away from her five sisters, all of whom stayed in Kentucky where she was born. Yet in her heart she was always a Kentucky girl who was the heart's desire of the handsome young preacher who snagged her away from another man. Today, long years after we laid her to rest in the small graveyard beside the old Morris home place, I am remembering my Mama with great love.

THE COUNTRY STORE

I lived in Gates County, NC from 1974-1982 though my family had lived there for a couple of hundred years (since about the time of the American Revolution.) I bought what was then known as the old Hudgins place on Highway 32 just north of the little village of Sunbury. The house had not been lived in for a dozen years and was quite a mess. It was 200 years old at the time, so I like to think we rescued it from decline. Much of the materials I got to work on the house came from my favorite store in the county - Rountree & Riddick. You could find anything there.

The floors had a nice wooden creak to them and the cash register was on a short wooden counter just inside the door. Stacked on top of the cash register were little bags of chocolate covered peanuts - heavenly! Canned goods and groceries of all sorts were on the first couple of aisles.

SCENE FROM SUNBURY, N. C.

Near the back of the front room was the meat counter where Billy Matthews, my friend from church (Middle Swamp Baptist) would slice and wrap whatever cuts of meat or cheese you wanted. I always got a hunk of hoop cheese from the round wooden box and then selected sausage from the glass refrigerated counter. I watched as he ground hamburger for me, carefully washing his hands first. Then he'd put it in a paper container, wrap everything in butcher paper and tie it with string and a slip knot.

Behind the meat counter was the hardware department where you could get most any kind of tools, plumbing supplies, nails, or screws you wanted. There was a huge nail bin that I always liked to spin. Mr. Hallet Hurdle worked for the store and could be counted on to install whatever you needed.

On the far left of the main room of the store, there were blue jeans, overalls, and boots. There were sizes to fit everyone from adults to children. I outfitted my son Tom in overalls and Red Ball Jet shoes from there. You could also find a few bolts of yard goods, sewing supplies and oil cloth. I remember my grandmother covered her kitchen table with a fresh oil cloth covering each year, tacking it to the sides of her round table. (She lived in an old house with no counters so this provided a ready substitute.)

In the next room, one could find appliances of all sorts. I bought a refrigerator, range and dishwasher from Rountree & Riddick, all in Coppertone. You could also find mop buckets and mops, rakes and hoes, shovels and, in the spring, a wide assortment of vegetable and flower seeds. Also available were huge bags of fertilizer, traps and the very necessary Sevin dust which I used under my daddy's instruction.

Outside the store, a porch roof shaded customers who wanted to sit and talk on the benches. There was a single gas pump where I filled up each week.

Every time I shopped there, I chatted with Billy or Rosa May or whoever was working. They picked up Tom from my arms and walked him around the store, giving him a piece of candy or cheese. It felt like home. Today I shop in well-lit, sterile grocery stores that offer more things than Rountree & Riddick could have stocked in a decade. But no one knows me there and I always spend too much. I would give anything to go back to shopping at Rountree & Riddick.

HOLDING THE ROPE

very day after learning that our grandson Camden would need heart surgery, I cried a little bit, dried my tears and thought a lot about how I could help Katherine and Shon. But one day shortly before Camden's birth, I was brought to my knees in tears of gratitude by an expression of solidarity from a friend.

Most of my classmates from Meredith College are familiar with the story of Rodney Cook, the husband of my classmate Sue Hammons Cook. Rodney developed heart disease and a couple of years ago, he was told that he needed a heart transplant. Rodney, Sue and the rest of us in the Meredith Class of '70 waited on pins and needles for the news that they longed for. Finally, a brave and generous family donated a heart and Rodney was given a new lease on life. The smiles on the faces of Sue and Rodney and their children and grandchildren in the photos we've seen since then are evidence of the great gift of life they received. Rodney goes back periodically to Duke to check for evidence of rejection but each time he gets a big fat zero - 0% rejection which is exactly the number he and Sue want to see. In the course of their waiting - waiting for a heart; waiting for the surgery; waiting for the results of testing for rejection, Sue and Rodney, huge fans of the University of North Carolina basketball program, received a big boost from Coach Sylvia Hatchell and the members of her championship women's basketball team. Upon hearing of Rodney's ordeal, Coach Hatchell sent him an inspirational message and a length of rope. The message is below:

"Every year a basketball team wins the NCAA National Championship. It's a long road, but the teams who are able to make that journey have one thing in common. No matter how tough it became throughout their season, they did one thing - they held the rope.

What is holding the rope? Imagine that you are hanging off the edge of a cliff with a drop of 20 thousand feet. The only thing between you and a fall to your death is a rope, with a person of your choice on the other end. Who do you know that has the guts to pull you to safety? Who will hold the rope? Who do you know that is going to let that rope burn her hand and not let go? How many people you know are going to withstand the burning pain and watch the blood drip from their hands for you?

If you can name two, that's not enough. The next time your team is together, look around and ask yourself, who could I trust to hold the rope? Who is going to let their hands bleed for me? When you can look at every member on your team and say to yourself that they would all hold the rope, you are destined to win a lot of games. You see, the teams that hold the rope when the going gets tough are winners. Down 4 with 30 seconds to go, don't give up. Yell at your teammates to hold the rope; let it burn but don't you dare let go.

Every year there are winners and losers in every sport. Every year winners hold the rope. You don't have to be the best team on the floor to win a game. You don't have to be the best player or even to play very much, but it is vital that you hold the rope. You must be committed to your team, and your teammates must be able to trust that you will be there for them, if and when they need you.

Don't let your teammates down; no matter how bad it hurts...HOLD THE ROPE!"

At the bottom of the page, Coach Hatchell had written by hand the message - "Rodney, We are holding the rope for you! God bless! Coach Sylvia Hatchell"

I mention this because of something I received in the mail one day which brought me to my knees in a prayer of gratitude for the support of our friends and family. I opened a brown paper envelope, and found within the following items: the message above from Coach Sylvia Hatchell to Rodney, a yellow burlap sack containing a length of rope and a message from Sue and Rodney for our Baby B [later named Camden] along with a stack of tags and yellow ribbons for others to write a prayer or message for B's healing.

In Sue's typical attitude of gratitude, she said she wanted to send some positive energy [like that she and Rodney had received in their hours of need] to my family and me. Sue's tender gift will forever be the metaphor for me for God's loving care. For Sue and Rodney and all of you who expressed prayers for Katherine and Shon's child are God's loving arms wrapping around us; you are the rope we held on to.

Camden's rope from the Meredith Angels

A DAY WITH MY FATHER

I was in Gates County, NC, my old country home, this week, for the funeral of a young man, John, the son of Rita and Roger, dear friends of mine. He was just 45 and passed away unexpectedly leaving a beautiful wife and two precious children. How sad, I thought, for those two children to be facing their first Father's Day without their daddy. I pray for them to make it through the days ahead. They will need God's strength.

While in the county, I stopped by to visit my daddy and leave a pot of flowers at the cemetery where he rests. So many thoughts swirled about me as I stood there, my hand on his tombstone. I was sad as always because of missing him but grateful for the 78 years I had him. We had such wonderful times together.

I remembered a cold day back in February, 1985 when he and I drove all over Gates County looking at the sites of his childhood and that of his parents. Daddy was 71 then - just a year older than I am now. He showed me the home of his cousin Elliott. He told me that on the day of Elliott's funeral, it was so wet and muddy the hearse would not go back in the field to the cemetery. So the coffin was put in a four-wheel drive pick-up truck and Daddy, who presided at the funeral, rode along in the truck. Seeing the cemetery set Daddy to talking about his ancestors. He told me of my great uncle Tobe Smith, Elliott's father who lived in a house nearby. Daddy told me that during the War Between the States, a Yankee cavalry patrol was encamped near Tobe's house and Tobe's father carried him through the woods to see the Yankees' beautiful horses. A Yankee captain came upon them and escorted them home where they met Tobe's mother. She told the Yankee captain that the one thing she missed most during wartime was coffee. So the captain went back to his encampment and brought her some coffee. But she was afraid the Yankee was trying to poison her so she wouldn't use it. She just put it in a can and set it upon the mantel where she could smell it every time she went by.

Daddy then took me to the house where my grandparents set up housekeeping after they married. Most of it had fallen in but there was enough left to see that it had been a nice structure. I explored an old cemetery nearby while Daddy stood at his truck waiting for me. When I got back to the barn, Daddy told me he had been thinking of how many times his father must have hitched and unhitched teams of horses or mules at that very barn. He told me his father had worked the farm alone, a big farm for a farmer with no tractor, only mules and horses. But Granddaddy had been a young man with a lot of ambition and a family to feed. So he did it. It was a sweet day with my father - one I will always remember.

On this day over thirty years later, I am thinking of my father as he thought of his father that day with me so long ago. I am grateful for the memories that he shared with me and glad I had the presence of mind to write them down at the time so I would remember them. I am grateful to my Heavenly Father for a Godly father who loved me and instilled in me a love for family and our heritage. And I pray that John's children will have memories enough to carry them through as my memories have sustained me. God bless them all. And thank you, God, for my Daddy.

SAYING THANK YOU

On a shelf in my basement I keep an old metal box that I received after my Daddy passed away. The box is black, dented and scarred and contains nothing more than a series of letters, and post cards, some of them tied with a ribbon. Most of them were sent to my Mama or Daddy when they were young adults, on their own for the first time. They were married and lived in a seminary apartment where Daddy was preparing for the ministry. The letters are from my grandmother to her boy or her new daughter in law, or from my aunts to their brother. All of them are yellowed and written with a kind of stiffness that would never appear in letters today. In fact, our children and grandchildren will most probably never see boxes of letters like this because the only way we communicate is by email. Sad, really, but that's how life is now – fast, a little shallow and definitely not sentimental.

That's why I was so moved by one particular letter I read from the box. It was in an envelope Daddy had labeled in red pencil "Letters Mama Received from Fairfield, KY" The letter I refer to was actually a tiny postcard from October 14, 1934 addressed to my grandmother, Daddy's mother, from a Mrs. O.M. Rogers. Daddy was a young preacher then, only 20 years old and just beginning his career in the ministry. According to the card, Daddy had just preached at her church and stayed in her home as was the custom of the time, there being no inns in the rural areas of the Kentucky knobs [as the hill country is called.]

Mrs. Rogers didn't know my grandmother but wanted to tell her how well her son had preached that weekend. She said, in part, "His message was from on high. He has a big heart and full of the love of God...He is a great boy and wants to be about his Heavenly Father's work. I also know the love and interest that a mother has for her children so I thought you might appreciate this bit of information. Yours must be a Christian home...with the prayers that come from your home, [he] will be a great soul winner. Congratulations to you and your husband for such [a] fine boy. Yours in Christ, Mrs. A.M. Rogers."

Of course, Mrs. Rogers, my grandmother and father are all passed away now. The work that each of them had to do on earth is over and their hands are folded in rest. But how wonderful to look back on my daddy's long life, a life well-lived, and see from hindsight that the promise Mrs. Rogers saw in my daddy at age twenty was fulfilled. But I am just as grateful that she took the time to send a note to my grandmother to tell her of her feelings. Very few people today take the time to say thank you or offer words of encouragement and support. We are too busy today with the minutiae of twenty-first century life. But there are still some people who take the time and I am thankful today for these, the encouragers.

OLD HYMNS

When my parents passed away, my three sisters and I inherited and divided among us their books. Several of the books I got in the division were old hymnals. Among these are the following titles: *New Worship and Song* – 1942, *Joy to the World* – 1913, *Gospel Hymns Nos. 1 to 6* – (no date given but it is at least 100 years old), *The Baptist Hymnal* - 1958 and two copies of *The Broadman Hymnal* – 1940. Turning the pages of these old volumes brings to mind sweet memories of days gone by.

Being a minister's daughter, I was in church a lot during my childhood and I sang so many of these hymns over and over. The old hymns like "Bringing in the Sheaves," "In the Garden," "Love Lifted Me," and "In the Sweet By and By," help me recall childhood days when the only minister I ever heard was my Daddy. He was literally the face of God to me back then. I knew (and still know) these old hymns by heart and only look at the hymnal because looking at the notes marching in order across the page reminds me of botched piano lessons from my past (Sorry, Mrs. Mendel, Miss Mendel, Mrs. Woodcock, Mrs. Burch and all the other piano teachers I failed throughout my childhood.) When I married Paul, he told me he only liked the hymns that were authored before we were born and I came to realize that I thought the same thing. There is no comparison, for example, between "On Jordan's Stormy Banks," composed by Samuel Stenett who lived from 1727 – 1795 and set to an American folk melody and the new "praise songs" whose words are projected onto a screen high above the sanctuary. I love the old hymns for their easy to sing melodies, for the comfort of their words and for the memories they call to mind. I love them for the promise they bring and the images they bring to mind. I'm thankful today for old hymns.

A VETERAN'S DAY ROLL CALL

My family is an average American family with the same hopes and dreams of the rest of you. Most of the time I forget what a great privilege it is to live in a country of such wealth and freedom. Living in America is a gift that I too often take for granted, but it is a gift that has been bought with a high price. On this Veteran's Day 2010, I want to honor the service of the following members of my family who served in various branches of the military:

- Great grandfather PHILLIP DEVER - Civil War, US Army Cavalry

- Uncle WILBUR MORRIS - World War I

- Cousin WILBUR MORRIS, JR. - World War II, Pacific Theater

- Uncle CORBELL MORRIS - World War II - Pacific Theater, briefly a prisoner of war

- Uncle GLADSTONE MORRIS - World War II - US Coast Guard

- Cousin JOE HOWARD - Viet Nam War - US Air Force and the USAF Thunderbirds, shot down over North Viet Nam

- Brother-in-law LARRY HESTER - US Army - Germany

- Son-in-law - BENJAMIN WILLIAM BOND - Lieutenant, US Navy

- Father in law – GLENROY PERSHING BELVIN – World War II, the Pacific theater - US Navy

- Cousin – LARRY MORRIS, Viet Nam

- Cousin – CLIFFORD MORRIS, World War II

- Cousin – R.G. MORRIS, World War II

and all other men and women who have served or are serving in the military so that I can live free.

BEING RETIRED

I'm thankful for being retired. It allowed me to take care of my granddaughter Leighton. Tom called last night to say she was running a fever. "Can you stay with her tomorrow, Mom?" Of course I could, so this morning, I arrive at their house around 8:00 am and find my normally bright, active, inquisitive 4-year-old granddaughter lying on the couch. Sick with a fever, she is listless and quiet. She watches TV wrapped in a crocheted blanket, her water bottle at her side. Her eyes are dull; their lids heavy. I ask if she wants to lie down and she leans wordlessly into her pillow, looking sad. Her cheeks are red and she runs a fever of between 99 and 100 all day. I suggest that she take a drink of water every time there's a commercial (an idea which my hilarious daughter-in-law Julie later suggests is Leighton's first drinking game taught to her by her grandmother!) Well-behaved little girl that she is, Leighton remembers to drink, even when I forget. She sleeps most of the morning until time to take her to her pediatrician who diagnoses "a virus – just Tylenol and fluids for a few days until the fever subsides." We get a milkshake at McDonald's on the way home which she barely touches.

After lunch she says "I want a story." Which one? She points to her story Bible with pictures and I read a few until she falls asleep. She sleeps for about two hours. I look at her and marvel at how tiny she is and what a little miracle she is. Often with her twin brother and sister around, I don't have much time to devote to Leighton – there are diapers to change or tantrums to quell or disasters to avert. But today, I got some quiet time to see (as if I didn't already know) what a gift from God our Leighton is. Julie told me what I already have felt myself when I was a working mother – that she wished she could have been at home for her. But right now when Julie and Tom have to be at work, I'm grateful for the freedom that retirement brings me to nurse my sweet granddaughter and wonder anew at how brief and fragile childhood is - and how lovely.

LAUGHTER

ife can be humdrum at best so I am always happy to take a moment and laugh at the inane, ridiculous, hilarious things that happen. I love watching comedians on TV. I am always amazed at their timing and ability to remember their lines. Our daughter Caroline introduced me to Brian Regan. When our children were small, we got a Pop tarts video which has become the gold standard of comedy in our house. We also love The Blue Collar Comedy Tour.

But my children also frequently provide me with comedy gems of their own. I will never forget the morning which in our family we called The Kramer Moment (after the Seinfeld character that did this move.) On that morning I woke up to a huge snowfall causing schools to be cancelled. I let the girls sleep in and was enjoying a quiet cup of coffee when Katherine came sliding in her socks fast and sideways beside the kitchen counter, her hair askew, and her pajamas twisted to the side.

Katherine: "Mom, I overslept!"

Me: "Look outside, Katherine – schools are cancelled."

Katherine: {rolls her eyes and heads back upstairs without a word.}

Finally, I have to laugh at some of the stuff I see in school. Two in particular stand out. Once I gave a vocabulary quiz and one of the words was "sagacity." Johnathan's [not his real name] answer was "a city which is sagging." No lie.

And I'll never forget the ultimate – my Turkish transfer student Ughur. Ughur had moved to the United States from Turkey and was quite a talker. I was teaching what I'm sure was a masterful lesson on diagramming sentences when I happened to notice that Ughur was what we teachers call "off-task." He was seated in the back of the room and had put his right arm into the left sleeve and his left arm into the right sleeve of his tee shirt. He was wiggling his wrists, Tyrannosaurus Rex-style to the amusement of the student next to him. I stopped my lesson and the room got quiet, except for Ughur who was not looking at me. He was still enjoying his routine and wasn't aware that most of the class was watching him.

"Ughur," I said, "Can you please come to order?"

Ughur tried and failed to extract his arms, his face turning a bright red. He turned to the student next to him, a tough-acting kid named Marcus and sheepishly said, "Can you help me, please?"

Marcus surveyed the scene, looked at my disapproving face, and said to Ughur, "Nah, man, you're on your own."

The class erupted in laughter and so did I. So many years later, I still enjoy that moment.

GRACE

ur lives have become so very complex that we often eat on trays in front of the television, a shameful thing which my mother almost never allowed unless we children were sick at home. Lying on the couch, the old navy blanket tucked around us, we sipped tomato soup and ate cheese toast while watching "I Love Lucy" reruns and thinking smugly of the schoolwork we were missing. But most times we ate dinner at the kitchen or dining room table, full meals with our father presiding at one end and our mother at the other.

Each meal was preceded by our father's sonorous voice thanking our Heavenly Father for the bounties before us.

One of the things I always liked about my daddy's grace was that it was never drawn out. Occasionally I've had dinners blessed by preachers so long-winded that the meal gets cold waiting for them to draw a breath. But my daddy was always purposeful, saying just enough so that the Lord Almighty knew we were appreciative but that we had a piece of work ahead of us and it was time we got to it. When the children were little, we allowed them to say the blessing. With their tiny dimpled hands folded, and their eyes closed, they lisped the words to "God is great, God is good, Let us thank him for our food. By His hands we are fed, Give us Lord our daily bread. Amen" By doing so, we hoped the foundation for a lifelong faith was set in their little hearts.

Now that I am married to Paul and the children are grown, we still say a simple grace before we eat. It was established early in our marriage that I would say the grace, Paul's feeling being that my prayers would have more efficacy than his. I ask the Lord's blessing on whatever and wherever we eat, even in a fast food joint. Once, years ago, after I quietly said a blessing in McDonald's, a lady came up to me. She looked at my girls and said, "My daughter and I were watching when you said your prayer. Not many other people do that. Thank you." It was the first time I realized that my actions might influence people I didn't even know. I've made a point since then to offer a brief, unostentatious prayer before every meal, no matter where I am. I'm glad to offer a prayer of thanks to God for His bounteous blessings before every meal and on my knees at night. It reminds me of what my daddy often said, "Even a hog looks up to see where his acorns fell from." Taking the time to pray is important – it makes us stop for a minute to consider Who sent us so many blessings.

PHOTO ALBUMS

I'm thankful for my photo albums. Marching across the bottom two shelves of the bookshelves in my home library are twenty-five burgundy clothbound notebooks (what my students now call binders.) On the spine of each one, to the hilarious delight of Paul is a tape with a date on it (1990 – 1992 or something like that,) made with my handy dandy P-Touch labeler. He says I am obsessive about organizing everything. And yet, he comes to me every time he needs me to find something. Ask me for any picture from almost any date and within a couple of minutes I can whip that baby out. I even fold my dust cloths. So yes, I guess I am kind of an organized neat freak.

But being organized has helped me keep all of my photos in a way that is usable – all except the ones from about the year 2006 to the present. That's when we got a digital camera and began storing our photos online. I know. I know. They're preserved better there from fading and other forms of destruction especially since our hard drive is backed up, whatever that means. But I just don't enjoy the ones on the computer nearly as much as I do the ones in my photo albums. I can't take each picture out and hold it in my hand to examine more closely my baby's tiny foot or my granddaddy's lined face. I can't turn pages, recalling the events of each day's picture or imagining what the people in each picture are thinking.

There's something about holding a picture or an album in your hand that seems to make a magical cord of connection to that day so far in the past. Here, for example, I see my daddy, aged about thirty, on a snowy street in Richmond, his overcoat buttoned up. In another I'm a five year old at a birthday party for Martha Randolph, a paper hat perched on my head. Here's me, a great big college girl sitting in my Aunt Thelma's lap, big smiles on our faces. In another, I'm back in my grandmother's old farmhouse in Gates County, not long before it was razed. I remember how cold it was that day when Jerry and I walked through the rooms snapping pictures and making memories.

In another, my mother and daddy, Jerry and I are standing at the front of the Ivy Memorial Baptist Church sanctuary on our first Sunday there. Mama is wearing a dress of pink flowers scattered across a background of white. Her white gloves reach nearly to her elbows. Her earrings twinkle. Daddy is wearing a suit and tie and a smile. Jerry and I look at each other and giggle in that silly manner of young, nervous teen girls. Here's another picture of Aunt Arie, my mother's aged aunt who lived to her mid-90s. Mama used to make us kiss her once a year when we saw her. She smelled of mothballs and had a scratchy chin because I'm pretty sure she shaved. And I see my own children in other photos, babies, pink and sweet, all of them now adults with children of their own.

My mama had albums, too - black oblong cardboard albums with thick black paper. Each photo was stuck in little black gummed corners glued onto the page. I loved those too and used to spend hours perusing the pages, wondering about those people too. I'm glad for all the photos that I have but most especially for these I can hold in my hand. A picture in the palm of my hand is almost like touching again one of these precious faces from my past.

HOLDING ONTO MEMORIES

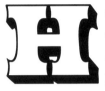ere in the South, we never give up on the past. Our long deceased loved ones, the places we used to live and love, and the memories of times we had are not locked in our heads somewhere. They are as alive as if our loved ones still walked this earth, as if we still lived in the old home place, as if the events of past times were still current.

I remember, for example, taking a ride on my Uncle Corbell's house-boat which he kept docked at his cottage in Tunis, NC on an inlet of the Chowan River. We stayed there occasionally for vacations and the whole clan gathered there for parties. I remember the amazement I felt that my cousin JC, a full year younger than me, was allowed to take me out on his little wooden boat. He paddled us up to the bait shop just up the creek from the cottage where we pulled cold Co-colas from the icy water of the drink box. You had to put in a nickel, and then pull the bottle along a channel in the cold water to get your drink.

I remember sitting at dusk under the spreading shade of the trees at my grandparents' home on Buffalo Creek in Kentucky. The uncles and aunts sat in aluminum folding chairs and told jokes, reminisced about old memories, and commented on how big we children were getting to be. I remember being upset that my mother sent me to bed before everyone left to go to their homes. I wanted to stay up to hear the stories. I wanted to savor every moment of my once a year visit to my Kentucky kin so I sat in my grandmother's kitchen to watch her make banana croquettes or churn butter from the cows on the hillside. Or I sat shyly beside my grandfather, a grand old white-haired gentleman, who didn't talk much. I wondered if he was different when my mother was a little girl like me.

Mostly I remember my parents. Mama and Daddy met when my daddy, a stripling Baptist preacher from North Carolina who was a seminary student in Louisville preached at my mama's church. Introduced to her by his brother, (another preacher,) my daddy proceeded to steal Mama away from the fellow she was seeing. That was in 1934. We found their love letters years ago, a treasure trove of sweet, innocent awakening love between the two of them. In all the years Mama was alive she kept them tied with a ribbon in her dresser drawer and refused to let us see them. Always a private person, Mama wanted to keep those sweet days to herself, it seemed.

After their deaths, I read them all, organized them by date and transcribed them for my sisters to see. They recorded happy days, lovers' quarrels, and sweet make-ups and all led to the 10th day of September, 1936 when Mama and Daddy were married in the parlor of the Rev. Gabbert in Lebanon, Kentucky. Daddy wore a suit. Mama wore a burgundy suit with mink tails on the collar. She remembered it for years afterward and wished she had kept her outfit. I'm just glad she kept the memory.

They are all gone now, of course, Mama and Daddy, all the aunts and uncles, even JC and his younger brother Walter, taken from us too soon by separate car accidents. But here in my heart, they are still alive, still vital, still making memories. I'm glad you married so many years ago, Mama and Daddy, and I'm glad for all the memories I have because of that day.